Covert Risk

Jane Blythe

Bear Spots Publications
Melbourne Australia

Paperback
ISBN-13: 978-0-6456432-4-4

Cover designed by RBA Designs

Also by Jane Blythe

Detective Parker Bell Series

A SECRET TO THE GRAVE
WINTER WONDERLAND
DEAD OR ALIVE
LITTLE GIRL LOST
FORGOTTEN

Count to Ten Series

ONE
TWO
THREE
FOUR
FIVE
SIX
BURNING SECRETS
SEVEN
EIGHT
NINE
TEN

Broken Gems Series

CRACKED SAPPHIRE
CRUSHED RUBY
FRACTURED DIAMOND
SHATTERED AMETHYST
SPLINTERED EMERALD
SALVAGING MARIGOLD

River's End Rescues Series

COCKY SAVIOR
SOME REGRETS ARE FOREVER
PROTECT
SOME LIES WILL HAUNT YOU

SOME QUESTIONS HAVE NO ANSWERS
SOME TRUTH CAN BE DISTORTED
SOME TRUST CAN BE REBUILT
SOME MISTAKES ARE UNFORGIVABLE

Candella Sisters' Heroes Series

LITTLE DOLLS
LITTLE HEARTS
LITTLE BALLERINA

Storybook Murders Series

NURSERY RHYME KILLER
FAIRYTALE KILLER
FABLE KILLER

Saving SEALs Series

SAVING RYDER
SAVING ERIC
SAVING OWEN
SAVING LOGAN
SAVING GRAYSON
SAVING CHARLIE

Prey Security Series

PROTECTING EAGLE
PROTECTING RAVEN
PROTECTING FALCON
PROTECTING SPARROW
PROTECTING HAWK
PROTECTING DOVE

Prey Security: Alpha Team Series

DEADLY RISK
LETHAL RISK

EXTREME RISK
FATAL RISK
COVERT RISK

Prey Security: Artemis Team Series

IVORY'S FIGHT

Christmas Romantic Suspense Series

CHRISTMAS HOSTAGE
CHRISTMAS CAPTIVE
CHRISTMAS VICTIM
YULETIDE PROTECTOR
YULETIDE GUARD
YULETIDE HERO

I'd like to thank everyone who played a part in bringing this story to life. Particularly my mom who is always there to share her thoughts and opinions with me. My awesome cover designer, Letitia from RBA Designs, who whips up covers for me so quickly and who patiently makes every change I ask for, and there are usually lots of them! And my lovely editor Lisa Edwards, for all their encouragement and for all the hard work they put into polishing my work.

CHAPTER ONE

October 13th
12:25 P.M.

This sucked.

Majorly.

But with the threat hanging over his head Christian "Surf" Bailey didn't see that he had any other choice.

Drawing in a deep breath, he forced himself to do this. Breaking Lila's heart would break his right along with it, but he couldn't let her know that. If he wasn't strong and didn't make a clean break of things, then he was painting a major bullseye on the woman's back, and he'd rather break her heart than get her killed.

Surf knocked on Lila's apartment door and schooled his expression into a mask of disinterest. If he didn't like the woman so much this wouldn't be so hard. When he'd met her, he'd been in the middle of a month-long sex binge. Falling for a woman had been the last thing he'd wanted.

After he and his team—Prey Security's Alpha Team—had been ambushed and held captive in Somalia, they had been beaten and tortured for two weeks before they'd been rescued. He'd found the only way he could cope with the mess of emotions and overwhelming helplessness the ordeal invoked was the high of an orgasm.

Meaningless sex was all he'd wanted. In and done as quickly as possible. Get the woman off, get himself off, then leave. He hadn't even known the names of the vast majority of them. Hadn't wanted to. It wasn't about them, wasn't even really about him, he just needed that high to survive.

Until Lila had changed everything.

"Oh, Christian, hi. What a great surprise." Lila's sweet smile greeted him like a beacon shining a light through a pitch-black night. She might not know it—would likely never know it—but she was what had saved him. Brought him out of that darkness, and he hated that this was how it was going to end.

All he could do was pray that once they found and eliminated the threat hanging over him and his team, he could come back, explain, and Lila might understand.

Not sure he would if he was her, but he could hope.

Had to hope.

"We need to talk."

At his tone, the smile slowly fell from Lila's face, and instead, uncertainty danced in her beautiful baby blue eyes. It had been a few days since he'd been able to come and see her, but they had talked on the phone and texted every single day since they had met. He knew this was going to come completely out of the blue for her, she wouldn't understand, and he absolutely hated that. But telling her the truth meant putting her in danger, and he hated that even more.

"Uh, sure, come on in." When she stepped back to let him enter her apartment, he felt that distance like a physical blow.

This was it.

In just a couple of minutes, he would rip out her heart and walk away like she meant nothing to him. She'd saved him, and she wouldn't know it. It seemed so unfair, and he cursed everyone involved in this plot to overthrow the government that now had him and his team marked for death.

"Umm, do you want something to eat? I was just about to make lunch. I can make you something too," Lila offered. She'd closed the door behind them but was watching him somewhat warily as though she suspected whatever he was there for wasn't something she wanted to hear.

"No, thanks anyway. I think it's best that I just do this."

Lila lifted her arms to wrap around her stomach, bracing herself for a blow, and he hated that he was the one who was going to deliver it. She wasn't usually the kind of woman he found himself attracted to. Usually, he went for outgoing, loud extroverts, people who liked to be the life of the party, but also women who had a great sense of humor and loved to have fun.

In contrast to that, Lila was quiet and contemplative. She had a steady confidence that you might not notice right away, but she held herself tall in a crowd, paid attention to everything happening around her, noticed details, and hadn't been afraid to stand up for herself or to him.

They'd met quite by accident.

He'd been leaving after having sex with a woman he'd already forgotten what she looked like. She'd been coming home from her job as a 911 operator.

Already losing that high he'd needed, Surf had been distracted, dropped his cell phone, and bent down to pick it up, not realizing a woman was walking by. She'd tripped over him and would have hit the hard pavement if he didn't have quick reflexes.

She had been understandably wary of him given it was early morning, the sun just beginning to rise, and had told him off for not paying attention to his surroundings. The spark of irritation in her eyes had immediately captured his attention, but the lurking sadness made his heart stir and take notice.

It had taken all of his charm and sweet-talking skills to get her to agree to go to a local diner with him for an early breakfast. Eventually, she had opened up and told him that it had been a rough shift at her job. She'd had a kid die of anaphylaxis and a woman kidnapped while on the line.

Seeing how deeply she cared about people she didn't even know, he knew then and there that she was something special.

Had he been thinking long-term?

No, not yet.

Too much had happened over the last few months, and he was wary of planning a future when he knew the future was anything but certain. But he'd been intrigued, liked her and wanted to get to know her.

Since meeting Lila, he hadn't had sex with another woman, hadn't even thought about it. Lila had been more than enough to satisfy him in every single way. Not just physically, although they were certainly burn up the sheets compatible, but emotionally and psychologically as well.

Without Lila's calming presence in his life, he feared he would resort back to having to chase that high with random women all over again.

"Christian, you're scaring me. Can you just tell me why you're here?" Lila's voice drew him out of his head, and he took one last look at her before he severed the connection that seemed to have bound them together from that very first moment.

"I'm sorry, Lila, it's over."

"You're breaking up with me? Just like that?" Lila's eyes widened with shock. And he hated how this had come completely out of the blue for her. When he'd last seen her a few days ago everything had been perfect, and when they'd spoken on the phone right before he and his team raided the Mikhailov estate to rescue Julia Garamond, they'd made plans for another date.

Now he was here ending things.

"Just like that."

Tears shimmered in those gorgeous eyes, and they almost had him breaking down and telling her everything. But Lila's life was what was important here, and he wouldn't put it in danger.

"But I don't understand, everything was going so well," Lila said. "I thought this was going somewhere."

"Well, it's not." Surf hated coming across as so callous. While he was every bit as deadly as the rest of the men on his team, he was the lighthearted one, the goofy one, who was able to put victims at ease, and charm anyone into doing what he wanted.

This wasn't him, but he didn't know any other way to end things and keep Lila safe than to shatter her sweet heart.

"But—"

"Look, babe, it's not up for discussion. We had some fun, but you knew when I met you that all I wanted was a physical relationship." It took everything he had not to cringe at the words coming out of his mouth.

Lila's eyes went almost impossibly wide. "So, I meant absolutely nothing to you but a warm body primed for sex?"

The incredulity in her voice told him that he would never have a chance to convince her that this had all been a ruse to protect her.

"Don't call me, Lila."

Anger shoved aside some of the confusion and hurt. "Oh, don't worry about that. I have no intention of calling. I don't want to see or speak to you ever again."

Mission accomplished.

Memorizing every detail about her, her long, wavy blonde hair that fell like a golden waterfall down her back, the soft dusting of freckles across her nose, and the way her plump lips quirked up when she was amused before her face bloomed into a full-blown smile.

She was everything he wanted.

Everything he needed.

It killed him to have to walk away like this.

"You should go now." Lila stalked to the door and threw it open, waiting expectantly for him to leave.

Because he was a weak man, a selfish one as well as it turned out, Surf paused at the door. Curling one hand behind her neck, he touched his lips to hers in one last kiss.

One last taste of paradise.

Then he turned and walked away leaving his heart in tatters on Lila's apartment floor.

* * * * *

October 29th
6:49 A.M.

"No, no, no, no, no."

Lila Angeletti groaned as she sunk back to rest against the side of her bathtub.

Another morning, another round of vomiting.

It was getting harder to pretend that nothing was wrong.

Harder, but still she clung to denial.

This couldn't be happening to her.

It couldn't.

It would be the most unfair thing in the universe.

She had turned thirty just a week ago, was single, and hadn't had any plans for marriage and a family until a sexy former Navy SEAL came barreling into her life. She had been perfectly content with her life. Her hard fight for freedom meant she could live where she wanted, have the job she chose, and live in her own cozy little apartment that was furnished the way she wanted.

Free from her family's influence, she had fled to the opposite side of the country, needing an entire continent between them to finally feel safe. A job that was tough but she loved, friends who knew who she had been but accepted she wasn't that person anymore, and a man she had been falling in love with.

Now she was sitting here, on the bathroom floor, drenched in sweat, no longer able to pretend that this was food poisoning or a stomach virus, alone, scared, angry, and hurt.

More than two weeks had passed since Christian "Surf" Bailey had broken her heart and she still didn't understand what had happened.

What had changed?

One minute they had been falling in love—well, at least she had thought they were, Lila knew she had been—the next he was showing up at her place out of the blue, ending things with no explanation whatsoever.

Christian had told her that first day they met about his issue. While he hadn't gone into details, she'd known that something had happened to him and his team a few months prior to their meeting and that it had been bad, and his coping mechanism was sex.

But she'd thought they had something more.

Stupid.

She should have known better.

Her track record with men was a disaster, although it wasn't her fault, it was her family's. Which was part of the reason she now lived in New York while they lived in Los Angeles. But this mistake had been all hers, and now she might have a constant reminder of said mistake growing inside her.

Could she do this on her own?

Juggling a demanding job with long hours and being a single mom sounded utterly terrifying. Plus, there was the financial aspect. She made enough to support herself, but herself and a baby?

Lila wanted her child to grow up knowing who his or her father was, but would Surf even want to be part of the baby's life? And if he did, would she be okay with him parading women through their son or daughter's life? That wasn't the environment she would want for her child, but Christian was the baby's father so he had as much right as she did to be part of its life, and she could hardly dictate how he lived when their child was with him.

What if he decided he wanted to take the baby from her?

His job with Prey Security's Alpha Team was unpredictable and dangerous, but he had more money than she did and could hire a nanny to care for the baby when he couldn't be there. Would he use his money to hire a lawyer, get full custody of their child, and cut her out of their lives?

Nausea churned in her gut only this time it had nothing to do with potential morning sickness.

Now it had everything to do with the fear of being cut out of her child's life.

"You're getting ahead of yourself, Lila. Calm down."

Easier said than done.

There was no point in panicking until she even knew if she was carrying a baby. There could be other reasons why she missed her last period and why she'd been getting sick in the mornings.

They had used a condom. Christian had been insistent, which she understood given he'd been sleeping around, and she hadn't wanted to wind up pregnant and alone anyway, so they had used protection every time they'd slept together.

But no birth control was infallible.

As she might be about to find out.

Using the side of the tub for leverage, Lila hauled herself to her feet. There was a moment when the world spun around her and she was sure she would hit the tiles when she collapsed in a heap, but somehow, she managed to remain standing.

In the bathroom cabinet—buried way down at the back—were the pregnancy tests she'd bought a week ago.

On her birthday.

When she realized she was late and that what she thought was a stomach bug could be something else entirely.

She'd been so excited to celebrate her birthday with Christian. It would be the first year she'd celebrated with a real boyfriend. Pathetic, she knew since it was her thirtieth, but the relationships she'd been forced into in the past made her want to steer clear of the whole thing.

Christian was different though. Lila had felt a connection to him the moment their eyes first met. Love at first sight? Maybe not. But a connection nonetheless. He had hinted he had special plans he was making for her birthday, and she'd thought the day was going to be the perfect way to usher in a new decade of her life. One where she learned to cut the final threads tying her to her past so she could finally be completely free and happy.

Instead, she'd spent the day curled in a ball in bed, feeling sick and so alone and heartbroken it had physically hurt.

Lila wanted to run from this, pretend she hadn't missed a period, that she wasn't throwing up every morning, and it didn't mean anything at all. But pretending wouldn't change anything.

If she was pregnant, she was pregnant.

She'd deal with it.

Just like she had dealt with everything else life had thrown at her.

If Christian wanted to be part of the baby's life, they would work something out. If he tried to take the baby from her she'd fight, and if he wanted nothing to do with the baby like he wanted nothing to do with her then she'd raise it on her own.

Her fear—over something she hadn't even confirmed existed—over losing her child proved that she did, in fact, want this. Maybe it wasn't what she had planned, maybe it wasn't what she had expected, but she would find a way to make this work no matter what it took.

Crouching down, Lila rummaged around until she found the box and pulled it out of the cabinet beneath the sink. Her hand trembled as she opened the box and took out the stick.

The trembling increased as she shoved her pajama bottoms down, along with her panties, and held the stick in place so she could pee on it. After she'd flushed the toilet, she pulled off some toilet paper and put it on the vanity beside the sink, setting the stick on it while she washed her hands.

Now there was nothing to do but wait.

Seconds ticked by, feeling like hours.

As terrifying as this was and as absolutely alone as she felt, Lila found she was already accepting the fact that this was just a formality. She already knew there was a new life growing inside her.

"Okay, Lila, it's time to see what your future looks like.

Whatever it is you can handle it. You've been through worse, and this time there isn't anyone controlling your life. It's just you and …" she trailed off as she reached out and picked up the stick.

Confirmation.

Pregnant.

She was pregnant.

"… a baby. Just you and a baby. Your baby."

Bursting into tears, Lila dropped the pregnancy test onto the vanity and ran into the bedroom, throwing herself onto the bed and burying herself beneath the covers.

How could this be happening to her?

Yeah, she knew she would figure it out, but right now it was so overwhelming. This wasn't how it was supposed to be. You were supposed to be happy and involved with a man who loved you. You were both supposed to be thrilled and excited about the new life you would soon bring into the world.

Of course, she knew reality often wasn't like that. She wasn't the first woman to find out she was pregnant and alone, but this was her life they were talking about.

Her life.

Only it wasn't just hers anymore.

She was pregnant and hopelessly in love with the baby's father. A man who had callously used her for sex and then tossed her aside when he got bored. A man who wouldn't be beside her as she raised this baby.

Curling her arms protectively over her stomach, Lila realized she was already falling for this child, already starting to love it. "Don't worry, little one, it might be just the two of us, but somehow we'll make it work."

CHAPTER TWO

November 9th
3:02 P.M.

The street looked clear.

How many times was he going to do this before he finally accepted it was over and walked away?

Surf shook his head and lifted his hands to massage his temples.

He knew the answer to that question, and it was never.

Even though it had been almost four weeks since he ended things with Lila, he couldn't stop thinking about the woman. Time hadn't helped, if anything it was making it worse. The more time that passed without being able to talk, touch, kiss, and make love to her, the bigger the chasm between them seemed to grow.

While he was every bit as into her as he had been when he'd ended things, Lila was no doubt starting to move on. Since she had no idea why he'd broken up with her or that he had been falling in love with her, she had no reason to think about him at all. And if she was, he doubted they were nice thoughts.

It physically hurt to know that she likely hated him and that the chances of him being able to fix this once the threat to him and his team was eliminated were so slim they were virtually non-existent.

Damn Kristoff Mikhailov and his mysterious and as yet unidentified Dark Beauty.

If the head of the Russian Mafia family hadn't concocted this crazy plot to overthrow the government, then none of this would be happening. Although he had to admit if it wasn't for the man's plans, none of the guys on his team might have ended up with their partners.

Luca "Bear" Jackson had met his now wife Mackenzie when they'd raided the island compound on Lake Victoria in Uganda of a man named Storm Gallagher. Storm was a survivalist with a grudge against the government and plans to destroy it and usher in his version of a utopia. Mackenzie was Storm's half-sister and had been abused by him all her life. In his delusional mind, she was to be the mother of the man who would bring in this utopia.

Asher "Mouse" Whitman and his wife Phoebe met when she saved his daughter Lolly from being abducted. When it became clear Phoebe was terrified, and on the run, they ended up learning her abusive ex was mixed up in a law firm that helped finance the plot that went deeper than Storm and his vision, by extorting money from wealthy clients.

Antonio "Arrow" Eden already knew his now fiancée Piper Hamilton because she was Prey's on-staff psychiatrist. Things changed between the two of them when Alpha Team was captured in Somalia and tortured. Determined to go after the woman who had caught his attention, things became complicated when Piper was being stalked by a former Prey employee turned weapons dealer.

This led Dominick "Domino" Tanner to meet his now fiancée Julia Garamond when they went back to Somalia to try to track a couple of the weapons dealers who had escaped the raid on Pete Petrowski's compound to rescue Piper. Julia was a reporter who had been caught in one of the explosions and decided to investigate.

When they learned that Domino was in fact a Mikhailov, firstborn son and heir to the Bratva family empire, all of them were completely shocked. Domino had kept his true identity from them for fear that they'd see him as evil like his family, but in reality, the most shocking thing about the whole mess was the way the hard, emotionless man had softened under the love of the woman he'd fallen for.

Domino and Julia deserved to be spending this special time at the beginning of their relationship enjoying getting to know one another and basking in their new love. Instead, they were living in an apartment in Prey's Manhattan building under constant fear that Domino's brother Kristoff's, who had been killed almost a month ago by Domino himself, Dark Beauty would come after them.

The woman had vowed vengeance for Kristoff and to continue his plan.

Which was why he'd had to break up with Lila.

How could he ask her to give up her life and have around-the-clock security when things between them were so new?

With a last scan of her street, when he saw nothing that looked suspicious, Surf turned the engine back on and pulled out into the busy Manhattan traffic.

Over the last four weeks, he had spent way more time than he should sitting outside Lila's building watching over her. Just because he had ended things with her as soon as they knew about Dark Beauty, it didn't mean someone from the Mikhailov Bratva hadn't already tagged Lila as being connected to him.

If they had, his ending things with her would have been for nothing.

But so far things had been quiet. Nothing appeared to be out of the ordinary. There was no one he could detect watching Lila or her building.

The small glimpses he'd gotten of her when he'd timed his near-daily check-ins of her building to coincide with when he knew she would be leaving for work weren't enough. How had he ever thought he could do this?

Cutting her out of his life—well, as much as he had been able to—felt like cutting a piece of himself away. While before being tortured in Somalia he had never been the manwhore he'd turned into afterward, he had dated his fair share of women. There had never been any intention of it being anything long-term, but it hadn't been a one-and-done thing either.

He dated because he liked companionship and having a pretty woman to hang out with and have fun with, but he wasn't looking for marriage and forever.

Not until Lila anyway.

Surf had no idea what it was about her. Her quiet strength, her intelligence, and her pretty baby blues that seemed to see deep down inside him to a place that not even his team could see into. Her cute freckles, adorable giggle, and stunning beauty combined into a woman who had managed to knock him to his knees and barge her way into his heart without even trying.

And now he'd lost her.

He could have undone the pain he'd caused her. She had tried reaching out a couple of times, but he never answered when she called, and he'd ignored both her voicemails and her texts asking him to call back. It was better for both of them if they made a clean break.

Maybe if he kept telling himself that it might become true.

A dark vehicle switching lanes behind him caught his attention.

Given the known threat to his team, Surf didn't hesitate, he called Bear immediately.

"I just picked up a tail," he announced without preamble when his team leader answered.

"Hold on," Bear said, and a moment later he could tell he was on speaker and the rest of the guys were there.

"Are you near Lila's?" Arrow asked.

"Yeah, picked it up not long after I left."

"Could they have been watching her?" Mouse asked.

"No. Definitely not. I didn't see anyone suspicious, and I don't recognize the vehicle from any that were parked outside her building."

"I hate that we haven't made any progress identifying Dark Beauty," Domino growled. Since he was the one to kill his brother, he blamed himself for all of Alpha Team having a bullseye painted on their backs.

"I took Phoebe and Lolly out for dinner last night because they were both getting edgy from being cooped up, and I'm positive someone was tailing us," Mouse said. "They didn't approach, and when I went to intercept them, they hightailed it out of there. Phoebe and I talked once we put Lolly to bed and decided to move into Prey."

"I want Mackenzie and Mikey there as well. She's been reluctant, but if she knows you guys are in, she'll probably be more amenable to the idea," Bear added.

"Piper is there basically all day anyway. I don't think it would take much to convince her to stay there. I know I'd feel better, especially with her lingering health issues," Arrow said. Piper had been badly beaten by Pete Petrowski, and some of her injuries were still yet to fully heal, going on four months later.

"Vehicle still following you, Surf?" Bear asked.

"Yep. Keeping its distance … hold on," he said as the black SUV switched lanes and began to gain on him.

"Surf?" Bear demanded.

"It's approaching," he said, keeping his attention focused on the vehicle.

A moment later it pulled up beside him, the back driver's side window opened slightly, and the barrel of a weapon appeared.

Preparing to perform evasive maneuvers right here on the busy road and hoping no innocents got taken out, before he could, the weapon withdrew, the window went up, and the vehicle sped off down the street.

A warning.

A reminder that the threat was still there, that Dark Beauty wasn't giving up.

He'd memorized the license plate, but the vehicle would turn out to be stolen, or rented under an alias, nothing that would lead anywhere.

Whoever Dark Beauty was she wasn't going away, wasn't backing down.

If there had been any doubt in his mind that he had done the right thing when he broke up with Lila it was gone now. As much as it hurt, and as much as he couldn't stand the thought of her hating him, at least she was alive and safe.

* * * * *

November 14th
9:32 A.M.

Okay, you can do this.

It's not that hard.

Not that hard.

Right.

Because walking into a man's place of work and informing him he was going to be a father was an absolute piece of cake.

And the fact that the man had zero feelings for her and had ignored her numerous attempts at reaching out to tell him made it oh so much easier.

Insert massive sarcasm there.

Lila knew Christian wouldn't be happy to find out that they were having a baby, but she was not going to cut her child's father out of its life. Christian deserved to know, but more than that, her child deserved for his or her father to decide for himself if he wanted to be part of their life. She was keeping this baby. She wanted this baby and was already falling in love with it. If Christian wanted no part of its life, then it would be because he chose not to be, not because he didn't know.

While she definitely hoped he wanted to be involved because it was a terrifying prospect to think about eighteen years of child-raising she would have to do alone, she was prepared to go this alone. Chances were, Christian wouldn't be thrilled. For him, their relationship had just been about sex, he hadn't caught feelings like she had. But she hoped that even though he didn't care about her, he would be willing—maybe even happy—to co-parent with her.

Prey Security was an imposing building, and Lila couldn't deny she was anxious as she walked through the front door.

There was a security guard who threw her a glance as she headed for the reception desk. It was unnerving to be so closely watched, but she had nothing to be ashamed of, she hadn't done anything wrong. On the contrary, she was trying to do the right thing. It wouldn't be fair for her to keep the baby a secret and take away Christian's choice. They had both made this baby growing inside her, and if he wanted no part of it, he would have to tell her that to her face.

"How may I help you?" the young woman at the desk asked as she approached.

"I'm here to see Christian Bailey."

Surprise flickered in the woman's eyes, along with a dose of wariness. Lila had no idea why. Had Christian told them not to let her see him if she turned up here? That seemed extreme. She was hardly some lovesick stalker, she was just trying to do the right thing in completely unexpected circumstances.

"Is he expecting you?" the woman asked.

"No. He's not, but it's very important that I speak with him," Lila said. She noticed that the security guard had sidled closer and his hand was resting just above his weapon.

What was going on?

This was crazy.

They were acting like she was some sort of threat.

Lila got that Christian worked for one of the best security companies in the world. No doubt his work was extremely dangerous, but she was just a woman he'd had sex with, she was no threat at all.

"Is he here? Can I see him?" she asked, her nerves growing.

The receptionist shifted her gaze to the security guard, then nodded slowly. "I can call him and ask him to come down. Your name is?"

"Lila. Lila Angeletti."

"Does Mr. Bailey know you?"

"Yes." There was no point in saying more than that. For whatever reason, these people thought she was here for some sort of nefarious purpose. It didn't matter why, and in some ways it was true. While her motives were good, she was about to upend Christian's world in a way that could never be undone. Even if he chose not to be part of their child's life, he was still going to be a father. Nothing would change that.

While the woman got on the phone the security guard hovered nearby, his attention focused on her. Did she really look that dangerous? As far as she could tell there was absolutely nothing threatening about her. She was wearing white jeans and a pink sweater, her coat was a darker shade of pink, her boots were black, and her hair hung loosely around her shoulders. She looked like pretty much every other woman in the city.

"Mr. Bailey will be down in a moment," the receptionist informed her, voice borderline cold and rude.

"Okay," she said, not sure what else to say. There was no reason for them to be rude to her, not even if Christian had told them who she was. And why would he? She was nothing but a warm body for him to use to satisfy himself. Get the high he claimed he needed to cope with being hurt badly a few months before they met.

Standing awkwardly by the desk Lila waited, twisting her hands together. This was hard enough as it was without having these suspicious looks thrown her way. If she had ever imagined having a child, this was not how she thought it would be. The father wanting nothing to do with her, ignoring her, likely either outright ridiculing her and telling her he didn't believe the baby was his, or just downright disinterested.

She wasn't sure what would be worse.

"Lila." At the sound of Christian calling her name, she turned to see him striding out of the lift. Only he didn't look like the man she had been getting to know. That man had been sweet, funny, and kind. This man looked cold and unfeeling, exactly what she suspected he looked like when he was on a mission to take down bad guys. Is that how he saw her? As some bad guy he had to get out of his life.

It sucked that her stupid, traitorous body reacted to Christian's as he came to stand before her. How could she still be attracted to him when she knew he didn't care about her at all?

Hardening her heart and reining in her hormones, Lila straightened and gathered her courage. She might not feel confident right now, but she was an expert at acting like she had everything together even when she didn't.

"We need to talk," she said.

Christian shot her a mocking smile. "Nothing left to talk about, babe. I told you it was over, and I don't appreciate you coming to my work to try to see me. I didn't answer your calls or texts for a reason. I didn't want to hear from you."

She did her best not to wince at his harsh words. It would be so easy just to turn, run, and keep her secret. Chances he was going to be happy to find out about his impending fatherhood were slim to none. But she hadn't come here for him. Or for herself.

The only reason she was here was for her child.

When her baby was old enough to ask about its father, she wanted to have truthful answers to give. She didn't want to have to tell her son or daughter that she hadn't told their father about them.

"If you don't stop calling and texting, I'm going to take out a restraining order, and I won't hesitate to have you locked up if you break it."

His harsh words made her flinch.

How had she ever thought she was falling in love with this

man?

Goes to show how a man would do anything to get himself sex.

Lila would have thought she had already learned that lesson, obviously she hadn't. This was a lesson that would stick though. She would never trust a man again. Not that she would have time for dating, she'd be raising this little one alone because no way did the man standing before her want any part of being a parent.

"I don't want to see you again, Lila." Christian nodded to the security guard who stepped up and grabbed her elbow, pulling her toward the door.

She wasn't going until she'd done what she came here for.

Jerk or not, Christian Bailey was the father of her child, and he would know that this baby existed.

"I haven't been calling and texting because I want you back, Christian," she said. "I'm pregnant. You have a right to know that I'm carrying your child even if I do think you're the world's biggest jerk and not who I would have chosen to father my child." Reaching into her bag she pulled out the pregnancy test which she had kept because she knew Christian would want proof, along with the results from her doctor when she'd gone in to confirm the pregnancy.

Yanking her arm free from the guard's grip, she shoved them at Christian then turned and walked away, head held high.

He knew the truth. Whatever he decided to do with it was on him.

CHAPTER THREE

November 14th
9:48 A.M.

I'm pregnant.

I'm pregnant.

I'm pregnant.

Lila's words rattled around inside his head, stuck on a loop.

Surf couldn't have been more shocked if Lila had walked in today to tell him that she was actually part polar bear.

On the heels of the shock was relief so great it almost took him to his knees.

Taking off after Lila who was almost at the door, about ready to fling it open and storm out of his life possibly for good, he shoved past the security guard who had been following her, ready to neutralize her if she turned out to be a threat and snatched her up into his arms.

Her pregnancy changed everything.

Keeping his distance to protect her was a moot point now. She was connected to him, carrying his baby. She was in as much danger as any of his teammates' women, and leaving her alone with no one watching out for her was asking for her to be hurt.

Clutching her to his chest, he spun around in a circle, happier than he'd been in the very long month since he'd broken her heart and walked away.

"Put me down," Lila ordered, shoving at his shoulders. "What are you doing? Are you crazy? One minute you're telling me you'd love to have me arrested, and the next, you're hugging me like you're happy to see me."

"Oh, honey, I *am* happy to see you. Happier than you could ever know."

When he set her on her feet and dropped to his knees in front of her, Lila's mouth dropped open in shock. He didn't care that he was making a fool out of himself in front of his team who he had no doubt were watching on the building's security feed—hell, probably the entire building was watching—all he cared about was Lila and making her understand.

"We're really having a baby?" he asked in wonder, placing a palm over her flat stomach.

"I brought the pregnancy test and results from my doctor as proof," she said defensively.

While he couldn't blame Lila for having zero faith in him, it didn't stop a shaft of pain from arrowing through his heart. "I don't need proof, sweetheart. I believe you."

"It's your baby," she added, still defensive. Despite the fact that he had one hand still on her stomach, his other wrapped around her thighs she was stiff as a board, wound tight with stress, anger, and uncertainty.

"I know that, honey. You don't sleep around, I know that. I remember."

Her cheeks flamed red with embarrassment. He'd known the second he kissed her that the woman was sexually repressed, not inexperienced exactly, but she had no idea how to let go and run with those emotions. Watching her blossom, her confidence grow, no longer fighting against the pleasure he gave her, had been a gift, one he hated he'd had no choice but to squander.

"We can do a DNA test to prove it. If you don't want to wait we can get an amniocentesis done. I'd rather not risk the baby by doing it but if you want to we can," Lila continued, obviously still believing that he wouldn't believe her.

"Again with the proof, sweetheart. How do I convince you that I already believe you?"

Lila tried to pull out of his grip, but he tightened his hold on her. It had been a very long month. Every day he had ached to touch her, hold her, tell her how sorry he was that he'd caused her pain. Now that she was here, he couldn't let her go.

Although there was every possibility he wouldn't have a choice in the matter.

Could Lila forgive him?

Could she understand why he'd done what he did?

"I'm sorry, honey, for everything. So very sorry for having to break your sweet, beautiful heart." Tugging her closer with the arm he still had hooked around her thighs, he curled his other arm around her waist and pressed his face against her stomach.

Pregnant.

Lila was having a baby.

They were having a baby.

He was going to be a father.

This was huge.

Huge, but he was thrilled. Excited.

A baby.

Surf had never really thought about having kids. He was excited to be Uncle Surf to his teammates' kids, but a kid of his own? Given how he'd grown up, having kids hadn't even been on his radar.

"We need to talk, but please know I am so sorry for hurting you," he said as he slowly released her and stood, immediately curling a hand around hers so she couldn't put distance between them. She wanted to, he could tell she did, and he understood why but these last four weeks had been hell, and now she was here and everything felt right again.

"You're sorry for hurting me? I don't know what that means." Lila's brow furrowed, her eyebrows drawing together in the most adorable little frown.

"Let's go in here, and I'll explain everything," he promised as he led her toward the nearest conference room.

He could tell by the way her cheeks pinked again that she had just realized they were still in the middle of the lobby and that the receptionist, the guard, and a couple of other people were all watching them with interest.

More relieved than he could express that she didn't fight him, he guided her into the room and pulled out a chair at the table for her. Once she was seated, he took the chair beside her and took her hands.

When she went to pull them away, he tightened his grip. "Please," he begged softly.

Confusion swirled in her baby blue eyes, and he longed to wipe it away. He wouldn't hold anything back, she deserved to know everything. Once she did if she wanted nothing to do with him, or she didn't believe he could keep her and their baby safe, then he would ask his boss, Eagle Oswald, to put her in a safehouse with around-the-clock security. Then once this was over, he would set her up anywhere in the world she wanted to go. If she didn't want him to be part of their baby's life, then he would at least provide financially for the two of them.

"I'm getting whiplash here, Christian. The man I was dating was sweet and caring, then you're all harsh, breaking up with me and telling me you were using me just for sex. You ignored my calls and texts, and just now you were so cruel, but now you're all sweet again." She pulled one of her hands free and rubbed at her temple like she had a headache.

Immediately he panicked. "Are you okay? The baby, the pregnancy, is everything okay with it? Is the baby healthy? Are you?"

Lila gave him a funny look, one that said she couldn't figure him out. "I'm struggling with morning sickness, but the baby is fine."

"Good. I'm so glad."

"You're … happy I'm pregnant?"

"Shocked but thrilled. Definitely excited."

"But …"

Touching a finger to her lips to silence her, Surf leaned over and touched a kiss to her forehead. "I'm going to explain everything and pray that you can forgive me. My team has been involved in trying to take down a plot to overthrow the government. The explosions set a few months ago were part of it, and we managed to find the man in charge of the plot. Unfortunately, he had a partner, one who vowed revenge on my team for the death of the man she loved. Until we find her, we're all living with a threat hanging over our heads. I like you, Lila. A lot. More than you realize. Enough to push you away to keep you safe."

"That's why you broke up with me?"

Surf nodded. "I couldn't tell you the truth because if I did, I know you would have said you were prepared to walk this road with me, but I couldn't risk you. You're too special, too important to me. It about killed me to do it, but ending things between us in a way that you wouldn't want anything to do with me was the only way I knew to keep you safe. I did it *for* you. I know you might not be able to forgive me, and if that's the case I understand, but I promise I will make it up to you if you're willing to give me a chance."

He held his breath as he waited to see what she would say. There was a wariness in her expression, and it was clear that she still had her guard up. Did that mean she couldn't forgive him?

"You and your team are really in danger?"

"Yes. Someone followed me a few weeks back, pointed a gun at me before driving off, and one of the guys on my team saw someone watching him with his wife and daughter. Two of the guys are married. One has a baby, the other a seven-year-old and another on the way. Another two are engaged. They've all moved into apartments here at Prey to keep their families safe. I want you to move here as well, where I can protect you and earn my way back into your good graces," he teased.

Lila cracked a smile. "You really want me to stay here with you and your team?"

"Sweetheart, when this mess was over, and you wouldn't be in danger by being associated with me, I intended to come after you, try to win you back. The day I was followed, I had been outside your apartment building. I spent most nights there, watching over you, making sure you were safe. Needing to be close to you," he admitted.

"I … I didn't know you did that."

"There isn't anything I wouldn't do to protect what's mine."

Her eyes widened. "Are you saying I'm yours?"

* * * * *

November 14th
10:09 A.M.

Her head was reeling.

Stomach tight with anxiety.

Hardly able to believe what Christian was telling her.

His forest green eyes met and held hers. "I'm saying that I like you a whole lot. Walking away from you was one of the hardest things I have ever had to do. I feel connected to you and loved every second we spent together. I want us to be together. I understand you probably need time to come to terms with everything and I'll wait as long as you need." Christian's hands tightened on hers. "But make no mistakes I am thrilled you're here."

Lila wanted to believe that so badly, but she felt like she had whiplash from Christian's attitude changes. First, he liked her, then he ended things, then he was cruel, and now he was telling her he had done it all because he cared about her enough to want to protect her.

But she had dropped a major bombshell on him, one that had taken her a whole lot longer to accept than he seemed to have taken. It was like they had just glossed over the whole they were having a baby thing.

"Don't *you* need some time to come to terms with everything?" she asked hesitantly.

Christian reached out and picked up the pregnancy test from where he'd put it on the large table. His grin was huge, his eyes sparkling as he looked at it in wonder. "A baby. Totally out of left field but I'm thrilled. How do you feel about it?"

"It was a shock, but I definitely want to keep the baby," she said, feeling defensive again. Just because Christian seemed happy didn't mean he was. He'd already played with her emotions once, and now she couldn't quite believe he wouldn't do it again.

"How far along are you?"

"About eight weeks."

"So, we pretty much got pregnant the very first time. That means I have seven months to make up for the last four weeks and earn your trust back."

"You want to be in the baby's life?" That was best case scenario as far as she was concerned, especially now she knew that Christian hadn't wanted to hurt her but had been trying to save her life.

"Sweetheart, I want to be part of *both* of your lives. Can you forgive me?" Christian's smile dropped, and he looked genuinely upset by the idea that she might say no.

"I have to be honest," Lila started, feeling Christian's hands tighten almost convulsively on hers. "It might take me a little while to trust you again, but I understand why you did what you did, and I won't hold it against you. We can get back to where we were." Lila knew in her heart what she'd just said was true. What he'd done had hurt her, but she honestly couldn't say that if their positions were reversed, she wouldn't do the exact same thing.

"I won't let you down again," Christian vowed. Lifting one of his hands, he cupped her cheek, and Lila found she automatically tilted her face into the contact. As his thumb brushed across her bottom lip his eyes met hers, the question in them clear.

When she nodded, he closed the distance between them, his lips capturing hers. The kiss was soft, sweet, and full of feeling, but she could also tell that Christian was holding back, not wanting to push her too hard too soon.

Wanting—needing—more, Lila grabbed his shoulders, dragging him closer and deepening the kiss. Following her lead, Christian tilted her head to get a better angle, his tongue sweeping inside her mouth.

The pain and anger of the last month began to fade, and Lila realized just how much she had come to care about Christian. Losing him had been like losing a part of herself, and now she had it back, and she was almost giddy with happiness and relief.

"I already love our baby," she whispered when he finally drew back.

"That's because you're going to be the best mama bear," Christian said, touching his forehead to hers. "This little baby bear is so lucky to have you as its mama."

Tears filled her eyes. He had no idea how badly she needed to hear those words. Her parents hadn't cared about her at all no matter how much they had pretended to the outside world that she was the sun, moon, and stars of their universe. Lila had major doubts about her ability to be a good mom, but nobody would love this little one more than she would.

Except maybe the man looking at her so tenderly.

"I know it's a lot to ask, but I need you to consider moving here to stay with the rest of my teams' families," Christian said, taking her hand in one of his while the other scooped up the pregnancy test.

"The threat is really that great?"

"Honey, the only reason I would have broken both our hearts was if I was afraid for your life. Yeah, the threat is credible, and I'd feel much better having you here where I know you and the baby are safe. If you're not comfortable with the idea, you can stay at my place or I can stay at yours. Bottom line is, you're not staying alone. If you don't want it to be me I'll ask my boss to assign you a bodyguard."

Lila shivered. He'd mentioned a threat, but she hadn't realized it was this dangerous. No wonder Christian hadn't wanted to drag her into this mess. There was no way she wanted some stranger watching over her. She'd had enough of that for a lifetime. So, it was either Christian's place with him, her place with him, or here with the other families.

Families she hadn't met yet because Christian hadn't wanted to introduce them when they'd been together. She'd thought it was a little odd, but she'd also thought that given the issues he was dealing with, he'd wanted to protect this special little spark growing between them.

"I would be prepared to stay here if that's what you think is best," she said.

Relief filled his face. "Thank you. I don't want anything to happen to my girls."

"Girls?"

Christian grinned and shrugged. "I have a fifty percent chance of being right. It's gotta be a girl or a boy."

"Ha ha." She rolled her eyes as she laughed at his lame joke, tension fading out of her body. This was the Christian she knew and had been falling for.

"Let's go meet the others." Keeping his hold on her hand, Christian led her across the lobby and into the lifts. They went up to the sixth floor and into an apartment that was bustling with people.

A pretty redhead lay on the couch, and a woman with wild dark curls had a gurgling baby balanced on her hip while she leaned over a little girl with long blonde locks sitting in front of a computer. Another woman, this one a blonde, was also watching over the child. Four burly guys and a pretty brunette were sitting around a table, and a man with dark hair and black eyes was fussing over the woman on the couch.

It was the redhead who spotted them first. She grinned, clapped her hands, and gently pushed away the man at her side. "You have to be Lila. I'm so glad you're here. Surf hasn't been the same since he broke up with you. We all hated to see him suffering, and no one liked the idea of you being hurt, but we also didn't want you in danger."

"Julia, hush, you're going to scare him off," the man beside her said, sounding bemused.

"Oh, come on, Dom, you can't tell me we haven't all been itching to meet her since she dropped her bombshell and literally got Surf down on his knees apologizing. I should have made you do that for me after you acted all stupid and pushed me away." Julia swatted playfully at Dom.

"I would have loved to see you down on your knees when you messed up with me," the woman with the dark skin and curls said to a big, burly, growly-looking man, who smiled indulgently at her and stood to go and take the baby from her arms.

"I think I would have been the one who had to get down on my knees for you, Asher," the blonde said.

"Daddy would have thought that was funny," the little girl said, giggling.

"My guy knows that's the only way to apologize," the brunette said, tweaking the cheek of the man sitting beside her.

"I don't remember that," he said, clearly fighting a grin.

"Well, I definitely remember you on your knees in my office, telling me how deeply you regretted …"

"Okay, okay," the man said, pulling the woman into his lap and silencing her with a kiss.

Christian rolled his eyes at his team and their families. "I think what these guys are trying to say is welcome to our crazy little family."

Lila smiled and introduced herself to everyone as they all came forward to greet her. Everyone was friendly. They all smiled, seemed genuinely happy to meet her, congratulated her on her pregnancy, and told her how Christian hadn't been himself this last month. While hearing that definitely helped her to believe he really hadn't wanted to hurt her and had been doing what he thought was best, there was a rock of fear sitting in her gut.

Her childhood had been difficult, even though no one would believe that, and even though she hadn't been planning on having kids, if she'd ever wanted to, she would have wanted them to have the complete opposite upbringing to what she had. But now she was pregnant, and her baby was going to be born into a world where it was being hunted just because someone had a grudge against its daddy.

How could she keep her baby safe when she hadn't ever been able to protect herself?

And could she trust her baby's father not just to keep them alive but also never to hurt her again?

CHAPTER FOUR

November 14th
8:24 P.M.

His gaze tracked her no matter where in the room she was.

Surf couldn't seem to keep his eyes off Lila.

Not only was she breathtakingly beautiful, but she seemed to have slipped into his team without a single bump along the way. It was so seamless he wondered why he hadn't introduced her to the guys and their partners before.

Maybe it was because what Lila gave him was so sweet, so precious, so important to his healing as he struggled to cope with what had happened in Somalia that he had wanted to keep it all to himself. It was selfish of him. Because he'd kept her separate from the rest of his life it had been easier to cut her out of it rather than risk her like Bear, Mouse, Arrow, and Domino were forced to risk the women they loved.

Now he realized he hadn't been protecting her, he'd actually left her alone and in potential danger.

If anyone had connected her to him, she would have been alone and vulnerable if Dark Beauty sent someone after her. If anything had happened to her, it would have been entirely on him, and he never would have forgiven himself.

"Relax, man, she's here and she's safe," Arrow soothed.

"She fit right in with all of us. She's quiet but intelligent, and she hasn't hesitated to assert herself when needed," Mouse added. "Lolly and Phoebe both like her already."

"Mackenzie too. And Mikey. She's been peppering Kenzie with questions about babies, pregnancy, and birth. Mackenzie loves sharing everything she's learned so far about being a mom," Bear said.

"Phoebe is excited that there will only be a few months separating our baby and yours, Bear's too, they'll all grow up together. You guys had better hurry up and get reproducing," Mouse said with a teasing smile to Arrow and Domino.

Domino looked horrified by the prospect of babies. The man had come a long way since he met his fiancée. Julia had helped him learn to face his emotions rather than run from them. Given the fact that Domino had been raised by the head of the Russian Bratva, it was no wonder the idea of kids scared him. "For now, I think I just want to focus on Julia healing from her injuries. Then maybe once we're married we can talk about kids."

"Piper and I talked about it," Arrow admitted. "We want to get married as soon as this mess is cleared up, then both of us would like to start a family. You guys are getting us all broody."

"Lila turning up pregnant when we used protection is a shock, but not a bad one. I can't believe that in seven months I'm going to be a father." It hadn't sunk in yet, but as it did, he found he was getting more excited. There was a lot to do, a lot to prepare for, but for the moment he wanted to keep his focus on regaining Lila's trust.

"If you need any practice with babies, you can babysit Mikey any time you want," Bear offered with a desperation that said their team leader was a little anxious for some alone time with his wife.

"I think Lila would like that. And I can get used to changing diapers," he said, making a face. Those things were perhaps the most disgusting thing God had ever created.

Brick laughed and slapped him on the back. "Good luck with that, brother."

Of all of them, Brick was the only one now not involved. Surf didn't even have to think about things to know that Lila was it for him.

To be honest, he had known it from the second he laid eyes on her.

Not love at first sight perse, more a deep cosmic understanding that this woman was the other half of him.

There was no other way to explain it. It was why he had been willing to risk losing her to protect her from the threat hanging over him. But now she was back and pregnant, and he would never let either of them go again.

"I don't need luck, dude. I already had the best luck in the world when that woman ran into me that day." There was understanding in the eyes of the other guys, even Brick's which surprised him. That man was like a vault, getting anything out of him was next to impossible. But if Brick had known love and it had slipped through his fingers, Surf had nothing but empathy for him.

He'd come so close to having the same thing happen to him, and he wasn't letting anything mess up this second chance.

"I'm going to go get her settled into our apartment, she looks exhausted," he announced as he pushed away from the table where he and his team had been doing another fruitless search for the elusive Dark Beauty.

"We'll get them, Surf," Domino vowed. As personal as this was for all of them since Domino's brother had set the whole plot in motion, Surf knew no one wanted this finished more than Domino. He had been the one to end Kristoff's life and so technically the reason why they were all now in danger from Kristoff's girlfriend, partner, lover, whoever Dark Beauty was. If any of them got hurt, he knew his friend would take it hard.

"Yeah, we will," he agreed. Crossing over to the couches where the women were talking, he rested a hand on Lila's shoulder. "You ready to go get settled in?"

"Sure. It has been so nice getting to know you all," Lila said to Mackenzie, Phoebe, Piper, and Julia.

"You're going to get to spend a *lot* more time with us over the next few weeks," Phoebe said with a grin.

"I'm kind of glad to have another pregnant woman here, it's scary. Exciting though," Lila said, glancing up at him. More of the wariness had faded from her eyes, and he felt the old Lila starting to come back to him. It might take a little time, but he was sure they could get back to what they'd had before.

After saying their goodnights, he led her out of Mouse and Phoebe's apartment and up a floor to the one he had been staying in. Prey had a total of ten apartments over five floors. Mostly they were used as safehouses, although from time to time they were also used for visitors or clients of Prey.

To give them all some privacy, each team member had taken an apartment on a different floor, with him and Brick sharing the same floor since neither of them was involved.

Now, not only did he have a girlfriend but a baby on the way.

"Eagle had someone go to your place and pack up some things. He said let him know what else you want or need and he'll have it brought here," he told her as he led her inside the apartment. She'd met Eagle and the rest of the Oswald siblings earlier. Hawk and his wife Maddy had been particularly excited to meet her because Maddy had also shown up at Prey out of the blue and dropped the bomb of a pregnancy on Hawk. Now the two were happily married with two-year-old Louie and were expecting their second child around Christmas.

Actually, a few Oswald babies were due over the next couple of months. Eagle and his wife Olivia were six months pregnant with their second child. Sparrow and her husband Ethan were also expecting their second, Irish twins because their son Ryder would be eleven months old when the baby arrived next month. Youngest Oswald sibling Dove and her husband Isaac were also due in a few months, the couple was expecting triplets.

"That was nice of him," Lila said. Things felt a little awkward between them. It was the first time they had been alone together since he introduced her to his team, and while he knew it would take time for things to go back to the way they'd been before he missed their closeness.

"I'm sorry, Lila. I hate that I hurt you." When he reached out to smooth a lock of silky blonde hair behind her ear, she didn't flinch away from him.

"I know that, Christian." She lifted her hand and covered his. "I understand why you did it, it sucked, but I can't fault you for trying to protect me. I just need to know you won't do it again. I can't let myself continue to fall for you if I'm constantly afraid that something will happen and you'll push me away again."

"Oh, baby. No. I would never do that again.. I couldn't. It about killed me last time. I don't want to be away from you again. Ever. I think you feel the same way."

"I do," she whispered.

"Life with me won't be easy. My job means I can get called away with no notice, what we do is dangerous, and there's no set timeframe. I could be gone a couple of days, or I could be gone weeks, or sometimes even months. I won't be able to talk about a lot of what I do, and I won't always be able to be here for special moments. Birthdays, anniversaries, holidays, recitals, or football games, I'll miss a lot of it. You'll be a single mom a lot of the time."

Lila gave him a one-sided smile. "You trying to convince me to walk away from this?"

His fingers tangled in her hair. "No, sweetheart. I just want you to be sure. Life with me will be hard, but I can promise you something. When I'm home I am one hundred percent yours. I will give you everything I have."

"You're talking like you already know what our future looks like."

"I do, Lila. I think you do too. You knew the moment you saw me, just like I did." Stepping closer, he slipped an arm around her waist and drew her against him. When her gaze dropped to his lips and the tip of her tongue darted out to wet hers, Surf groaned. "I need to taste you."

"What are you waiting for?"

Nothing.

There was nothing between them anymore. She was his, he was hers, and as he touched his lips to hers it felt like the entire universe shifted into place around them.

This was exactly where he was supposed to be.

* * * * *

November 15th
5:57 A.M.

Lila woke with her stomach churning.

Great.

Another morning another round of morning sickness.

Stumbling from the bed, it took her a moment to realize she wasn't in her bedroom at her apartment. It took a moment longer to remember that she was at Prey Security, in the apartment that Christian had been staying in. And another precious moment to remember where the bathroom was.

Her stomach revolted, and Lila pressed a hand to her mouth, praying she would keep everything down until she reached the bathroom. Not bothering to waste seconds closing the door, she flung up the toilet lid and dropped to her knees seconds before last night's dinner came back up.

This was not fun.

At all.

Morning sickness was supposed to ease by the second trimester, which was still four weeks away. Right now, it didn't feel like she would make it.

The sound of running water drew her attention, and Lila turned her head. Looking through blurry eyes, she saw Christian standing at the sink, running a washcloth under the water.

"What are you doing?" she asked blearily. Her head was throbbing, her stomach screaming that it wasn't finished with her yet, and she felt unrested. Last night Christian had suggested they stay in separate bedrooms until he'd earned her trust back enough that she was ready to take the next step.

That all sounded good in theory, but that kiss they'd shared—a kiss that managed to be both sweet and fiery at the same time—had left her turned on and her body needy, desperate for the touch of the man who had brought it so much pleasure. It had been on the tip of her tongue to tell him that she was ready to sleep with him—in every sense of the word—but she'd held back only because she wasn't really sure that she was. Understanding why he'd done what he did and coming to terms with it and trusting he wouldn't do it again were two different things.

Still, all night she had been restless, her dreams filled with sexy times with Christian. Each time she woke unfulfilled and more desperate for his touch than she'd been the time before.

"Taking care of you," Christian replied, crouching beside her. "You done?"

"For now."

Helping her move back a little away from the toilet, he blotted at her sweat-streaked face with the washcloth, then draped it over her forehead while he moved behind her and pulled her hair back into a ponytail for her. He was so sweet, her heart clenched, her stomach fluttered, and instinctively she leaned toward him.

"I got you, mama bear," he murmured, voice low and soothing, washing over her in a wave of tranquility. Wrapping an arm around her shoulders, he touched his lips to her temple before scooping her into his arms.

"I don't think I can go back to sleep," Lila told him when he carried her back into the bedroom.

"That's okay. You just rest here and let me take care of everything else." Setting her on the mattress, he leaned her forward against his arm as he fluffed the pillows and propped them against the headboard. His touch was gentle as he eased her back to rest against them, and any lingering doubts she still had melted away.

How could she not fall for a man who was warrior enough to protect her any way he had to—and she truly believed it had been as hard for him as it had for her—and gentle enough to take care of her?

Christian pulled the covers up, tucked her in, then switched on the lamp on the nightstand. "Be right back."

When he went to leave, Lila caught his hand, holding him in place. Feeling emotional and a little weepy, she couldn't stop a couple of tears from falling free. "Thank you."

With warmth in his eyes, he sat beside her. "You never have to thank me for taking care of you. That's my job. Mama bear, baby bear." One of his large hands covered her stomach. "Papa bear. There isn't anything I wouldn't do for either one of you."

His sweet words made her tears tumble faster down her cheeks. "I know you said I don't have to thank you, but I'm going to. Thank you. For caring about me, for wanting this baby. Sorry I'm a weepy mess."

"Hormones, babe. You got this, and I'm here every step of the way. You're not doing this alone. You have me, and you have my whole team. We're a family and we have your back."

Unlike her own family.

She didn't fit in there, but maybe she could fit in here.

Everyone had been so nice and welcoming. The guys were a little scary en masse, but beneath the muscles and the warrior attitudes, she sensed they were softies who cared about their family. A family they were willing to make her part of.

Her heart swelled with love. Not just for this man watching her so tenderly, but his whole extended family too. They were all wonderful people, and she was excited to have a real family for the first time in her life.

She and Christian hadn't talked about their families in the

month they'd spent together, but she knew they were going to have to sit down and she would have to tell him who she really was. Well, who she had been, she wasn't that woman anymore, never really had been. Lila had played the role she'd been given until she'd found a way out.

Now she was out, free, and had a future with Christian and their baby.

"Can I say it?" Lila asked softly. It was so soon, and yet she'd known from the moment her gaze met Christian's that he was hers. She didn't even believe in love at first sight. Hadn't even been sure she believed in love at all, but then she met this man, and Cupid shot an arrow straight through her heart and everything else was a forgone conclusion.

"Unless you want me to beat you to it." Christian's eyes sparkled with a mixture of love, affection, and cheeky amusement.

"I think I'm falling in love with you. I think I started falling that very first day. Does that make me crazy?"

"If you're crazy then I'm following you onto the crazy train."

"Really?" It was comforting to know she wasn't the only one developing such strong feelings so quickly. The weeks they'd spent together had been the best of her life. Not what people who knew her in the past would believe. They hadn't been glamorous or elegant, filled with expensive gifts or trips. But they had been real.

More real than anything else she had experienced.

There had been genuine talks, connections forged, and they'd played games and had picnics in the park. Christian had been funny and romantic. He'd taken her out for pizza and ice cream dates, snuggled on the couch watching movies, brought her flowers and chocolates, and even endured a marathon shopping trip with her. Everything that Christian gave her was exactly what she had always wanted.

"More than really, darlin'. What we have is real. As real as it gets. It wasn't something I was expecting to find or even wanting to find, but it found us, and I couldn't be happier. I didn't know I wanted you, sweetheart, but I know that I need you." He curled a hand around the back of her neck and lowered his head.

Quickly she pushed him away. "We can't kiss, Christian. I just threw up, will probably throw up at least a couple more times this morning."

Christian laughed and kissed her forehead instead. "Nothing could make me not want to kiss you, darlin', but you wait right here, rest, call me if you're going to be sick again. I'm going to go and make you some breakfast."

"I might not be able to keep it down," Lila warned.

"I missed out on four weeks of being there for you, I have a lot to make up for. But I am here by your side from here on out. Wild horses couldn't drag me away from you."

"No wild horses, huh?"

"None. If you can't eat that's fine, but I need to take care of you. I already looked into remedies for morning sickness, ginger, crackers, there are these acupressure wristbands that relieve seasickness that have been shown to reduce nausea and vomiting during pregnancy, I ordered some." There was a thread of desperation in his tone like this need to be there for her ran deeper than she could understand.

Maybe he had his secrets like she had hers.

Secrets she was going to have to share with him sooner or later.

It wasn't like she could keep them forever.

Assuming he proposed to her at some point, they would need to get a marriage license, and when they did, he would learn her full name and who she really was.

Once he did it could change everything.

Maybe she could keep her secrets just a little longer.

Enjoy this journey as long as it lasted.

"Of course, you can take care of me. Nothing would make me happier."

CHAPTER FIVE

November 15th
2:40 P.M.

"So, is there some hidden meaning to your nickname? You never told me what it was before so I never really thought about it."

Surf took his eyes off the road for a second to throw a glance at Lila. Even though he hadn't liked the idea, she'd asked to go to her apartment to pack some more things since she'd be staying with him and the rest of his team and their families at Prey until this was over. Security wise it wasn't the smartest move. He wanted Lila and their unborn baby where he knew they were safe and protected. Realistically, she had been extremely accommodating, even agreeing to take leave from her job, so he hadn't thought it was fair to tell her no when she asked.

"Sorry to disappoint you, darlin', but there is no hidden meaning. I grew up in California and taught myself to surf when I was about six. I loved it, even thought about going pro for a while as a teen." Surfing had been more than just a hobby for him, it had been the only thing that had kept him sane. Alone out there, surrounded by nothing but the wildness and freedom of the ocean, it had been the only place he'd felt safe. That was all that had kept him … alive, if he was completely honest.

Without those hours out riding the waves, he would have succumbed to the pressures of gangs, drugs, and a life of crime.

Instead, he'd gotten out, and Surf truly believed it was because of his love of surfing and the ocean.

Lila didn't know about his past, about how he'd grown up, no one did. Sooner or later, he would have to tell her. He wanted a future with this woman and their baby, wanted to marry her and grow old by her side. It was only fair that he not keep any secrets from her.

"Aww, that's a shame. I was kind of hoping there was some great story behind it," she teased, amusement dancing brightly in her blue eyes. Things had been getting better between them with each hour they spent together. They were teasing one another, laughing, and talking. It felt like it had before.

Before he'd broken things off with Lila, he'd been trying to keep things simple, move slowly. He hadn't been ready to tell his team he'd met the woman he knew he was going to marry, and they hadn't known each other long, he hadn't wanted to scare her off.

Now that they were having a baby, he didn't feel like he had to hold back.

It was time to offer her everything he had.

When they got back to the apartment, he was going to sit her down and tell her everything. It was time to stop hiding from his past. It was what it was, he couldn't change it, but running from it was a never-ending battle. You couldn't change who you were or where you came from, but he liked the person he was now. He had nothing to be ashamed of.

"You have any nicknames, darlin'?" he asked, switching his attention to the rear-view mirror. So far, they hadn't picked up a tail, but that didn't mean they wouldn't. Dark Beauty knew where they were staying, she had to, and she'd had him followed just a few weeks ago. She was biding her time, waiting. But for what?

"Umm, not really," Lila said slowly.

Something in her voice had him turning to look at her. Anxiety had replaced amusement, and suddenly instead of being relaxed the atmosphere in the vehicle became tense.

Why would a simple question about nicknames make her so upset?

Splitting his attention between the road, their surroundings, and the woman beside him, Surf reached over and covered her hands with one of his. She had hers twisted together so tightly he was sure she was going to dislocate her fingers. "Lila? What's going on, sweetheart? What has you all upset?"

"There's something I need to tell you," Lila replied in a small voice.

"You can tell me anything, honey. You know that. I won't ever judge you, and nothing you say can change how I feel about you. Nothing." Surf felt that deep in his soul. The only thing she might be able to say that would change anything was that she was already married. He didn't do married women. Ever. Not even when he'd been on his sex binge. But Lila wasn't married.

Was she?

She hadn't gotten upset until they'd started talking about nicknames. Was she afraid to tell him that her name wasn't Lila Angeletti? Or that Angeletti was her married name and not the one she'd been born with?

"Christian, I know I should have told you, I meant to, but I was scared of losing you, so I didn't. But I want to be completely honest with you now." Lila drew in a long, ragged breath that had tension coiling tightly in his gut. "Lila is …"

The hit came out of nowhere.

His attention diverted from watching for a tail because he had been so worried about what Lila was about to tell him, Surf hadn't noticed the other vehicle until it slammed into them.

A horrible sense of déjà vu hit.

Two months ago, he had been driving Julia when they'd been ambushed by the Mikhailov Bratva. He'd fought them off for as long as he could, killed over a dozen of them, but it hadn't been enough.

Julia had been taken. Kristoff Mikhailov had assaulted and tortured her before he, Domino, and the rest of their team could get to her. Julia had then been injured further when Dark Beauty blew up the building with Julia and Domino inside it.

He had failed her that day and was yet to forgive himself for it.

No way was he failing again today.

Not when the life of the woman he loved was hanging in the balance.

"Get down," he ordered, already pulling out his weapon. They'd been hit in the side, shoving them sideways and into a parked car, which blocked his door. Someone would have already called 911 to report the accident, and they weren't far from Prey.

Help would be here soon. All he had to do was hold them off until then.

"Christian?" Lila's terrified voice called his name, and he spared a quick second to toss what he hoped was a reassuring smile at her.

"It's going to be okay. I won't let anyone hurt you. You just hold on for me, okay, mama bear?"

"Okay." Her voice was shaky, but she was holding it together. She'd got down between her seat and the dashboard, curled into a small ball.

Men piled out of the vehicle that had rammed them, and several other black SUVs with tinted windows had pulled up around them as well.

An ambush.

They'd been waiting for him.

Which meant they knew he had left Prey at some point today. The first time he or his team had been out of the building in two weeks.

Coincidence?

No, he didn't believe in coincidence.

Had they been watching the building or had someone tipped them off?

Was someone at Prey working against them?

Everyone who worked at Prey was thoroughly vetted, but it had happened before, and it could happen again.

Their vehicle was as bulletproof as a vehicle could be, but the men approaching were firing relentlessly at them.

Hurry up and get here, he silently yelled at his team.

A man walked up and stuck something to the front of the car.

A bomb.

Damn.

Thirty seconds.

As soon as they strapped it to his vehicle the men retreated.

They'd left him no choice.

It was either stay here and get blown up or run.

"Lila, get out of the car," he ordered.

"Did they go?" she asked, not hesitating to do as he asked.

"Just run." The last thing he needed was for her to panic.

Lila scrambled out of the car, and he followed her out her door, not wanting any distance between them. He hated being forced into this position, but he had no choice but to take her out into an ambush they would likely not survive, but at least this gave them a chance.

Snatching Lila into his arms, Surf ran, knowing they'd never make it.

The blast would be big enough only to take out the immediate area around the vehicle. He could see where the men had positioned themselves but knew he'd never make it there in time.

He was mere yards away from safety when it hit.

Curling his body protectively around Lila's he prayed that she and the baby would survive. Surf would give his life in a heartbeat for theirs, but he had no control over what happened next.

They were both lifted into the air by the concussive blast and then slammed down again into the concrete.

The world began to fade to black, and Surf's last conscious thought was that once again he had failed.

Failed the woman he loved and his unborn child.

* * * * *

November 15th
6:19 P.M.

Groggy.

Confused.

Heavy.

Lila felt so heavy.

Like her blood had been turned into concrete.

Pain drummed through her head, and when she tried to blink open her eyes, she found everything around her was fuzzy.

There was an insistent humming that felt like a bug trying to burrow inside her brain, and with a horrible realization, Lila found she was on a plane.

The world spun around her, making her nauseous, and instinctive fear for her baby yanked her out of the fog she was engulfed in.

Memories flooded her mind. She had been about to spill her secret to Christian when all of a sudden, their car had been hit. Men had been shooting at them, and then they'd put a bomb on the car. Christian hadn't told her that, just to get out of the car, but she knew from what she'd been told that Kristoff Mikhailov had used bombs, and these people were carrying on his plans.

Plus, she remembered the terrifying sensation of being lifted into the air and slammed back down into the ground.

Christian had done his best to protect her, but the force of the blow had knocked them both unconscious.

She knew that because unconsciousness was the only thing that would have prevented him from saving her.

Was he dead?

At the thought, her breathing quickened to the point she was hyperventilating, and the world began to spin around her all over again. The spinning seemed to get faster and faster until it felt like she was on a carousel, and it wanted to throw her right off.

"Would you shut her up? That panting sound is annoying," a female voice snapped. Was this Kristoff Mikhailov's Dark Beauty? The woman and her vow of vengeance was the reason that Christian had broken things off with her so Lila hated her for that fact alone.

"How exactly do you expect me to do that?" a male asked. There was something familiar about that voice. Something that had the churning in her stomach growing worse.

"I expect you to figure it out," the woman growled.

"Fine," the man huffed, and through her blurry vision, Lila saw him rise out of the seat opposite hers.

He was coming toward her.

She shrunk back into her seat as though it had the power to protect her and blinked to clear her vision.

Immediately she wished she hadn't.

The man coming toward her was someone she knew.

Not just someone.

He was the man who still haunted her nightmares. Haunted a lot of her waking moments as well. He was why she had fled from her home and the world she had been raised in, seeking freedom and a new life.

A new life she'd built for herself, a life that was slipping through her fingers, disappearing as her old life dug its claws into her and pulled her back.

Why was he here?

Did this have nothing to do with Dark Beauty and the plot to overthrow the government?

Was it about her and her past?

Was it her fault Christian had been hurt or even killed?

If that was the case, Lila knew she would never forgive herself. Without Christian and everything she had worked so hard to build for herself, how would she resist being sucked back into the life her parents had wanted for her?

No.

She had to be strong.

For her baby.

She had to do whatever it took to get away, to get back to Christian. No way would she allow her baby to be thrown into the world she had fought so hard and for so long to escape.

This baby was everything to her and very possibly all she had left of the man she was falling in love with.

Air was still wheezing in and out of her chest. Lila was powerless to do anything about it, especially as the man leaned down so his face was close enough that she could feel his hot breath against her skin. The feel of it and the smell of it threw her back in time, to months of her life she desperately wanted to forget.

When he reached out to lay his disgusting hand on her shoulder, her swirling nausea peaked, and she threw up.

"Eww, she vomited all over herself!" the man shrieked, sounding very much like a little girl instead of a fully grown man in his late sixties.

The woman laughed, and Lila realized that she recognized that voice too.

Turning her head, she saw the man's wife sitting in a plush leather seat next to the one the man had occupied. Jet black hair hung down her back, huge eyes as dark as midnight, and long black lashes fanning out against paper-pale skin. Was it possible that this woman was in fact Dark Beauty, and that Lila's own past was somehow connected to this plot?

Her head spun, and when the man backhanded her, she plummeted dangerously close to unconsciousness.

Valiantly she clung to consciousness, the idea of being completely vulnerable to the pair was enough to make her almost throw up again.

"I'm not sitting here with her stinking like that for the rest of the flight," the man snapped.

The woman merely continued to laugh.

"Stop it," he growled. "I mean it, she stinks."

"Then take her clothes off," the woman said like it was the most obvious thing in the world.

"I'll have to remove the cuffs."

"So? We're on a plane. Where exactly is she going to go?"

"I suppose," the man whined. Had he been this pathetic when she'd known him before?

Lila honestly couldn't remember. Back then she had just been terrified of him, of what her parents wanted her to do with him, of what he wanted to do to her. Nothing else had registered.

"I don't want to touch her," the man whined again. "Can't they do it?" He nodded at two other men, big burly men dressed all in black who occupied seats in the row behind where the woman was sitting.

"They're bodyguards nor nursemaids. Stop being such a baby. Cut the cuffs off her and have her take her own clothes off. She can put them in one of the garbage bags," the woman told him.

"We don't have anything else to dress her in."

"Who cares?" Apparently losing interest in the whole thing, the woman lifted her iPad and turned her attention to it.

Old memories had her drawing away as the man leaned over her, his fingers lingering on her skin as he cut the zip ties binding her wrists together. The plastic had cut into her skin, and her wrists were smeared with blood.

The sight of it brought back more horrific memories.

Memories of blood smeared between her legs as this man climbed off her assaulted her mind, adding to the raging pain in her head.

It might have been fourteen years ago, but from the strength of her fears and emotions it felt like only yesterday.

Worse than this man raping her had been knowing that he was in her life because her parents had decided to marry her off to him. She'd been only sixteen, he'd been in his fifties. The absurdity of that hadn't occurred to them because they were concerned only with perceptions, appearances, and what the wealthy man could do for them. They hadn't cared about her at all, she wasn't even a consideration.

She'd never been a consideration, just a prop.

A prop to be used to further her parents' goals.

A prop for this man and his sick fantasies of having a young wife. A teenage wife.

His hand curled around her elbow, pulling her up and out of her seat. The fact that his touch was gentle, almost sensual in the way his thumb brushed across her skin, it felt like a lover's touch, and that churned her stomach up all over again.

Freaking out, Lila slapped at his hands and yanked herself away. Tripping over her feet, she went down on her knees in front of the woman.

Lifting her gaze, the woman fixed her in a glare, then lifted her foot, touched the heel to Lila's shoulder and shoved, sending her sprawling backward.

"Get up," the man ordered, standing above her, holding out a trash bag. "Strip and put your clothes in here."

The very last thing Lila wanted to do was make herself more vulnerable by removing her clothes, but what choice did she have? They were on a plane, going who knows where. Christian, if he was still alive, and his team would be looking for her but who knew how long it would take them to find her. There was zero chance of escape right now, zero chance anyone was coming riding in to her rescue.

If she wanted to live, to protect her baby, then for now she had to do as she was told.

Tears trickled down her cheeks as she removed her sweater, sneakers, jeans, and socks, dropping everything into the bag, leaving her in just her bra and panties.

Lila shivered when the man's eyes roamed over her near-naked body, and it had nothing to do with being cold.

She was trapped with the man who had stolen something from

her she could never get back when he had raped her, and a woman with plans to take over the world and a vendetta against the man Lila loved. She was pretty sure it wasn't possible for things to get any worse than this.

CHAPTER SIX

November 16th
4:37 A.M.

Guilt and terror dug their claws into Surf's skin.

With each second that ticked by his anxiety racked up several degrees.

How much longer could he go on before he completely lost it and fell apart?

No.

He couldn't afford to fall apart.

Lila was out there somewhere, alone and scared, possibly hurt, wondering where he was and praying he would come for her.

There was no way he could let her down.

No way.

Failing her meant losing not just the woman he already knew he wanted to spend the rest of his life with but also their unborn baby. No way could he live knowing that he lost both of them.

"Why don't you sit," Bear suggested in a voice that made it sound more like an order.

"Can't. Too wired."

After he'd regained consciousness on the street after the explosion to find that Lila was gone and the cars with the men who had attacked them were speeding off down the street, he'd tried to pursue them. With a concussion and cuts and bruises all over his body, he hadn't made it far.

By the time his team and cops had shown up it was already too late.

They were long gone.

Refusing to waste time at a hospital while Lila and their baby's lives hung in the balance, he had been patched up by Arrow and all of them had returned to Prey. They'd been here ever since, going over security footage. Eagle Oswald, founder and CEO of Prey Security, had pulled in everyone on his cyber team, run by his sister Raven and wife Olivia. There wasn't a single person at Prey who didn't take this plot to overthrow the government personally. The second Storm Gallagher had gone after Dove Oswald—now Dove Anderson as she'd married Isaac a few months back—it had become personal to Prey. With each attack it only made them more determined to take down everyone involved.

Even though Surf was surrounded by people he had never felt this alone in his life.

Loneliness wasn't a new feeling to him. His childhood had been brutal. Ruled by gangs and addictions, father murdered in front of him when he was four, men in and out of his drug-addicted mother's life. Abuse on a good day, what could only be considered torture on a bad one. It had taken everything he had to fight his way out of that life. He'd wanted more from his future than dying in a gang war or overdosing.

Joining the military was his salvation, but Lila had brought something into his life that he hadn't experienced before.

True love.

They might have tiptoed around their feelings, chosen their words carefully, claiming they were only falling in love, but they both knew it was more than that. They had already fallen.

The love he had for his teammates was different. He would die for them. They shared a deep friendship, a brotherhood, a bond that had been born in blood and bullets, one that could never be broken. But what he had with Lila ran so much deeper.

Now it could be gone.

"Surf, sit," Bear ordered.

"Can't," he repeated. "Something isn't right here."

"We'll do everything we can to find her," Arrow assured him.

"We're reviewing footage searching for anything that will tell us who they are," Raven Oswald assured him. The woman was a warrior if ever there was one. She had battled armed men as a teenager to protect her younger siblings, survived losing her three-year-old daughter, and scoured the globe to get her child back and taken down a human trafficking ring in the process. And now she was happily married to the man she loved with two beautiful children.

If there was anyone who could find a clue that would help them find Lila it was computer genius Raven.

Yet he wasn't reassured.

"The answers aren't out there," he said, restlessness flowing through his veins. "They're in here somewhere."

"Here at Prey?" Eagle asked, his blue eyes sharp, anger simmering beneath the surface of his calm exterior. The man was heavy on responsibility and very protective of everyone at Prey. Since he and Lila were together that made her one of them, and Eagle would go all out to get her back.

"What are the chances the first time we leave the building in weeks we get ambushed?" he demanded.

"They were likely watching the building," Mouse said.

"No, we didn't pick up a tail when we left, and it would have been easier for them to take us out at Lila's apartment," he countered.

"Would have been safer too," Domino said slowly. "My brother's men were highly trained and smart. An ambush on the street like that had way too many variables. Too many people, could have been cops nearby, we were close by. And using a bomb like that was risky. They could easily have taken themselves out as well."

"It was like they threw together a plan on the fly because they knew I wasn't here," Surf said, glad Eagle and his team were starting to catch on.

"Okay, let's say you're right," Eagle said slowly, "then that means we have a bigger problem than just Kristoff Mikhailov's Dark Beauty. It would mean we have another mole at Prey."

"I can't think of anyone who would turn, everyone is thoroughly vetted," Olivia Oswald protested, leaning back in her chair to stretch her back. Six months into a difficult pregnancy and there were lines of exhaustion on the woman's pretty face and dark circles under her big blue eyes.

"*You* were a mole at Prey," Eagle reminded her, slipping an arm around his wife's shoulders and touching a kiss to her temple.

Olivia rolled her eyes. "I was working for Falcon, not the same thing. Seriously though, we're so careful with everyone we hire."

"Who's the newest hire?" Brick asked.

"Vivienne Waters," Eagle replied.

"The receptionist," Arrow said thoughtfully.

"What?" Surf asked. If he had a theory, he had to talk it out. They needed to figure this out sooner rather than later because otherwise it would be too late for Lila and their baby.

"She was there when Lila showed up here to tell you she was pregnant, and she wasn't happy about it," Arrow said.

"Vivienne has been flirting with Surf since she started here," Mouse added.

"You've been flirting back," Bear said.

Shoving his fingers through his hair, he didn't want to think of another woman while the one he loved was out there somewhere needing him and he wasn't there for her. "Not seriously flirting. She was here when we got back from Somalia. I slept with her. Sorry, man, I know that's against policy," he said to Eagle, "but I needed sex. It was the only thing keeping me sane." Until Lila.

"Don't care," Eagle said, waving off Surf's apology. "Could she have a grudge against you and want to get rid of the competition?"

"Could make sense," Arrow said. "After all, they took Lila but left you."

"So maybe this is about Surf and Lila, not Kristoff's plot and Dark Beauty," Mouse said.

"I don't think so." Raven's words drew all their attention to the woman staring intently at her computer. "Here, you can all see." After a few taps at her keyboard, Raven brought up an image on the large screen that took up most of one wall.

The image was of the street where he and Lila had been blown up moments before the explosion. They had all already seen the footage, so he had no idea why Raven was showing it to them again. A moment later she brought up a picture of the inside of what looked like a car rental place.

"This was earlier this morning," Raven said. The footage began to roll, and they watched as Vivienne Waters walked up to the counter. "She called herself Layla Waters."

Olivia was the only one who didn't look confused. "It's of Arabic origin, means dark beauty."

"Whoever this Dark Beauty is she has the resources to access a fake driver's license that passed the rental company's checks," Raven added.

"Can you track her through the fake ID?" Eagle asked.

"Raven and I can track anything, but it will take time," Olivia replied.

"Getting answers from Vivienne is your best bet right now," Raven added. "That is Lila's best chance."

Breaking Vivienne might be Lila's *only* chance. And by default, his only chance.

This woman hadn't just wriggled her way inside his heart, she *was* his heart.

It killed him that he had no one to blame but himself. This was all his fault. He should never have allowed her to leave the property. Ever since Olivia had been snatched from the premises security here wasn't just tight it was impossible to breach.

But obsessing over his guilt and what he should have done wasn't going to get Lila back. All he could do was focus on what needed to be done to make sure he got her back home alive and in one piece.

"Let's go pay Vivienne a visit."

* * * * *

November 16th
11:02 A.M.

Falling.

The sensation of falling snapped her out of a drug-induced slumber a second before she hit the ground.

Pain zinged up through her knees, bound wrists, elbows, shoulders, and hips as her already bruised and battered body, limp as it fought its way out of unconsciousness, had no way of protecting itself.

Lila groaned as she rolled onto her side, immediately chilled to the boned. Only then did she realize she was actually on the ground, not the floor of the plane. When the pilot had announced that they were beginning their descent, the man from her past had produced a syringe. After running his hand over her bare skin, he had injected it, and it had been lights out for her.

Until now.

Still dressed in only her bra and panties, she was lying on what felt like hundreds of rocks. It was light, daytime, she could feel the sun on her, but it provided no warmth. Lila was chilled down to her bones, and she knew it wasn't just because she was all but naked and outdoors in the late fall weather.

Where in the world she was she had no idea.

If Christian would find her, she didn't know that either.

Neither could she count on it. For all intents and purposes, she was alone. If she wanted to save herself and her baby, she had to do it herself.

"Get up," the voice from her nightmares ordered. Lila couldn't even bear to think of him by his name. There wasn't a single redeeming quality this man possessed, and if the rest of the world knew that Ross Duffy wasn't who he portrayed himself to be, they would be shocked.

But no one knew. No one ever cared about the truth, only about perception.

"Would you hurry up," the woman called out from somewhere nearby. Lila knew who she was as well. There likely wasn't a single person alive who didn't know either of the couple. Not that it would help her, no one would think to look for her here with them.

"Where are we?" Lila asked as she tried to push to her feet. Near naked as she was, she needed to get inside before the cold made her hypothermic. Right now, she needed to hold on to any advantage she could get, and not succumbing to the cold meant she could at least keep her wits about her.

"So, she speaks after all," the woman sing-songed as though all of this was highly amusing. Was it possible she really was Dark Beauty?

"Switzerland," Ross replied as his hand gently grasped her elbow and helped her to stand.

As badly as she wanted to yank herself free from his grip—his touch, even in a non-sexual manner made her feel ill—right now she wasn't steady enough to stand unassisted let alone walk. The last thing she needed was more injuries. She knew where in Switzerland he meant, and her only hope was to make it out of the house and into the surrounding mountains. From there, she would have to pray she could make it to a town before the elements claimed her.

Her feet were cold and numb, barely feeling the rocks as he led her up the driveway. When they entered the house, the sudden warmth to her frozen skin felt like a million tiny knives stabbing into her.

The contrast of warmth on the outside and cold on the inside threw her body's system into a meltdown. Add in the fact that she had been blown up and knocked unconscious, possibly had a concussion, and had been drugged and she began to tremble violently.

Ross shoved her through the large entry foyer and into the living room on the right. It had been a long time since she'd been here, but she knew there were six exits on the ground floor, Lila prayed she got a chance to use one of them.

As she was pushed into a chair by the fire, she did her best to still the shaking that made her feel like she was going to be shaken apart. The more she fought against it the more her body trembled. Lila clamped her jaws together and pulled her knees up to her chest, wrapping her arms around herself in an attempt to physically hold herself together.

"Would you like to get dressed, darling?" Ross asked, standing before her with a pair of jeans and a cashmere sweater.

The way he said darling made her shivering increase. It sent another wave of nausea rolling through her cramping stomach. When Christian called her darlin' it made her all warm and soft inside, like her blood was heating and desire building. When Ross said it, it made her cold and scared, made her skin crawl.

It took effort to shove away the sensation and nod her head.

"Words, darling, you know I don't like it when you're sulky," Ross said, his tone reprimanding and condescending, making her feel like a child and reminding her of the vast age difference between herself and the man her parents had all but sold her off to.

"Yes, please," she replied. It grated to have to do what Ross ordered, but she wasn't a teenage girl anymore, she was an adult, one who had been free for thirteen years now. This was a long game, not a short one. It wasn't about being belligerent and fighting him every step of the way, it was about getting herself as strong and prepared as possible so that when it was time to act she could.

Lila reached for the clothes, but Ross moved them back, just out of her reach. The smile he gave her was both creepy and sickening, and she knew he was going to take advantage of having her here at his mercy.

Thirteen years ago, he'd had no choice but to let her go. Her threats to go to the cops with proof of her rape had bought her freedom, and she'd enjoyed thirteen years of being in control of her life.

Now she was back.

His victim once again.

"You want the clothes you have to let me dress you," Ross said.

The woman who may or may not be Dark Beauty had followed them into the room. She had a glass of wine in one hand, a book in the other, and was sitting on the other side of the fireplace. "Really, Ross? You are so childish."

He shrugged, not bothering to look at the woman she knew was his wife. It was obvious that he had no issue with lusting after another woman right in front of her, so she had to assume that their marriage was not one of love.

Not that she would have expected differently. Ross wasn't the kind of man who fell in love in the traditional sense of the word, he developed obsessions. If his wife was Dark Beauty, she had been involved with Kristoff Mikhailov. From what she'd said before setting the explosion that had almost killed Domino and Julia, she had been in love with the leader of the Russian Bratva. She didn't seem to care what Ross did any more than Ross cared if she watched.

Everything in her wanted to refuse. Lila would much rather stick to her principles and refuse to let this disgusting lech of a man touch her, but she needed to be dressed. If an opportunity to run presented itself, she would take it.

Practical.

That was the only thing she could afford to be right now.

Principles were only going to get her hurt and if she was too badly hurt she couldn't escape.

All on you, Lila.

That was what she had to keep reminding herself.

Being alone wasn't something new to her but never had it been this hard. The stakes were so high. It wasn't just about her, it was about this little baby she was carrying. Christian's baby.

Maybe her papa bear had imparted a little of his warrior spirit into their baby bear. If she didn't believe in herself then she couldn't do this. Christian would believe in her. He would encourage her, uplift her, and tell her she could do this.

If she didn't believe in herself then she was already dead.

If she was already dead, then her baby was dead too.

And with both of them gone, she had a horrible feeling in her gut that Christian would have nothing left to live for.

Her man and her baby depended on her, and she was not going to let them down.

Jutting out her chin, Lila didn't shy away from meeting Ross' gaze. "You can dress me." She didn't flinch as lust flared in his light brown eyes, and when his hands roamed her body in completely unnecessary touches to put clothes on her, she steadfastly endured.

Lila prayed she had what it took to endure whatever else was coming.

CHAPTER SEVEN

November 16th
2:09 P.M.

This was taking too long.

Every second that passed without a solid lead on who had taken Lila and where they were holding her was another second where she could be hurt.

Surf was nearly paralyzed by thoughts of what could be happening to her.

What could have already happened to her.

Lila's fate all depended on who had taken her and why. If Vivienne had organized this to get Lila out of the way to clear the path for her to make a move on him, then Lila could already be dead. But this being all about him and Vivienne didn't fit with the number of men who had been there and the fact they had used an explosion. They already knew Kristoff was into explosions, and it all seemed too elaborate to be about a girl wanting to get a rival out of the way to get a guy.

As much as he hated to admit it, Lila being taken by Dark Beauty was her best chance of still being alive, giving them a chance to find her.

"If this doesn't work …" Surf started, unable to finish the sentence as his throat closed up on him.

"We'll find her," Arrow assured him from the front seat of the SUV.

"Vivienne wasn't at her apartment and didn't show up at Prey today," he reminded his teammate. They couldn't waste time driving around the city hoping they might stumble upon Vivienne

Waters. Yet he wasn't sure what else they could do. They had no leads on Dark Beauty and no way of making any progress any time soon. Already they had been trying for weeks to figure out the woman's real identity.

"We'll find her," Bear repeated fiercely.

His team was his rock right now, and he didn't know what he would do without them.

As though their team leader's words brought it to fruition, Mouse's voice came through their comms. "Got a lock on her. She's at the park by the lake."

Immediately, Bear turned the vehicle around, narrowly avoiding colliding with a cab, and they headed for the lake. Central Park had been their last immediate hope of finding Vivienne. She talked about the park all the time, often walked there in her lunch breaks, and jogged there after work. It was the only other place they could think of that she might be.

If she wasn't there, chances were she'd realized she had made a mistake and fled the city.

Then they'd never find her.

"There she is," Arrow said, pointing out the front window.

Anger flooded his system in a rush as he spotted the woman standing calmly staring out at the lake like she hadn't just had two people nearly blown up and one of them abducted.

"Play things cool, man," Bear reminded him as he parked the vehicle and they all jumped out.

It wasn't the reminder that had Surf reining in control of his emotions, it was the fact that they weren't alone at the park. The last thing he wanted to do was cause a scene, get the cops involved, and waste time. Eagle would get everything sorted out, but precious seconds would be lost, seconds they couldn't get back.

All that mattered to him was Lila and their baby, and he would set everything else aside to get to them in time.

The rest of his team got out of the other SUV, but they all

stepped back and allowed him to take the lead as he approached the woman who had ripped everything he loved right out of his grasp.

"Vivienne," he said as he reached her.

For a moment the woman didn't react, then she turned very slowly to face him. A pair of devastated brown eyes looked up at him through thick lashes, and some of his anger melted away.

Whatever Vivienne had done he suspected it wasn't by choice.

"I'm so sorry," she whispered. A soft broken sound that cracked away another piece of his anger.

"What did you do, Vivienne?" he asked. His team had formed a small circle around him and Vivienne, both to make sure she didn't try something stupid like running or pulling a weapon, and also to watch for threats in case they had been lured into a trap.

"I wasn't given a choice."

"We always have choices."

Vivienne nodded slowly. "Then I chose my family over yours."

"What do you mean?"

"I don't know how, but they knew I worked at Prey. Somehow, they even knew I slept with you, that I liked you." Guilt was written into every one of her features making her look much older than the beautiful young woman he had used for sex.

"I never promised you anything."

"I know. And I thought I could do one night with no strings attached. But I couldn't. I kept hoping you would realize we could have had something special. I let myself dream about it, that you'd see something in me, see how much I cared. But then Lila showed up." There was no heat in her voice as she said Lila's name, no anger or jealousy, and he truly believed that she had been coerced into betraying them. "I saw the way you looked at her. It was the way I had dreamed you would look at me. I knew then that you would never care about me like that because you were already in love."

"What happened? Who came to you? What did they tell you to

do?" he demanded. Just because Vivienne had been coerced didn't absolve her of guilt, nor did it get him Lila and their unborn baby back.

"There was a man dressed all in black with a balaclava covering his face waiting for me in my apartment when I got home. He showed me a picture of my sister's house and a guy sitting in a car right outside it. Told me I either helped them or they would kill my sister and her two little kids. I'm so sorry, Surf, but I had to do it. I couldn't let them hurt my family." Vivienne's voice pleaded for absolution he couldn't give her. While he understood her position, she could have come to Prey and told them what was going on. They would have found a way to keep her family safe and use the situation to their advantage.

"What did they want you to do?" he asked.

Vivienne closed her eyes for a moment and drew in a deep breath. "Just contact them if one of you left the building."

"Do you know who they are?"

"No. I just took the burner phone they gave me and called the number I was given when you and Lila left to pick up some of her things." Vivienne dropped her gaze again, this time to the cell phone she held in her hand.

On the screen was a woman, some celebrity he vaguely recognized, and it looked like she was doing some sort of televised appeal. The volume was turned down low, but an image of Lila popped up beside the woman who was talking. Snatching the phone from Vivienne's hand, he turned the sound up to hear what was happening.

"If anyone has information on the disappearance of Liliana Angeletti we implore you to call the hotline immediately," the woman said. She sounded sincere, but there was a vibe about her that had him on edge.

"Liliana Angeletti?" Brick asked. "The child star?"

Was his Lila the former child actress Liliana Angeletti? Was that why she had freaked out when they'd been talking about names and nicknames?

"How do they know she's missing?" Mouse asked.

"Eagle got her name held back when the story about the explosion and abduction was picked up, but someone probably had cell phone footage and recognized her," Arrow said.

"That's Zara Duffy," Mouse added. "She's a well-known actress, married to that billionaire movie producer Ross Duffy. Does all those kids' movies, you know the ones, wholesome, funny, family fun. Lolly loves her."

"Lila is such a wonderful woman, and her family is frantic for news on where she is and who abducted her," Zara spoke onscreen. "She's also a dear family friend who doesn't deserve this. She spent her childhood bringing joy to millions, and now we ask that you help her in return. If you know anything, no matter how small, don't hesitate to reach out, *pozhaluysta*."

Domino stiffened. "That was Russian."

"Zara Duffy has black hair and dark eyes," Brick added.

"Dark Beauty," Surf said, a flicker of hope igniting inside him. If this was Kristoff Mikhailov's Dark Beauty, then not only did they have a lead on finding Lila before it was too late, but they could also end this whole plot. The danger to him and his team and their families personally would be gone, and the lives of millions of innocent people would be saved.

Selfish or not, right now his priority was finding Lila and getting her safely back where she belonged.

In his arms.

* * * * *

November 17th
8:27 A.M.

Courage came and went in waves.

Some moments Lila was positive that she had this, that she

possessed what it took to survive, to get through this, and to find a way to escape.

Other moments she felt like curling up on the floor, closing her eyes, pressing her hands to her ears, and giving up.

Right now, she was kind of hovering between the two.

All night she had been building herself up, trying to catch snippets of sleep when she could, but mostly too wired and afraid to do more than doze off for a few minutes before the tiniest of sounds—most of which she was sure she had imagined—ripped her awake. Thankfully, she had been brought up to a room last night and left alone. The room was on the third floor so climbing out the window was out, and her door had been locked so she was trapped inside, but at least she was alone.

Other than touching her inappropriately as he dressed her yesterday when they arrived at the Swiss villa, Ross hadn't laid a hand on her. His wife had gotten a call, insisted he go with her to a different room, and they had spent most of the day there dealing with whatever they were doing.

Not that she was complaining.

The reprieve had been welcome. She'd been fed and left alone to sit in front of the fire. At dinner, she had been escorted to the dining room and given dinner, then taken up to this room. The bedroom had a bathroom attached so she'd been able to take a shower. No one had put cuffs on her again, so she was free to move about, clean herself, go to the toilet, and get dressed. There was a dresser and a closet full of clothes that she assumed were for her use, so she'd chosen some pajamas for the night. This morning, she'd dressed in jeans, thick socks, comfortable boots she could walk in if she got a chance to run, and multiple layers so she could survive the elements if she escaped.

Now someone was at the door, and it was time to summon every ounce of courage she possessed.

Channeling her inner Christian "Surf" Bailey, warrior extraordinaire, her very own sexy SEAL, she stood ready and waiting to face whatever was going to happen next.

When the door opened it revealed Ross. Dressed elegantly in black pants, a crisp white shirt, with a blue silk tie, he looked the picture of sophistication. Too bad the man had a penchant for young girls and had no problem physically holding them down and raping them, stealing their innocence.

"Good morning, darling," he drawled as though she were a guest in his home instead of a kidnap victim. "Did you sleep well?"

"Not particularly," she shot back. No way was she going to cower at this man's feet. Not this time.

Ross' brow creased. "You've certainly grown an attitude since I last saw you."

"I'm not a sixteen-year-old girl anymore, Ross," Lila reminded him. It had been a mistake bringing her here to this place she knew far too well. Fourteen years ago, when she learned that he had left proof of the rape growing inside her, she had been shipped off to his home in Switzerland so no one would learn that he had impregnated her.

For eight months she had basically been left on her own here with just the staff to run the house and the doctor who came weekly to check on her. There wasn't a single inch of this house and the land it sat on that she didn't know like the back of her hand. That was her advantage and the way she was going to escape.

All she had to do was be patient.

"No, you're not." His eyes roamed her body in a way that made her want to lift her hands and cover herself, curl in so he couldn't see her, but instead, she stood tall and proud. She had nothing to be ashamed of and would endure whatever he did to her because all she cared about was getting home to Christian. Anything else she could compartmentalize and deal with later.

She hoped.

No. She would.

"You would have made a stunning wife," Ross said, still leering at her like she was nothing but a piece of meat.

"I never wanted to marry you, Ross. I was a sixteen-year-old girl. My parents arranged the marriage because they wanted you to restart their flagging careers. All I wanted was to be free to make my own choices about what I wanted to do with my life. I wanted to go to school, date boys, dream about the future, and be a normal kid. I certainly didn't want to be betrothed to a man in his mid-fifties."

"I would have given you everything. Fame, fortune, millions of adoring fans."

Been there. Done that.

Hated it.

Acting wasn't who she was. She was introverted, quiet, and contemplative. She liked to problem solve, help people, and keep private things just that, private.

Lila had nothing against acting, it just wasn't for her.

Her parents were acting royalty. Their families had a long history in the industry. Both sets of grandparents and all four sets of great-grandparents had been actors. From the golden age of cinema onward, her family had been entertaining the world in movies and then later in TV shows.

She was the odd one out.

The only one of all her aunts and uncles and cousins who didn't want to continue on that tradition.

It had been forced on her as a child. From birth, she had been made to follow in her parents' footsteps. Ironically, it wasn't until she was sixteen and the man standing before her had raped her and left her pregnant that she had found freedom and the confidence to use her voice and dictate her own life.

Now she needed to find that same confidence.

"I never wanted fame and fortune. I hated acting, hated having fans. Hated that people thought they knew me, hated that people wanted to be me even though they had no idea what being me was really like. I wanted a quiet, peaceful life where I could help others."

"You don't think bringing joy to millions is contributing to society?" Ross asked with a sneer.

"Oh no, I do. I think the arts are a wonderful gift. But it wasn't for me, it wasn't what I wanted to do, and wasn't who I was. I finally found the real me, I found peace and happiness. Then you and your wife came along."

Zara Duffy—formerly Zara Vasiliev—was another child star. Born to Russian immigrant parents, she was the only member of her family to enter the world of acting, and Lila had filmed a movie with the woman when they were both preteens. She had never liked Zara. There was a cunningness and ruthlessness about her that hadn't sat well with her.

It shouldn't surprise her that somewhere along the way, Zara had met up with Kristoff and the two had conspired to devise a plot to rule the world. Zara had always been ambitious, and add that to her ruthless and cunning sides, and she seemed like the perfect candidate to be Kristoff Mikhailov's Dark Beauty.

"Zara has her own plans, her own reasons for doing this. I simply want what was mine."

"I won't ever be yours, Ross," Lila said softly. Her heart and soul already belonged to someone else. It wasn't possible for him to take something from her that was no longer hers.

"Sixteen years ago, I was promised a future with you." Ross took a step toward her and the darkness, the evil that had been in his face that night when he had snuck into her bedroom and held her down while he raped her, was practically bleeding out of his every pore.

"Not by me," she reminded him.

"I held up my end of the bargain. I produced the show that relaunched your parents' careers, but I never got my payment. Now I do. That was my deal with Zara. I let her use this place, and I get to keep you for as long as I want. In her mind, you're nothing but bait to be used for her own purposes. In mine, you belong to me. I will use you however I choose. You will submit because you have no choice. I will touch you whenever I want, kiss you whenever I want, have you whenever I want."

Ross stalked toward her, backing her up until she was pressed against the wall. Using his knee to nudge her legs apart he ground his erection against her stomach. His large hand grasped her face, his fingers digging into her cheeks, forcing her mouth open so he could crush his against hers, his tongue plunging between her lips.

Be strong.

Don't give up.

You can do this.

Please, Christian, please be coming for me.

CHAPTER EIGHT

November 17th
8:58 A.M.

Revenge was within her grasp.

Zara Duffy relaxed back in her chair at the dining room table, content in the knowledge that soon everyone who had played a part in the death of the man she loved would be punished.

It wasn't enough just to kill Dominick Mikhailov and the rest of the members of his team, she wanted them to suffer.

She *needed* them to suffer.

A quick death was more than they deserved.

You will be avenged, moya lyubov.

Kristoff's death would not be in vain. She wouldn't allow it. For now, their plans to destroy the government would have to be put on hold. Kristoff was her everything and nothing mattered more to her than avenging him.

Glancing up as she heard footsteps, Zara smiled as the first step in getting revenge for Kristoff entered the room.

A part of her understood that what she had planned for Liliana Angeletti wasn't what anyone with a conscience would consider to be fair. The woman had nothing to do with any of this. Nothing other than being involved with one of Dominick's teammates.

Still fair or not, the woman would suffer.

One by one, Zara intended to capture the wives of Kristoff's brother's teammates. Once she had all five of them in her possession, only then would she lure Alpha Team into a trap and kill them all. She wanted them to know what it felt like to watch the person you loved most in the world die right before your eyes.

Then once the women were dead, she would have Alpha Team executed.

There was probably a way to use that as a springboard to launch her plans to take over the government. There was always a patsy who could be found, a puppet to be used, a lunatic like Storm Gallagher who had delusions about a utopia where everyone lived off the land. She would find a terrorist and frame him for Alpha Team's deaths, use that to destabilize the government, then swoop in and take over.

"Sleep well, old friend?" Zara asked with a smirk as she lifted a glass of pineapple juice and sipped it.

Liliana glared at her in a way she wasn't used to seeing the woman look at anyone. Lila was too soft to survive in the world where they had grown up. It was no surprise that she had run like a coward.

You didn't run from pain, you learned to embrace it.

That was what her childhood had taught her.

Pain was part of life. If you ran, in the end, it found you no matter how hard or how fast you ran, so what was the point?

A chance meeting with Kristoff Mikhailov had changed the entire trajectory of her life, and she had found what she had been searching for.

Someone who understood pain and the freedom that came from accepting it. Kristoff understood, and he delivered her the most amazing painful sensations. Feelings that made her come alive. He'd saved her from a life of emptiness and filled it with everything she had needed. He had held nothing back, offering her every dark, twisted crevasse of his black heart.

Kristoff was her everything, and now he was gone.

Gone and never coming back.

All she could do was avenge his death, continue their plans, and bring them to fruition. Maybe then she would be able to sleep through the night again.

"No, I didn't sleep well," Liliana said as Ross—who had what looked like a tight grip on her elbow—shoved her down into a chair at the table, taking the one beside her.

It didn't bother Zara in the least seeing her husband infatuated with another woman. There was no love between her and Ross, she didn't even like him. The man was disgusting and had a thing for teenage girls, but he was wealthy, influential, and the most well-known and respected director in Hollywood. There were a lot of benefits to the marriage, and they had agreed that what she did in private and what he did in private had nothing to do with the other.

"You'll sleep better tonight, darling, with me by your side," Ross said to Liliana, leaning in to kiss her cheek.

The woman leaned away from him, and Zara knew it was a bad move even before Ross snarled and grabbed Liliana, dragging her out of her chair and onto his lap. Ross had changed the last few months, getting angrier, more violent, and struggling to control his urges. A couple of times she'd seen him coming onto young girls on the sets of his movies right out in the open where anyone could see.

She'd been covering for him, not because she cared but because she still needed him and didn't want anything to mess with that. When he'd served his purpose and she no longer had a use for him, then she might have him declared incompetent and locked away in a nursing home, for his own good of course.

Zara smirked as she watched Ross curl his fingers into Liliana's hips and grind her center against his thick erection. Although it had never done anything for her, she had to admit that Ross was well endowed, and for a man in his late sixties he still had amazing stamina, was fit, and reasonably good-looking.

"Stop, Ross," Liliana said, struggling against him. "I just want to eat breakfast."

"Hungry, are you?" he snarled, shoving her off him and onto the floor on her knees before him. "Someone get me zip ties," he hollered.

One of the staff hurried to do as he ordered. There was no reason for anyone to suspect her and Ross in Liliana's disappearance, after all, she hadn't been a part of their lives in thirteen years. Switzerland was the perfect place to hide their prisoner, and the staff here were paid to keep anything they saw or heard to themselves.

"I have all the breakfast you need right here, darling," Ross said as he was handed the plastic ties. Taking one of Lila's wrists, he bound it to one arm of his chair, then did the same to her other wrist. Unzipping his pants his erection burst free, the man always went commando.

Liliana tried to pull back, to get away from it, but with her wrists bound as they were there was nowhere for her to go.

His length prodded at her lips as though it had a mind of its own and sought out the wet heat of her mouth.

"Come on, darling, you said you were hungry." Ross tangled his hand in Lila's long blonde hair and forced her to take him inside her.

As she watched, Zara felt a stirring between her legs.

Memories of being naked and tied spreadeagled to Kristoff's bed as he straddled her face, thrusting into her mouth, filled her head and made her shift in her chair as sensations built.

Since her lover's death, she hadn't been able to get off no matter how much she tried. She all but lived in the special chastity belt he'd had made just for her, and more often than not, she had the toy attached to it turned on. But the vibrating inside her did nothing to turn her body on.

Not without Kristoff in control of it.

In control of her.

Zara had always needed someone to control her in order to orgasm. As a young teen, it had been sleeping with much older more experienced men. But that had quickly grown old as she grew more experienced. Rough sex had worked for a while, but then no one could give it to her rough enough to satisfy her.

Then one night of passion with a man at the time she had known only as Scar had given her the most powerful orgasms of her life.

She had feared that with his death she would never experience pleasure like that again, but now, watching her husband thrust into the helpless and unwilling woman's mouth, pleasure began to build inside her.

Ross cried out as he found his release, and a moment later Zara found her own pleasure crescendoed into a powerful orgasm that had her gasping, her hips thrusting at nothing as wave after wave of pleasure ripped through her.

Revenge.

Blood.

Pain.

That was what she needed.

That was what she would have.

CHAPTER NINE

November 17th
9:12 P.M.

Switzerland.

Of all the places in the world he would have thought Lila was being held the beautiful European country wasn't one of them.

Surf had never been here before, most of his work as a SEAL and then with Prey led him to places in Africa or the Middle East, and his family certainly didn't have the money for international vacations when he was growing up. Most of the time, they barely had money for food and clothes. It hadn't taken him long to learn to take any bills he found floating around the house so if no one fed him he could go and buy himself something before the money was spent on drugs or alcohol.

Now he was here in a beautiful country, displaying its autumnal glory with everything it had, to rescue the woman who had done the impossible and captured his heart. With a past like his, Surf hadn't wanted to believe in happy endings. Love was a somewhat foreign concept to him, even though he'd seen his bosses all fall in love, along with most of the guys on his team.

But that was different.

They were different.

They hadn't grown up on the streets, surrounded by gangs, drugs, alcohol, abuse, prostitution, and poverty.

They weren't ruined like he was.

No one knew the truth about how bad things had gotten for him as a kid. His teammates knew he'd bounced back and forth between his mom and the foster system. They even knew there had been drug and alcohol addiction in his family. It was likely they could guess there had been some abuse, but there was no way they could guess just how terrible things had been, and there was no way he was going to tell them.

That was a secret he intended to take to his grave.

It wasn't even something he wanted Lila to know, and he wanted a future with her and their baby.

As they drove through the quiet streets up in the mountains near Geneva, he tried to wrap his mind around who Lila had been and why she hadn't told him. They'd been together for a month before he'd broken things off to try to keep her from winding up in the very position she now found herself in.

That was more than enough time for her to have dropped that bombshell.

Unlike his own past, being a child star was nothing to be ashamed of. On the contrary, it must have been an amazing way to grow up. Her family was cinema and TV royalty, four generations dominating the film industry. She'd been lighting up the screen since she was only a couple of months old, working well into her teens. She'd been talented, and once he found out who she was he actually remembered watching her in one of the TV series she'd starred in when he'd been lucky enough to spend the night at a friend's house or while he was in the system, the only time he had access to a luxury such as a TV.

Lila had to be loaded, and she was used to movie stars and celebrities, mansions, fancy cars, and designer clothes. She'd traveled all over the world, flying first class and staying in five-star hotels. What was she doing with a man like him?

"Hard to believe that's our girl," Arrow said, leaning over Surf's shoulder to glance at his phone where he had an episode of one of Lila's shows playing.

"I … feel like I don't know her anymore," he admitted. His feelings for her hadn't changed, and he was sure there was a reason she hadn't told him who she was like he hadn't told her everything about where he'd come from, and he wasn't angry with her about it. It was just that he didn't see how the former child star and the guy from the wrong side of the tracks could ever be together. They came from two different worlds.

"She's still the same woman who thought she meant nothing to you but was determined that you deserved to know you were going to be a father," Arrow said quietly.

"You mad she didn't tell you?" Mouse asked from the front seat of their rental SUV.

"No," he answered honestly. If he was it would make him a hypocrite. "Just confused. Why wouldn't she want me to know? I mean, she grew up in front of the cameras, millions of adoring fans, and money to have everything she could ever want. Why wouldn't you want people to know? She had talent. Could have made a lifetime career out of acting. Yet she lives in a small apartment in Manhattan and works as a 911 operator."

"Sometimes things seem different on the outside looking in," Brick said cryptically, and Surf had to wonder if they were just talking about Lila or something else as well.

"You think she wasn't happy with her life?" he asked.

Brick shrugged. "What other reason would there be for walking away from it?"

"That why you left your old life behind?" Mouse asked Brick.

"Partly," the man said tightly. Brick never spoke about his family or why he had chosen the military instead of following his father into politics, and they all knew better than to push.

Sometimes you couldn't open up until the right person came along.

Was Lila the right person for him?

He had thought so up until he learned who she was, and he still wanted that life with her and their child. He just wasn't sure that they would work out.

Was he setting himself up for major disappointment?

What if she decided she wanted to go back to her old life and take their baby with her? There was no way he could survive living in the limelight like that, and his job often required him to fly under the radar, a difficult thing to do if the paparazzi were splashing his face everywhere.

"You know what I think?" Domino asked.

"What?"

"That you're creating problems that aren't there. Like I did with Julia. I was so convinced she had to be somehow working against me because my feelings for her scared me. Maybe you're a little scared right now. You've only known this woman for a couple of months, and now you're going to be tied to her forever through your child. A kid is a big responsibility, especially when you weren't planning one."

Was Domino right?

Was he just scared because everything was happening so fast and there was a very real possibility that he could lose both Lila and their baby?

They needed uninterrupted time to really get to know one another without death threats hanging over their heads. He needed to understand more about her, and as much as he didn't like it, he needed to let her understand him too.

That month they had spent together had been special and he'd fallen hard and fast, but neither of them had mentioned the future. Then he'd broken up with her, and she'd found out she was pregnant. Now they had been thrown back together neither of them quite prepared for what that meant for them and their future.

But it was a future he wanted.

That much Surf was sure of.

One he would fight for.

Lila and their unborn child meant everything to him. He didn't want to lose them, not to a psychopath with delusions of grandeur or to the unresolved issues he still had from his childhood.

Nothing in his life had been easy, but he had fought to get out of the hellhole that could so easily have claimed him. He'd fought through BUD/s and Hell Week to become a SEAL. He'd fought to get a place on one of Prey's teams. He would fight for Lila and the future he wanted with her.

And it started here, tonight.

It had been a mistake to break up with her, to not bring her in and offer her the same protection the rest of his teammates had given their wives and fiancées. It was a mistake he wasn't going to repeat. No matter how different their childhoods had been, it didn't change one simple and very important fact.

He was in love with the woman.

Hopelessly and eternally in love with her.

The SUV pulled to a stop in the forest surrounding the estate of movie producer Ross Duffy and his wife Zara. They were positive that when the couple had orchestrated Lila's disappearance, they'd brought her here. He had no idea why Ross had agreed to go along with his wife's plans, but they were all convinced that Zara was Kristoff Mikhailov's Dark Beauty which meant this had something to do with Zara and Kristoff's plan to overthrow the government.

Surf couldn't help but feel there was more to it, something personal as well. Zara and Lila had worked together as kids, and Ross had produced several movies and TV shows that both girls had worked on, as well as other movies and TV shows Lila's parents had been in.

As he looked through the trees and caught sight of the lights glowing inside the mansion, Surf sent up a silent prayer.

Hold on, mama bear. I'm coming for you.

* * * * *

November 17th
9:44 P.M.

Numb.

Lila had progressed to the stage of feeling completely empty inside. She wasn't angry, wasn't scared, wasn't upset, wasn't finding her reserves of courage, but neither was she paralyzed with fear.

She just felt nothing.

Maybe that was better.

It was so unlikely that anyone was going to find her here. According to Zara, she had been officially reported missing, so the cops would be looking for her. Given who she was and who her family was, she had no doubts that the police would go all out to try to find her. But why would they think to look for her in Switzerland?

Prey likewise knew she was gone, and they had the added advantage of knowing that she had been taken by the woman they knew only as Dark Beauty, but they didn't know that the woman's real identity was the famous actress Zara Duffy. Without knowing who Dark Beauty was, they could never know that she was here in Switzerland at the house belonging to Zara's husband, Ross.

No one was coming.

Her chances of escape seemed improbable at best.

There wasn't a second where she wasn't being watched. If not by Ross, then by the men who seemed to be here to patrol and protect the property.

Without a moment to herself, there was no way she could slip away out into the forest. The forest was her only hope, but she couldn't see any way to get to it. Even if she could, it was no guarantee that she wouldn't be stopped as she tried to run.

"Almost time for bed, darling," Ross said, appearing before her.

Most of the day he'd left her alone. She assumed he still had work to take care of so nobody knew he and his wife had a kidnap victim in their vacation home. Lunchtime had been a repeat of breakfast, and … Lila wasn't ready to process any of that yet.

Accepting what Ross had made her do would crack her shell of numbness, and she was pretty sure not in a good way.

Anger.

She needed to find some anger to cling to. Right now, she needed an infusion of strength and power, and she was pretty sure fury was the only thing that could give her that.

"I thought since you have been such a good girl today, you had earned yourself a little pleasure."

Nausea rolled through her stomach at Ross' words.

Unfortunately, she knew exactly what he meant.

If there was anything in her stomach to throw up, she would likely have vomited it up right then and there, but she hadn't been given anything to eat since dinner the day before, so instead, bile just burned her throat.

"Are you going to be a good girl or do I need to use these?" Ross held up more plastic zip ties.

Already her wrists were red and raw, the skin torn from hours of being cuffed on the plane and then when Ross had sexually assaulted her earlier today. She didn't want to lie still and let him put his disgusting mouth on her, but an idea began to form.

It was late, completely dark out, a perfect time to disappear into the forest if she could just get out of the house.

If Ross left her free, all she needed was one second to make her move.

Dropping her eyes in the picture of submission, Lila forced her body to remain lax in the armchair she had been curled up in even as adrenalin flooded her system. "I'll be good," she murmured.

"I knew you were smart enough to see reason," Ross said as he petted her head like she was a dog.

Lila nodded, already working scenarios in her mind. While she didn't have a lot of self-defense training she knew a little, the basics, enough to know that she had to aim for a weak spot. Eyes, throat, groin, they were the best to go for, and she would be hitting him with everything she had.

She wasn't just fighting for herself but for Christian and their baby too.

Failure here was not an option.

"Move forward to the edge of the seat," he ordered.

It took everything she had to meekly comply.

The war, not the battle.

The reminder was enough to have her shifting in the seat, so her hips were perched on the edge, and she was reclining against the seat back.

Greedy hands reached for the zipper of her jeans, and he fumbled as he tried to simultaneously unzip it and pull it down over her hips, bearing her panties.

Panties he literally ripped off her body.

Pain from the material tearing at her skin barely registered because then he was forcing her legs apart and settling between them.

When his head moved toward her center, close enough that she could feel his hot breath against her most intimate flesh, Lila closed her eyes and counted slowly to ten. She needed him to believe she wasn't going to fight him, that she had been scared into submission, that he was finally going to get what her parents had promised him fourteen years ago.

Only she had no intention of giving him that.

His tongue had just darted out to touch her when she sprang into action.

Simultaneously, Lila rammed her foot up connecting squarely with his groin, while she whipped out a hand and slammed her palm up and into his nose.

Caught completely by surprise, Ross howled in pain and sagged down against her, pinning her to the armchair.

Panic added extra adrenalin, and she shoved frantically at Ross' much larger body and managed to scramble out from underneath him.

"You broke my nose," he howled, blood dribbling between his

hands as he staggered to his feet.

Ignoring him, Lila scanned the room looking for a weapon of some sort. Just because she had avoided what he'd had planned she was by no means safe.

Yet.

Her gaze settled on a vase, and she didn't hesitate to grab it. When he came storming toward her, she said a quick prayer and swung it at his head.

Luck was on her side, and it connected with a very satisfying thunk.

Ross dropped.

She ran.

Adding to her lucky streak she had hidden herself away in a small study with an exterior door. The door was almost hidden from the outside because it opened into a walled garden that then had a door hidden in the ivy growing over the stone fence.

All day she had kept her boots on just in case she got a chance to run. As she fled out the door and into the garden, she wished she'd had a coat as well. It was cold out, and she had no idea how long it would take her to reach a town. Her t-shirt, blouse, and cashmere sweater were going to have to do, and if she kept moving, she was sure she would stave off hypothermia.

No, she was determined she would.

There was no time to worry about the fact that she was cold, hadn't eaten in over twenty-four hours, was already thirsty and hadn't slept properly in days. She had one goal, one focus, and that was to survive.

There was no sound from the house behind her as she left the walled garden and entered the forest. When she'd been staying here as a teen and pregnant with Ross' baby, she had spent hours roaming through the forest. It had helped her process the rape and the fact that her parents weren't going to allow her to keep her baby.

Even though she had been torn between loving it because it

was part of her, and being terrified she would hate it because it was also part of the man who had violated her, in the end love had won. But at only seventeen with no skills or ability to care for an infant on her own, she had tearfully kissed her baby boy goodbye and prayed he wound up in a loving home where they would treat him right and give him all the love in the world, something she had never had.

She'd also prayed he wouldn't hate her for giving him up.

Her baby boy was a teenager now, yet today she was back in this same forest, pregnant again, only this time she was older, wiser, free of her parents, free from the paparazzi, and had the love of a man who would do anything for her.

It was love for Christian and their baby that spurred her on and gave her energy when her legs wobbled and threatened to give out beneath her.

She wasn't giving up.

She wasn't going to let Ross and Zara destroy her or use her as bait for Christian and his team.

Her baby deserved a life.

After being forced to give up her first baby, she hadn't thought she could ever handle having another. But already she loved this little baby bear growing inside her. This time no one was going to take it from her.

Whatever it took, she was going to give this child everything she hadn't had, everything she wished she had been able to give her son. She and Christian would raise it together in a home full of love, laughter, happiness, and freedom. Freedom for her child to be whoever they wanted to be, not molded into an image she or Christian had of it.

"Lila."

Her name echoed through the forest.

She panicked, sure she was about to be caught and hauled back to that house.

Lost her footing.

Then she was falling, tumbling down the side of a sharp drop.

There was no time to worry about pain, about injuries that would prevent her from running, about Ross and Zara getting her, or even about whether the fall would claim her baby, because she slammed into something and was knocked unconscious.

CHAPTER TEN

November 17th
10:23 P.M.

The unmistakable sounds of someone falling sent a wave of panic through him.

Lila.

Out here alone, possibly injured, running for her life, Surf was so proud of her for finding a way to save herself, but now he needed her safe and in his arms.

When he and his team had stormed the property, he had just expected to find her there, maybe locked up, restrained, hopefully still alive and in one piece. Instead, when they'd made it through the men guarding the outside of the property and into the house it had been empty.

Completely empty.

No signs of life at all. No Lila, no Zara Duffy, no Ross Duffy.

There had been blood though.

In a small study off to one side of the house, there had been a small amount of blood. Surf had been terrified it was Lila's blood, and even though it wasn't anywhere near enough to suggest that anyone had sustained life-threatening, or even serious, injuries, not knowing who it belonged to and fearing that it was Lila's a million scenarios had played out in his head.

None of them good.

An exterior door had been open, and he'd hoped it was because Lila had found a way to save herself and escape.

When no one had shot at him, and he'd made it through a walled garden and out into the forest there were clear signs that someone had fled this way on foot.

Leaving his team to search for Zara and Ross Duffy, he'd followed the trail out into the forest, praying every step of the way that he was tracking Lila. His girl was a fast runner, and she'd cleared a lot of distance. They had to be several miles at least from the mansion. Fear and adrenalin were powerful motivators that could carry her a long way, but not that would keep her going indefinitely.

He had caught a glimpse of her up ahead, but when he yelled her name, he must have scared her, and she'd fallen.

It took more seconds than he liked to get to the spot where he'd seen her, and when he did his stomach dropped.

Surf was standing at the top of a fifteen-foot almost sheer drop. Rocks and trees covered the ground, meaning it wasn't a smooth drop, there were too many obstacles she could have hit to believe she had made it to the bottom unscathed.

Below him, he could make out her form.

Her unmoving form.

"Lila?"

There was no answer, and his fear ratcheted up several notches. They were out here alone, several miles from the house and his team, Zara and Ross were unaccounted for. There was no way the couple wasn't protected by a team of well-trained men, and Lila was hurt.

"I found her," he said into his comms, already beginning to make his way down to Lila.

"And?" Bear asked.

"Unconscious, she fell. I'm not going to be able to get her back up." He'd need a c-collar and a litter to get her back up to where she'd fallen from so they could backtrack to the house. Surf was sure there was another, likely longer, path back but Lila was hurt, and he wanted her safe, warm, and receiving medical treatment sooner rather than later.

"Understood, we'll—"

Bear's words were cut off as an explosion ripped through his comms.

Things just got a whole lot worse.

Kristoff Mikhailov had had a thing for explosions, they should have assumed that Dark Beauty—Zara Duffy—would as well.

Torn between getting to Lila and going back to check on his team, Surf knew it wasn't really any choice. His team was all highly trained. He had to believe that they had anticipated the explosion and got out of the house as soon as it was cleared until it could be swept for explosives. Lila had no training and she was unconscious. She'd been kidnapped and likely hurt. There was no way he could leave her out here alone and go back to his team.

As he climbed the last few feet down to where Lila lay, he tried contacting each of his teammates, but all he got was emptiness. Whether they had been caught up in the blast, were injured, killed, or had escaped unharmed, the explosion had obviously messed with their comms rendering them useless.

Leaving him and Lila alone out here.

Dropping down to his knees at her side, Surf immediately touched his fingertips to her neck in search of a pulse.

Which he found.

At least she wasn't dead.

But she could have neck or spinal injuries, she could have broken bones, internal bleeding, or any number of injuries that would make moving her risky, and the chances of him getting her back to the house any time soon were non-existent.

For now, it was just the two of them.

"Lila, honey. Can you hear me, mama bear?" he asked as his fingers brushed a lock of hair off her cheek. She was dirty, there were leaves and sticks in her hair, bruises and scratches on her face, but the pressure in his heart touching her, seeing her, told him there was nothing in this world that could drag him away from this woman. He would protect her with his life, do whatever it took to keep her safe. Whatever it took to make her smile.

When he got no response, he began to run his hands over her body searching for injuries. There were two lumps on her head, one on the right side near her temple. The bruising around it suggested she'd sustained it in the explosion the day she was abducted. There was also a lump on the back of her head, and when his hands touched it, they came away wet with her blood.

Moving on, he worked down her torso, along her arms, and then down her legs. When he reached her left ankle, Lila suddenly jack-knifed up, a weak scream falling from her lips.

"Lila, it's Christian, sweetheart. You're okay," he said, immediately releasing her ankle and placing his hands on her shoulders to steady her.

With his night vision goggles on he could see her eyes glazed with pain and fear, it took a second for them to clear, and then she looked at him, hopeful relief in her expression.

"Christian?"

His name on her lips made his eyes blur with unshed tears. This woman had him all tied up in knots but in a good way. In such a short space of time, she'd become everything to him, and even though they had both kept a lot of secrets and had a lot to talk through, he already knew everything would work out.

"Right here, darlin'," he murmured.

"You came for me." With a sob she launched herself at him, wrapping her arms around his neck in a way that reassured him that while she might be hurt, she wasn't going to die on him.

Her death wasn't something he thought he could handle.

His very lifeblood was tangled up in Lila Angeletti.

Because he needed this moment just to hold her every bit as much as Lila needed it, he shoved aside the NVGs and buried his face in her hair as he held her tight against his chest. There were so many things he needed to do, tend to her injuries, worry about how he was going to get her out of there when it was obvious she had an injury to her leg, ask her what Zara and Ross Duffy had done to her, but right now, all he could do was hold her and thank God that she was alive and in his arms.

After a full minute, he carefully eased her back, slipping the NVGs back on so he could see her better. His hands on her shoulders gently kneaded, and he could feel her shaking beneath his touch. She didn't have a coat on, and winter was fast approaching, he wouldn't be surprised if snow wasn't very far away. Hypothermia was added as another concern.

One of many.

"Thank you," Lila whispered, her hands lifting to curl into his tact vest.

"Baby, there is nowhere in the world you could be that I wouldn't come for you."

"We're in Switzerland," she said like she couldn't quite believe it.

"I know, sweetheart, and I'll get you back home, but right now I need to know how badly you're hurt."

It took her a moment to answer, and he wasn't sure if the sluggishness was because of the head injury or the cold. "I … hurt all over, but … my ankle."

Even if it wasn't broken, it was hurt badly enough that she wasn't going to be ambulatory, or at least they would have to move very slowly. Staying out here wasn't an option, even if Zara and Ross were long gone, his team was hurt, Lila needed a hospital, and hypothermia couldn't be staved off forever.

Her shaking was intensifying, likely shock as well as the cold, and there was no way he could expect her to walk out of here tonight. What she needed was some rest. If they were lucky, after elevating her ankle overnight, it would be useable in the morning.

"Christian?"

"Yeah, honey?"

"So tired," she mumbled, and he could see she was fighting to keep her eyes open. Her system was crashing and what she needed more than anything else right now was sleep.

Cradling the back of her head in his hand to support it, he

eased her back against his chest. "It's all right, sweetheart, I have you."

As though his words were all she needed to hear to know she was safe enough to let go, Lila slumped against him as she passed out.

Nothing about this situation was good. Lila was hurt and exhausted, Zara and Ross could be nearby with some of their men hunting them. His team may or may not have been killed in an explosion but either way he was cut off from them.

For now, it was just the two of them alone out here, and as Surf gathered Lila into his arms and stood, he vowed he would do whatever it took to get her home safely.

Nothing else was acceptable.

* * * * *

November 18th
1:32 A.M.

Cold.

Pain.

Dark.

Thoughts flitted through Lila's mind, but they felt disconnected.

Snippets here and there, but nothing coherent.

Jostling.

Something hard shoved into her stomach.

Bouncing.

Lila drifted in and out of consciousness.

Unaware exactly where she was or what was happening.

She was so tired.

Still.

Cold.

Pain.

Something pressed against her head making it scream in agony.

A soft voice murmured soothingly, and she found that the sound of it calmed her enough that she slipped away again.

Cold.

Shivering.

Shakes wracked through her in an unrelenting stream. No matter what she did, she couldn't make them go away. They came at her one after the other until her aching muscles felt stiff and tight.

Then something warm curled around her. A voice whispered in her ear. Lips touched her temple.

Once again she felt safe, and as heat slowly infused her and her shaking tapered off, Lila finally fell into a deep sleep.

The next thing she knew she was blinking open heavy eyes, her mind felt clearer, and she could see again. The dark wasn't completely gone, but instead of being heavy and black now it was lighter and gray.

When she turned her head, she found the thing that had curled protectively around her wasn't a thing at all but a person.

Christian.

Somehow, he had figured out that she was in Switzerland and come after her. Snippets of memory returned. She remembered fighting off Ross and fleeing into the forest. Remembered running until her legs ached and her stomach cramped. Then she'd fallen, been knocked out, then woken to find Christian kneeling over her.

It was over now.

She was safe.

Brow furrowing, she looked around and realized they weren't in a hospital, or even in a house at all. It looked like they were in a small cave. She could see the rock curving up and around them and the light streaming through the opening a few yards away from their feet.

Why were they in a cave?

"You back with me, darlin'?" Christian asked as he propped himself up on his elbow and leaned over her. One of his hands swept across her cheek, lingering for a moment before it dipped to touch the pulse point in her neck.

"I think so," she whispered, suddenly filled with a need to have his touch all over her. She needed something to wipe away the feel of Ross and his disgusting hands on her body. Lila wanted to get as far away from Switzerland as she could get and never come back. "Why are we in a cave?"

Something darkened his gaze, and she sensed his worry even though when he spoke his voice was smooth and even. "Couldn't get you back up the side of the cliff on my own."

Why were they on their own?

Where was his team?

Had something happened to them?

She didn't have to ask to know that Christian wouldn't have come after her on his own. There was no way Alpha Team didn't have one another's backs. If he was here then his team was in Switzerland too, so why weren't they *here*?

"Is everything okay? Are your team all right?"

A smile wiped away a little of his concern. "You know that's one of the things I love about you. How you care about others more than you care about yourself."

"Not an answer."

His smile grew for a moment before he sobered. "You weren't in the house, it looked like someone had run so I came after them hoping it was you. Just when I found you, I heard an explosion."

Lila gasped. "Are your team …?"

"I don't know," he answered tightly. "I'm hoping they weren't in the house when it blew, but for now, we have to proceed under the assumption that we're on our own."

"What does that mean exactly?" This was all new to her. She had no idea about traipsing through the forest, how far they were from the house, if Ross and Zara were in custody, or if they were still a threat to them.

"It means we're going to have to take the long route back to the mansion." As he spoke, Christian uncurled his body from around hers, and she saw that he'd tucked them under a crinkly silver blanket. Lila assumed the blanket was some sort of thermal one, meant to stave off hypothermia, but it hadn't been the material that warmed her last night it had been the man who was now settling down by her feet.

As though thinking of her feet restarted that memory, Lila remembered the horrible pain last night in her ankle that had ripped her from unconsciousness.

Was it broken?

If it was, how was she going to walk out of there?

Even as she wondered, Lila knew she would do it. The only alternative was that Christian carry her, and she wouldn't make him do that. Besides, if Ross and Zara were still out there somewhere, he would need to keep his focus on protecting them, not having to carry her useless self around.

"You were too cold last night for me to ice your ankle. That's not going to be good, but I had to prioritize. If you can't walk, I can always leave you here and come back for you."

"No." The word burst out with more force than she had intended. No way was she sitting here alone while Christian went for help even if he could move faster without her. After all, she couldn't have run all that far from the house last night, she wasn't a runner. They couldn't be more than a couple of miles away. Even hurt she could make that in a few hours.

"I can leave you with a weapon," Christian said like he was seriously considering the idea.

Terrified by the thought of being left alone again, Lila frantically scrambled out from underneath the blanket and grabbed hold of Christian's hands. "I don't want to be alone. Please don't leave me."

"Aww, sweetheart." Christian's voice was rough as he dragged her into his lap and held her tight.

After everything she had been through, fighting Ross off on her own and getting herself away, she didn't want to be weak. Didn't want to beg. But more than anything she didn't want to be left here. "Don't leave me, please. I won't slow you down."

They both knew she would, but instead of calling her on it, Christian eased her back enough that he could frame her face with his large hands. They were rough against her skin, and she felt their strength and capability. Leaning down he pressed a kiss to her forehead, then his eyes met hers, and holding her gaze like a magnet he moved lower and feathered his lips across hers.

"What did they do to you, honey?"

Not ready to tell him about being forced to perform oral sex on Ross and how close she'd come to him doing it to her, instead she said, "Ross was my fiancé. My parents weren't happy their careers were waning." Since he'd found her in Switzerland at Ross' house, she had to assume he knew who she really was. "They made a deal with him. He liked young girls so they'd let him marry me on my eighteenth birthday if he wrote a movie for them that would relaunch their careers. He couldn't wait. When I was sixteen, he raped me. I got pregnant."

Her hand drifted to rest on her stomach, praying that the fall hadn't hurt the baby in any way. She loved this baby, wanted it so badly, and a future with Christian. How would she survive losing this child as well?

A growl rumbled through Christian's chest, making her smile despite everything. "I gave birth at that house. My family hid me away there so the scandal wouldn't hurt their careers. They didn't let me keep the baby. I know it was for the best for him, but I hated giving him away. I can't just sit here on my own. I'm sorry, I don't want to be weak—"

Christian growled again and then crushed his mouth to hers. This time the kiss wasn't a delicate touch, it was hot and hungry, and it conveyed everything he felt for her without him needing to say the words.

"You are not weak. You got away. I saw the blood. You hurt someone and ran. Saved yourself. Don't ever let me hear you call yourself weak again."

The force behind his words startled her, and she found herself nodding gravely. He was right, she had blackmailed her parents into giving her freedom, and she had fought off Ross and escaped all on her own. If Christian and his team hadn't already been there, she likely would have been found and brought back, but still she hadn't given up.

"Sorry I didn't tell you who I was. It's just people judge you differently when they realize you were a child star. I was never really that person. I hated acting, never wanted it to be my life. It's been thirteen years since I got away. The paparazzi aren't interested in me anymore. I look different, people don't recognize me, and I got my freedom. I didn't want you to think I was some spoiled actress princess. I wanted you to like *me*. The real me, not the me I had to pretend I was growing up."

It felt good to say that out loud, to have that secret cleared away. She really did want Christian to like the real her, and to do that he needed to know who she had been and how her childhood had shaped the woman she'd become.

His hands framed her face again, and when he kissed her it wasn't with gentleness, and it wasn't with fiery passion, this kiss was one of love. Again, it conveyed his feelings for her but in a different way. This kiss said it wasn't just attraction, it wasn't just sex, it wasn't even just that they were having a baby that would always tie them together.

It said he loved her.

Her.

The real Lila Angeletti.

The one she never let anyone see.

No holding back, from here on out, she wasn't keeping anything from Christian. She wanted to be his partner in every way that mattered, and it started with not being a burden.

They were getting out of here, eliminating the threat to him and his team, and then they were going to give this baby the very best life.

CHAPTER ELEVEN

November 18th
6:14 A.M.

Pure determination glowed in Lila's baby blue eyes, and Surf knew she had what it took to do this.

Actually, he had never really doubted that she did.

His protective instincts wanted to tuck her away here where she would be relatively safe. He would leave her his pack. She'd have food and water, medical supplies, he'd even leave her with his backup weapon so she could protect herself. On his own, it wouldn't take him long to scale the cliff she'd tumbled down last night and make it back to the mansion.

He needed her safe, but she needed not to be alone right now.

Her needs won out every time.

Lila was pure strength. She had more than proven she could handle anything life threw at her, and she'd been forced to deal with a lot.

Maybe that was why he'd known the second he saw her that she was strong enough to survive anything. His past, his job, and the strains it would put on a relationship, even the danger cloaking him and his team. His girl could take it all in stride.

She had been honest with him. Told him the darkest and most tragic things she'd been forced to endure, and he owed her the same. Not here, now he had to be focused on their survival, getting Lila help, and getting to his team, but later he would tell her. She didn't know, but despite their vastly different upbringings, they had gone through something similar.

Something he wouldn't wish on his worst enemy.

Even though the last thing he wanted to do was let go of her, they needed to get moving. Slowly, he slid her off his lap and set her on her backside so he could get access to her feet. "Okay, darlin', this is going to hurt."

"I can take it," Lila assured him.

"Never doubted it, honey." Never would he doubt Lila's strength. He only hated that he hadn't given her a chance to handle the whole Dark Beauty mess. Acknowledging and expressing his regret at pushing her away when he should have brought her close didn't negate the fact that he'd hurt her. Surf was so thankful that she'd wound up pregnant and was the kind of woman who wanted the father to know no matter what she thought of him.

If it wasn't for the way she'd so lovingly placed her hand on her stomach when telling him about the child she'd been forced to give up, he would have worried that she might not want their baby. But it was more than clear she already loved their little baby bear, as did he.

"All right, here we go." As carefully as he could, he blocked out her pained gasp as he eased her boot off her left foot. Last night he'd wanted to examine the injury, but he'd been afraid that icing it would do more harm than good given she was already borderline hypothermic. The boot had provided as much stability as bandaging it would have, and he'd been concerned that if he pulled the boot off swelling would mean he'd never get it back on again.

Now as he removed her sock and pushed up the leg of her jeans, he wished he'd followed his instincts and put an ice pack from his first aid kit on it.

There was absolutely spectacular bruising around the joint, a display of black and blue that he hated seeing on her soft, smooth skin. Trying to be as gentle as he could, Surf probed the joint, aware of Lila stiffening and clamping her lips together so she didn't cry out. There were no obvious breaks, and thankfully no protruding bones sticking through her skin. If anything was broken it was likely a hairline fracture or just a bad sprain.

Either way, walking on it wasn't going to be easy.

"Lila …"

"I'm not staying here, Christian."

"All right." He didn't like it, but then again, he wouldn't like leaving her alone and vulnerable either. "I'm going to bandage this and put your boot back on. It's going to be tight, and I'll have to keep checking that we're not cutting off circulation." With the cold she was already at risk of damage to her extremities, this just made it worse. "I'll give you an MRE and some water, then go and see if I can make you a crutch."

"What's an MRE?"

"Meals ready to eat. They're not terrible, not great but edible. The spaghetti is always my favorite." Opening his pack, he pulled out a bottle of water and tossed it to her. Last night he'd tried to get some water into her, but Lila had been too out of it. Shock and exhaustion had taken their toll, and she'd needed the rest. Although it wasn't until he had her settled in the cave and slipped under the blanket, wrapping himself around her small body, that she had finally slipped into a peaceful sleep.

Finding a spaghetti MRE, he handed it over and got to work bandaging up her ankle. Once he found this cave, he tended to the wound on the back of her head and checked her again for injuries. There were likely bumps, bruises, and scratches under her clothes, but removing them and risking letting her body temperature drop further had been out of the question. There had been a deeper cut that probably required stitches on her arm that he'd cleaned through the tear in her sweater and bandaged, but nothing he was worried about.

So long as he got her out of there quickly before infection became a concern.

His heart broke as he watched Lila eat the MRE as though she were starving, and he wondered if she'd even been given food since she was abducted.

"I'm going to put your boot back on," he warned, watching as she gave a tight nod and braced herself for the coming pain.

It was a much tighter fit than he would have liked, but he was able to get the boot on and the laces tied, so long as they didn't overdo things she would likely be fine.

"I'm going to go find something you can use as a crutch. Take this."

Her face paled a little when he handed her his backup weapon, and he suspected she'd never touched a gun before. One of the first things he was doing when they got home, and she was healed, was teaching her to shoot. When he and his team were away, he needed to know that she could protect herself and their child if she had to.

Leaving her to finish eating, Surf slipped out of the cave and into the early morning. The forest was beautiful, particularly with its display of fall leaves, but with the cold, Lila's injuries, fear for his team, and worry that Ross and Zara might be nearby there was no way he could enjoy it.

Chances were, Zara and Ross were long gone. When they realized they were under attack, they had probably escaped into the forest with some of their guards. They'd get to a nearby town and then flee the country. As soon as he got back to the mansion, he'd make sure that Eagle had other Prey teams search any other properties owned by either Zara or Ross.

Spotting a large fallen branch a few yards away that looked about the right height for Lila to use as a crutch, Surf hurried toward it, not wanting to be away from Lila for any longer than he absolutely had to be.

As he crouched down to pick it up something caught his attention.

To the average person, it would be nothing, but to someone with his training and skills he immediately noticed the signs that someone had recently walked here.

Not just one someone.

Multiple someones.

If it was his team, they would have known he'd have looked for shelter to bunk down with Lila overnight. They would have followed the same trail Lila had made that he'd followed last night and found the spot where she fell. As he'd carried her, he'd been careful not to leave any signs behind, but his team would have searched for caves or crevices and found him.

Had Zara and Ross Duffy passed this way?

Were they still in the vicinity?

If they were, it meant they were more determined than he would have expected to get Lila back and go after his team.

Survival instincts usually meant people did whatever they had to do to keep themselves safe, but staying meant they were no longer interested in just self-preservation. That made them so much more dangerous.

Logical people could be understood and their behavior predicted, but once someone stepped outside of that zone, they became a wild card.

Wild cards did the unexpected.

Alone out here with an injured and pregnant woman, the last thing he needed was to deal with an unpredictable couple, one of whom was obsessed with Lila, the other who had an obsession with revenge against him.

* * * * *

November 18th
1:11 P.M.

Christian was keeping something from her.

As they trudged through the forest, Lila tried to figure out what it could be and not be hurt that he was keeping secrets.

She had no doubt that he had found something when he'd left

their little cave to go and find her something to use as a crutch because when he had returned, he'd been different. Colder, harder, sharper, he was in special forces operator mode.

Something had spooked him.

Enough that she was almost positive that they were not in fact walking toward the mansion. Her sense of direction wasn't great, but it also wasn't terrible, and even though she'd been all but unconscious when he'd carried her to the cave so she didn't know exactly where it was, she would bet anything that they were walking in the opposite direction right now.

He'd been vague when she'd asked him about it, giving her non-answer after non-answer until she'd stopped asking. While Lila appreciated that he wanted to protect her, the wondering and worrying about it were doing more harm than good.

Although at least it was distracting her from the pain in her ankle.

Before leaving the cave, Christian had given her some painkillers. She couldn't take anything too strong because she had to be able to walk, and the paracetamol hardly did anything to dull the throbbing pain in the joint. Each step she took felt like a burst of fire set off inside her ankle. It was hell, but no matter how bad it got she wasn't stopping.

However long it took.

No matter the danger surrounding them.

Whether it continued to get colder or if snow came.

She was going to do whatever it took to get home.

"Time for a rest," Christian announced in his brisk near-emotionless voice.

Lila couldn't take it anymore.

Tears burned her eyes. She was hungry, thirsty, dirty, cold, and in pain. She was worried about her baby, about Christian, his team, and herself. Scared that Ross and Zara were nearby. Worried about why they weren't heading for the mansion and what that meant for them and his team.

With an exhausted cry, she dropped right where she stood, not bothering to check that there was nothing dangerous she might land on.

In an instant, Christian was by her side, his handsome face creased with concern. "Honey, what's wrong? Are you hurt? Is it your ankle?"

A sob built in her throat, but she shoved it back, not wanting to worry him more by bursting into tears. Why was she being so hard on him in her head? If he was keeping something from her it was because he believed it was for the best. This was his area of expertise, not hers, and she was filled with the realization that she should have stayed in the cave and let him handle things.

"Sweetheart, you're scaring me," Christian said as his hand cupped her cheek.

The soft touch broke the dam.

Tears flooded out in an unstoppable torrent, streaming down her cheeks even as she did her best to blink them away.

Gathering her close, Christian settled her in his lap, his strong arms folded around her feeling like a shield that could keep all her fear, terror, and pain away. Instead of fighting it, Lila sank against him, pressed her face to his neck, and allowed herself this moment to fall apart.

"Shh, baby, it's going to be okay," Christian crooned in her ear as he rocked her gently.

When he said it, she believed him.

This was what he did. He'd been a SEAL, and now he worked for the best security contractor in the world. If anyone could get her out of this and home again, it was the man holding her like she meant everything to him.

Time to toughen up again.

"Sorry," she murmured, lifting her head. Her eyes felt puffy and gritty, but no more tears trickled out.

"It's all right, mama bear, you're doing awesome. Toughing everything out like a champ, took care of yourself and our baby, didn't even need a knight in shining armor," he teased.

Huffing a small laugh, Lila wiped at her wet face. "I'm so glad you're here," she admitted. They both knew she had needed him and his team to come to her rescue. She'd fought for herself and her baby and gotten away, but without Christian and Alpha Team she would likely already be back at that house. "What's going on, Christian? I know you think you're protecting me by not saying anything, but it's making it worse."

Indecision was evident on his face as he looked like he was battling internally, deciding how much to tell her to put her mind at ease without adding further stress.

"I can handle it," she assured him.

Tenderness wiped away the indecision. "Yeah, you can. I told you about the explosion. Well, when we got to the house it was empty."

"Ross and Zara …?"

"Gone. We took out all the men outside guarding the perimeter, but there were likely men inside with them."

"There were." It seemed like there had been at least a dozen heavily armed men watching over Ross and Zara all the time.

Christian nodded. "They were likely using comms just as my team and I were, so the men in the house with the Duffys would have known an attack was underway. They got them out before we got inside."

"So, they're still out there?" It would have made her feel a whole lot safer to know that Alpha Team had taken Ross and Zara into custody, or even that the couple had been killed in the explosion, although that would have meant Christian's team would be dead too. So definitely the in-custody option was the best one.

A small shudder rippled through the big chest she was resting against, and Lila reached for Christian's hand, entwining their fingers. "When I was looking for a crutch, I saw signs that someone had walked past our cave last night."

"Your team?"

"No. They would have expected me to hole us up somewhere to spend the night. They would be looking for caves like the one we were in and would have approached, giving a specific whistle to let me know they were there so I didn't shoot them."

Understanding dawned. Now she knew why he had been so focused and intense today. "If it wasn't your team then it had to be Ross and Zara. They didn't go far, probably waiting to swoop in and grab any survivors of the explosion. And find me."

He offered up a small smile. "I knew you were too smart for your own good. That's exactly what I think. It's why we're going to circle down and around and then approach the mansion from the opposite side. They know you ran this way, so they'll be looking over here, hopefully we can sneak past them."

Exhaustion was taking a heavy toll on her. When she'd opened her eyes to find that Christian was here, Lila had thought everything was going to be okay. Instead, they were separated from his team and alone. Zara and Ross would have at least a dozen men with them, possibly more.

Not good odds.

Easing her off his lap, Christian shrugged out of his pack. "You should eat something and drink some water. I'll check your foot then we'll get walking again."

Taking the offered energy bar, she opened it and took a bite. It didn't taste very good, but it was food, and she needed the boost it would give her. "How long will it take us to get back to the mansion?"

"I want to go far enough away that they aren't expecting it. I'm thinking late the day after tomorrow. If we maintain this speed," he added as he peeled off her sock and examined her foot to make sure her toes were still getting adequate blood supply.

The prospect of spending two more nights out here in the forest, two more full days of walking was almost more than she could cope with. Lila quickly took another bit of the energy bar, it was either keep her mouth occupied or burst into tears again, and she didn't want to subject Christian to another crying jag.

"Drink some water, sweetheart," Christian prompted as he put her sock back on and then maneuvered her heavily bandaged foot back into the boot.

Lila sipped unenthusiastically at the water, rubbing her arms, chilled now she'd stopped moving. Maybe she shouldn't have run. If she'd just endured what Ross wanted to do to her, she would have still been in the mansion when Christian and his team got there. The two of them wouldn't be alone out here now. Although Ross and Zara probably would have taken her with them when they ran. And if she hadn't been gone Christian wouldn't have been chasing her, he might have been in the house when it exploded.

"Take some more painkillers." Christian held out the bottle, but she shook her head.

"They're not really doing much," she said before she thought. The way more lines of tension marred his already worried face she immediately regretted that she had added to his concerns. He was doing everything he could to keep them both alive and get them to safety, all she had to do was walk and not complain, and she hadn't even achieved that.

"I'll carry you for a while," he announced as he took a drink and then stood.

Lila clumsily got to her feet, using a nearby tree for support. "I can walk."

"I'll carry you," he repeated firmly, shrugging into his pack, his voice tight, body tense and she hated part of that was her fault.

His shoulder connected with her stomach, and then he straightened and started walking again.

She wasn't going to let him down.

She'd let him have this moment to make himself feel better, but then she was going to pull her own weight.

It was only two more days and some hours.

Fifty-five hours maybe.

Three thousand three hundred minutes.

Almost two hundred thousand seconds.

It felt like a lifetime.

How was she going to do this?

CHAPTER TWELVE

November 18th
5:39 P.M.

As much as he wanted to keep walking, the need to get Lila to safety near consuming, Surf was aware that she was way past flagging. She'd given it everything she had but was about ready to tap out.

Not that his girl would tap out.

Nope, not Lila.

She would keep walking until her body physically collapsed from exhaustion. If he let her push herself that far, she wouldn't be able to walk again tomorrow or the next day. As it was, he was expecting them to hit the mansion around twenty-two hundred day after tomorrow. That was more than forty-eight hours away from now, and if he wanted to make it, then his girl needed food and sleep.

"Okay, Lila, let's call it a night," he said when he spied what looked like a cave just up ahead.

"I can keep going," she protested immediately, making him smile.

There was only one pair of NVGs, and as the one with the skills and training to keep them alive, and the one who wasn't injured, he needed to keep them. With a possibly broken ankle, the last thing Lila needed to do was stumble along out here in the dark. While he could carry her and keep going for a few more hours, he believed their best bet was to get a good night's sleep and start again fresh tomorrow.

"I don't doubt you, honey, but what you need now is real rest.

We need to give your body a chance to do some healing and the only way for that to happen is for you to sleep."

As she opened her mouth to no doubt protest again, a giant yawn stole her words, completely proving his point.

Scooping her into his arms, Surf cradled her against his chest and carried her the last couple of dozen yards to the cave. There were no predators they had to worry about in the Swiss forests, and he'd seen no signs that Zara and Ross Duffy and their men had been in the vicinity, so he stepped inside the dark, dank space and set Lila on the ground.

Immediately, she groaned in relief and rested her head back against the rough rock wall. She had been such a trooper, and he was so proud of her. Considering the terror of being blown up and kidnapped, especially by someone she had a history with and who had done such despicable things to her, add to that the physical and mental exhaustion and being injured, and it was a wonder she hadn't already hit a brick wall.

Tough as any SEAL he'd ever known his girl was.

"Hey, I just realized something," Lila said as he grabbed them both MREs from his pack.

"What's that?"

"I've been so stressed out and preoccupied with everything else that I haven't had any morning sickness these last few days." Lila's eyes widened suddenly. "You don't think the explosion, drugs they gave me, and the fall hurt the baby, do you?"

"No, mama bear," he soothed as he moved to sit beside her. "There's been no bleeding, so I don't think you miscarried. Once we get you to the hospital, we'll have the doctors check out the little one."

"It'll be the first time we hear the baby's heartbeat." She smiled, but then it faded away. "I remember the first time I heard my son's heartbeat. I was so overwhelmed, and the whole pregnancy became so real."

"You were a traumatized teen, Lila. I hope you don't feel guilty about giving the baby up."

"It wasn't really my choice. My parents weren't going to let me keep him. And I know I wasn't ready to be a mother, but … they never told me what happened to him. I hope he's okay. I hope if he knows he was adopted he doesn't hate me for giving him away."

"If you want, when we get home, we can ask Eagle to have Raven and Olivia see if they can track him down."

"I don't want to unsettle his life if he's happy. I don't want to cause him pain," she said softly, and he could hear her own pain bleed into her voice.

"I don't think it can hurt your boy to know his mom loved him very much but was in a no-win situation. But we can do whatever you feel comfortable with, sweetheart. I'm sure Raven and Olivia would be happy to do it if you decide it's what you want."

"I … I think I'd like that."

They lapsed into silence as they ate and watched as the last light drained out of the sky, and stars began to twinkle in the inky blackness. When this was all over, and the threat hanging over his team was eliminated, when their little one was old enough as well as any other kids they might have, Surf would love to take his family camping. It would be so nice to sit out watching the stars, surrounded by nature, and this woman snuggled at his side.

After sitting around a campfire roasting marshmallows, making s'mores, and telling ghost stories, they would tuck their kids into sleeping bags in their tents, then the two of them would make their own fire. He would stroke his fingers through her silky folds until she was drenched for him, then slide inside her and take her until they both couldn't hold back any longer. Then he'd capture her screams of pleasure with kisses as they both tumbled over that peak of pleasure.

As though her thoughts mirrored his own, Lila reached out and stroked the bulge in his pants.

"We can't, sweetheart, not here, not now," he reminded her.

He might be turned on, hard as a rock, but his job right now was to protect her, not ravish her.

"We don't have to take our clothes off, I know we're not safe, people are hunting us, and we're tired and dirty, but I need this, Christian, please." There was an urgency in her tone that matched his own desperation, and with a growl he grabbed her and lifted her so she was straddling him.

His hand found its way inside her jeans, but it froze, his hard-on fading when he found she wasn't wearing any underwear.

Stifling a curse, he shifted her further down his legs and pulled her jeans down enough to bare her hips where he could see red marks similar to carpet burn.

Lila had frozen, too, and even in the dark he could see her deer in the headlights expression.

"Why aren't you wearing any underwear, Lila," he asked, his voice low and dangerous.

He suspected he knew why she had nothing on beneath her jeans.

Her swallow was audible, and her fingers curled into his tact vest. "Ross he … he made me give him oral a few times, and he was going to go down on me. That's how I broke his nose and got away."

A feral roar rumbled through his chest at the thought of his woman being forced to put her mouth on her rapist.

Her fingers stroked his chest, soothing him when he was the one who should be soothing her. "I know there's a chance we might die out here, and if we don't survive, I don't want the last sexual experience I have to be that, memories of him touching me and making me touch him. I need you, Christian. Please."

That whispered plea shattered him, and Surf dragged a finger across her core, then found her little bundle of nerves and began to swirl the tip of his finger across it. He would wipe away every bad memory the man had given her and replace them with good ones. Ones where she and she alone was in charge of who touched her and when.

As he increased the speed and pressure of his touch, Lila's hips began to undulate. One finger went inside her, then another. He curled them so they stroked that spot hidden inside her that was guaranteed to make her fall apart.

Lila's breathing became ragged. He could feel her internal muscles begin to quiver as she got closer to release. His fingers pumped in and out, grazing that spot inside, while his thumb kept up a steady pace on her tight little bud.

"Christian," she said on a gasp as pleasure hit. Her muscles clamped around his fingers, and he didn't stop touching her, drawing out her orgasm until he was sure he had given her every last drop of pleasure she deserved.

With a content sigh she collapsed forward, their fronts pressed together. Keeping her locked against him with one arm around her waist, his other hand withdrew from inside her pants, and he brought his fingers to his mouth sucking her juices off.

Her eyes flared with molten desire, but when she reached for him to return the favor, he gently grasped her wrist. "No, sweetheart, not tonight. Tonight was just for you."

"But …"

"No buts, baby." Bringing her hand to his lips, he touched a kiss to the tip of each fingertip, then her palm, and then to the inside of her wrist where he could feel her pulse fluttering against his lips. "I wish I could take away all your pain. All the horrible things you've had to endure."

"I know." Her smile was tender, and her kiss soft when she touched her mouth to his. "I feel the same way about you. One day you'll feel safe enough to tell me about your own pain, and when you do, it will shatter a part of me, knowing how badly you were hurt, but it will also heal a part of me because I'll have every piece of you there is."

Her words were everything he needed to hear, and Surf knew that when he did share his dark past, he too would heal. Not only would he let go of the power it still had to hurt him, but Lila would still be right there beside him. Knowing everything, his deepest shame, she wouldn't leave him.

They were two souls joined forever.

Reaching into his pack, he pulled out the blanket, then without releasing his hold on Lila, he laid them both down. Turning so they were lying on their sides, he moved to the other side of Lila, so he was between her and the entrance to the cave. Spooning her, he covered them both with the blanket, then touched one last kiss to her neck.

"I love you, my fierce, strong, sweet mama bear," he whispered, the first time he had told her he loved her out loud even though they had danced around it, admitting it without outright admitting it.

Lila pressed back against him. "I love you too, my knight in shining armor, papa bear."

Everything.

This woman was everything.

* * * * *

November 19th
10:50 A.M.

Another hour another mile.

Another step, another inch closer to safety.

To home.

To the life she wanted with her sexy knight in shining armor.

Lila was utterly exhausted. There was no other way to describe it. Not only did pain shoot through her ankle each time her foot hit the ground, but her hand and arm were red, blistered, and aching from using the crutch.

Both her feet also had blistered, her muscles were overused, overtired, and borderline cramping, and she was chilled to the bone, but she wasn't giving up.

She would do this. She would walk side by side with Christian until her body physically gave out on her. Even then she would crawl on her hands and knees if she had to. If it came to it, she would lie on her stomach and drag herself through the forest.

Whatever it took, she was getting home.

Because apparently, the universe liked to taunt her, Lila placed her bad foot on the ground, and it immediately rolled on something, a root, a rock, she didn't know, but it rolled, pain spiked through it, shooting up her leg and into her hip, and she went down hard.

"Lila?" Christian dropped to his knees at her side.

"Rolled it," she gritted out, clamping her teeth together so she didn't cry. The last thing she wanted was for Christian to feel like he had to carry her again. He'd exhaust himself, and it was so much harder for him to protect them if they happened to stumble upon Ross and Zara with her slung over his shoulder. Not impossible though. Nothing seemed to be impossible for her knight in shining armor, papa bear.

"Let me see."

When he reached for her foot, she pushed his hands away. There was a sense of urgency in her this morning. She didn't know why, but when she'd woken, she'd just felt this need to hurry up and get going, put as much distance between them and the last place Christian had seen evidence of the Duffy's men. "We need to keep walking."

"Won't take me long to check it out."

"But there's nothing we can do about it so we may as well just get going again."

Lila tried to push to her feet, but Christian easily held her down as though sensing she was balancing precariously on that ledge between holding everything together and falling apart completely.

"Come here, baby."

"We have to go," she protested, trying to push him away as he folded her into an embrace.

"Shh, it's okay. We're making progress right on my schedule, we can take a minute or two."

Relenting, Lila sunk into his arms, allowing him to hold her up. She hated that she kept being weak, she felt like she was letting him down. Feeling impotent and completely out of sorts, she fisted his jacket in her hands.

Cold, tired, hurting, suddenly it all felt like too much.

"What's going on?" Christian asked. His hands smoothed down her back, and his breath was warm across her forehead.

"I don't know. I just feel … unsettled." It maybe wasn't the right word, but she was too tired to think about how to explain what she was feeling.

"I know what's wrong."

Lifting her head, Lila looked hopefully at him. Needing answers as to why she felt so out of sorts this morning when she'd slept well in Christian's arms. It was still reasonably early, and while her energy was flagging, she shouldn't feel this out of sorts this early in what was going to be a long day of walking.

"It's your gut."

"My gut?"

"Telling you something is wrong."

Lila stiffened. "Is your gut saying the same thing?"

"Yeah, honey, it is."

"Ross and Zara?" She looked around, expecting one of them to jump out from behind a tree, laughing and mocking them as their men surrounded them.

"I don't think so."

"Someone else?" Who else could be out here? There were a few remote towns in the area, and she supposed there could be a few tiny houses hidden away in the forest. But if there were, why would anyone care about them?

"Just got this feeling of being watched. Hunted."

The fact that Christian's gut—which she trusted a whole lot more than she did her own—was also saying something wasn't right made her a whole lot more edgy.

If someone was out there and didn't mean them harm, then surely they would come to see if they could offer help. It was pretty clear with her hobbling along using a branch of a tree as a crutch that something was wrong. If they were being hunted as Christian put it, then another threat was out there.

As if they needed that.

"We should get going," she said, shivering, the hairs on the back of her neck standing up.

"First, you take some painkillers."

Because she knew Christian wasn't going to budge until she agreed, she nodded, took the bottle and water he offered, and quickly swallowed two pills. She didn't think they were going to do much. Walking on her ankle like she had to was too much for it. But the only alternatives were to take the morphine and make Christian carry her, or hide somewhere and let him go on without her.

Neither of those worked for her.

Once she'd taken the pills, Christian stood, pulling her up with him. He kept his hands on her until she got her balance, then passed her the crutch.

"We're getting closer now. Today and then tomorrow night we should hit the house," he assured her, leaning in to drop a quick kiss to her lips.

Pasting on a smile to reassure him that she could do this, Lila followed after him when he started walking.

She knew she could do this. It was mind over matter, so long as they kept their speed relatively slow, and she was careful that when she put her bad foot down it wasn't on anything that would make her roll her ankle again then she could do this.

Only seconds continued to tick by.

Turning into minutes.

Each step got harder and harder to take.

Despite the chill in the air, sweat was dripping off her. In theory, the body heat she was generating should help stave off hypothermia, but in reality, it helped only temporarily. The sweat against her skin and the moisture in her clothes left her icy cold.

Her use of her crutch increased with every hour—every minute—that passed. Instead of it just being there to help keep her steady and take a little of her weight, she was now using it to bear almost all her weight, her bad foot barely touching the ground.

A blister on her hand rubbed raw, and she bit her teeth into her bottom lip so she didn't whimper and alert Christian to this new level of discomfort.

Wasn't like things could get a whole lot worse, so all she had to do was suck it up and keep walking. The sooner they got back to the house the sooner she could get off her feet, get properly warm, real rest, and proper pain relief. And Christian wouldn't worry so much because he'd find out if his team were okay.

Lila prayed they were. How would she ever forgive herself if they died because they'd come after her? How would she face Mackenzie and Mikey, Phoebe and Lolly, Piper, and Julia if the men they loved died because of her?

Because once again all the universe seemed to care about was kicking her and Christian when they were already down, a crack seemed to slice right through the air.

Before she could even process the sound, Christian had launched at her and tackled her to the ground.

Pain speared through her body, and she couldn't help but cry out as her ankle twisted awkwardly as she fell.

Another crack followed the first, and then another.

After the third, Lila finally realized what was happening.

They were being shot at.

Something wet puddled beneath her right shoulder.

Blood?

Had she been shot?

Above her, Christian shifted, lifting his weapon and firing back at whoever was shooting at them.

Whether it was Ross and Zara or some random stranger, it hardly mattered. Bullets were bullets and could kill just as easily no matter who was firing them from a gun.

The sounds were so loud.

She'd never known a gun firing sounded like this. It was like a mini explosion each time Christian pulled the trigger. Before Christian put that gun in her hand yesterday morning, she'd never even touched one before, but she definitely wanted to learn.

Never again did she want to feel as helpless as she did in this moment.

When things suddenly went deadly quiet Lila startled.

Was it over?

Had Christian killed whoever was shooting at them?

"Christian?" she asked when what felt like a full minute passed without him moving.

"Lila?" His voice was strained, and he moved slowly off her like his body was heavy.

He staggered to the side, rolling to his side with a thunk that seemed to reverberate through the ground and into her.

Blood.

His shoulder was soaked in blood.

She hadn't been shot, Christian had.

CHAPTER THIRTEEN

November 19th
11:55 A.M.

Blood flowed down his shoulder.

Damn, that hurt.

Wasn't the first time he'd been shot, and Surf doubted it would be the last, but this had to be about the worst possible timing.

Who was going to protect Lila if he passed out from blood loss?

Already his clothes were soaked with blood, and he was feeling the effects. His limbs felt heavy, and his head stuffy, like someone had stuck a whole bunch of cotton wool in there.

He had to shake it off and pull it together because they still had miles to go before he got his girl to safety.

Not only were Zara and Ross Duffy and their bodyguards still out in the forest somewhere, but now some crazed mountain man was hunting them as well.

Yeah, this sucked big time.

"Oh my … you were … there's blood everywhere …" Lila stammered. Her blue eyes were huge in her much too pale face.

"It's going to be okay," he assured her. The bullet hadn't nicked an artery because if it had, he'd have bled out already. His arm was usable, and his wound needed to be stitched, but he had the supplies in his first aid kit. This would slow them down, he'd need time to recoup before he was capable of going any further, but they'd be okay.

"Okay?" Lila spluttered. "How can you say that?" Tears brimmed in her eyes, and the sight of them tore at his heart. She'd been through enough, seen enough, and now to add to everything she'd also been shot at. When he'd taken her to the ground, he hadn't had the luxury of doing it carefully. No doubt he'd given her more bruises when he crushed her against the hard ground and made the injury to her ankle worse.

"Lila, I will get you home. I promise."

A shudder rippled through her, and she closed her eyes for a moment, dragging in a ragged breath. When she opened her eyes again determination was back, and he knew she had stowed her fear and pulled herself together. "What do you need me to do?"

"There's my girl." Grabbing her hand with his good one he squeezed it, encouraging her to keep doing what she was doing. "First thing we have to do is check if the bullet is still in there."

"And how do I do that?" Lila asked, looking way out of her league here. This might all be new to her, but she was strong enough to handle it, of that he had no doubt.

"We need to take off my clothes and check for an exit wound." Removing his clothing from the waist up wasn't ideal. With the cold and blood loss it would put him at greater risk for hypothermia, but getting the bullet out if it was still in there was more important.

"Okay, that doesn't sound so bad," Lila agreed. Carefully she helped him shrug off his pack, then his tact vest, and several layers of clothing until his chest was bare.

"Looks like the bullet went in here." Her fingers traced along his skin right near the top of his shoulder. "It's so close to your neck. If you'd been just a little further over, you'd be dead." For a moment terror stood out starkly in her pale face, but then he saw her compose herself again. "It's bleeding a lot, but I see where the bullet went through. It's not still in there."

"Didn't get the bone either, I can still use the joint." That was all that mattered. A few hours and his body would recover from the blood loss, and he'd be good to go.

"There's so much blood." Lila sounded distressed as though

she felt his pain and was suffering right along with him. Same way he felt about her. Her fingers continued to gently caress his pecs, and the touch worked better than any painkillers he'd ever taken.

"You're going to have to stitch the wound."

Her fingers stilled. "Stitch it? Me?"

Surf smiled to encourage her. "You're the only one here, darlin'. You got this. I'll talk you through it, okay?"

Lila gave a shaky nod.

Talking her through cleaning the wound, stitching it, and bandaging it up, Surf gave himself a shot of antibiotics as Lila packed everything away.

They weren't going to make it any further today. They'd have to find a place to bunk down and spend the night. He needed to regain some strength, and Lila looked cold and shaky. She was in pain, but he knew she wasn't going to take anything stronger than paracetamol, which wasn't nearly enough given what he suspected her pain levels were.

For now, they both needed to rest.

It would mean adding another day to their trek. Possibly more. If Lila's ankle had been reinjured, she'd be moving slower than she already was. Assuming his team was alive and uninjured, they'd be looking for them, but they didn't know that Zara and Ross hadn't left the area and that he'd had to circle way around to get safely back to the mansion.

There was no way his team would leave Switzerland without him and Lila, but he hated knowing it would be another day before Lila got somewhere safe. She was flagging, hanging in there, giving it everything she had, but her body only had so much to give, and he feared her tank was already almost empty.

"What now?" Lila asked when she'd finished packing up and had helped him put his clothes back on.

"Now we find somewhere safe to rest."

She nodded, then looked at his weapon. "Should I take that?"

"No, honey, I can still aim and fire."

"Did you hit the man shooting at us?" Like it had just occurred to her, she looked nervously around as though the man might pop out from behind a tree and kill them both.

"Didn't kill him," he replied. He would have, but by the time he'd taken Lila to the ground, protecting her body with his own, the man was behind a tree, using it as protection as he continued to fire. Likely he hadn't expected them to be heavily armed, and when Surf fired back, he'd run.

Would he come back?

Possibly.

But not right now.

"Looks like a small cave over there," he said, moving to stand.

"Here, let me help." Lila reached for her crutch and used it as leverage as she pushed to her feet and reached for him, but since she was barely steady on her own feet and his added weight would likely knock her over, Surf took her hand but didn't do more than hold it as he stood up under his own steam.

Together they limped toward the small rocky space, and Surf wasn't pleased to find the short walk left him breathing heavily. The wound might not be life-threatening, but it had taken more out of him than he liked.

Positioning them at the back of the cave, Surf pulled out the thermal blanket, tucked Lila against his side, and covered them both. For several long minutes they sat in silence. Lila had her head on his good shoulder, their combined warmth with the thermal blanket was enough to stave off the cold, and if it wasn't for the pain in his shoulder he could almost believe they were just a couple out enjoying the quiet forest.

But they weren't just out here for a vacation or a day trip.

They were fighting for their lives.

With nothing else to do right now, Surf felt compelled to talk, to unburden his soul. "My father was a gangbanger," he said into the silence. Beside him Lila stiffened. Her hand found his beneath the blanket and she laced their fingers together. "He was murdered in front of me when I was four. My mom was an addict, drugs were her life although she drank too, there wasn't anything she wouldn't do to get her next fix. She had a parade of men in and out of her life. Some boyfriends, some men who paid her for sex. When she got really desperate, she offered up the only thing she had."

"Christian," his name was a harsh whisper as it fell from her lips, understanding exactly what he was saying.

"Men paid good money to have sex with a little boy." Pain and shame mixed inside him. His first sexual experience was when he was eight years old. Scared, confused, held down by men four, five times his size. He'd been fourteen the first time he voluntarily had sex. He couldn't even remember the girl other than she was in one of his classes at school. It hadn't been because he particularly wanted to do it but because he desperately needed to be in control.

The same way after he'd been held captive in Somalia, beaten and tortured, and held against his will, he'd needed to be in control. Meaningless sex was how he convinced himself he was in control of himself and his life, hence the sex binge he'd been on after they were rescued and came home.

That all changed when he met Lila.

"I'm so sorry. I hate so much that happened to you." Lila's voice was rough, and when she turned her face against his neck, he could feel it was wet with tears.

"I fought hard to get out of that life. Never took drugs, never even drank. Worked hard in school. Made friends who weren't part of the gang scene. When it all felt too much, and I was afraid I'd get washed away into the life my parents lived, I went out on the water and surfed."

"You did more than just get away from that life, Christian," Lila told him, lifting her head to meet his eye. "You're a hero. You fought for your country, protect the innocent, and risk your life every day to make the world a better place. You're my hero."

Peace settled over him at Lila's words, and he realized he wasn't surprised by her acceptance of him, even knowing the dirty secret he'd kept from everyone in his life.

Lila knew.

She understood.

She'd lived through something similar.

Two halves of a whole.

Gathering her close, he ignored the pull on his wound, needing to hold his woman in his arms. Needing to know that he wasn't alone.

"I've got you, Christian," she murmured as she held on tight.

Surf wasn't embarrassed to admit his eyes blurred with tears as he cradled his heart in his arms.

* * * * *

November 20th
6:39 A.M.

Lila felt off this morning.

Sluggish.

Cold.

Sore.

It wasn't just her ankle—although the constant throb of pain was becoming almost more than she could bear—every muscle and joint in her body ached.

And she was cold.

The kind of chilled down to her bones cold that made her feel like she was never going to be warm again.

"You okay?" Christian asked.

"Mmhmm." She nodded, keeping her gaze fixed on the MRE she was supposed to be eating for breakfast before they started another long day of walking. Now instead of reaching the mansion late tonight like the original plan, they wouldn't get there until tomorrow.

If nothing else went wrong.

She couldn't quite forget Christian telling her yesterday about her gut. That feeling she'd had that something wasn't right had turned out to be true when they'd been shot at. Not *at,* Christian had been shot, and she was terrified of him getting hurt again. Was this weird feeling she had now her gut again?

Was that man still out there? Were Ross and Zara nearby? Would one of them get injured today? Or maybe the weather would get worse, and storms and snow would roll in. So many things could go wrong, and she was feeling totally overwhelmed.

An arm slipped around her shoulders, pulling her close against Christian's strong, solid frame, and lips touched her temple. "Your gut acting up again?"

Lila nodded. "What is yours saying?" She trusted his a whole lot more than hers because she wasn't convinced hers wasn't anything more than nerves and exhaustion.

"It says nothing is going to stop me from getting you home."

His non-answer did nothing to alleviate her anxiety. She knew him well enough to know when he was trying not to worry her.

If he felt it too, then there was definitely danger in the air.

"Trust me, honey," Christian said.

"I do," she assured him. "I just … I feel … I don't even know."

Lifting his hand, he touched the back of it to her forehead. "You're a little warm."

"I'm freezing."

His brows knit together. Obviously not what he wanted to hear. "One of your wounds is infected. Probably the deeper one on your arm. You need to take some more antibiotics."

Lila grabbed his hands when he went to open his pack. "No, we should keep them in case you need them. Your wound is worse than mine and if we get delayed again its more important you stay healthy. You're the one with the weapon who knows how to defend yourself."

She could tell he didn't like it, but they both knew she was right. Christian was the one who could protect them if the man who'd shot at them came back or if they ran into Ross and Zara and their men. If she got sick, he could always leave her behind and go on himself, but if he got sick, she couldn't do the same.

"Take the antibiotics, Christian," she urged.

Reluctantly, he took the pills, then winced as he repacked everything and stood. He might have been shot but other than the small wince you wouldn't know it. His movements were smooth as he slipped his pack on, and he was steady on his feet when he reached out to help her up.

In contrast, Lila felt like she was a straw man, clumsy and uncoordinated as she took Christian's hand and allowed him to help her stand. It took a moment for her to get her balance, and she tried to summon an encouraging smile so Christian didn't worry about her too much. In truth, her ankle was screaming in agony, and she wasn't sure it would last the rest of the walk back to the mansion, but Christian had more than enough on his mind already.

After everything he had been through, she didn't want him to hurt anymore.

She had always thought that her life had been rough, and it definitely had been. Parents who didn't want or care about her, being forced to act even though she hated it, the paparazzi following her all the time, and printing made-up stories about her and her family. Then being basically sold off to a man old enough to be her grandfather just so her parents could advance their careers. Raped and left pregnant, forced to give her baby away. Her life had been rough, but she'd also had the luxuries that came with wealth. It wasn't enough to make up for what she had endured, but at least it was something.

Christian hadn't even had that.

Where she'd had a nice house to live in, good food to eat,

brand-name clothes, a private tutor when she wasn't working on set, toys, a pony, and her own car when she turned sixteen, Christian had been hungry, dirty, basically living off the street. She had lacked love and people to care about her but not material possessions. Christian had lacked both, and she desperately wanted to make it up to him.

As he took her hand and guided her out of the cave they had spent the night in and they began another long day of trekking through the forest, she wondered how she could do that. She had access to all the money she'd earned on various TV shows and movies. When she'd run from her old life Lila had wanted to make it on her own, so she hadn't used it. It had been well-invested, and she'd made a lot more.

She could buy them a house, take them on vacations around the world, buy him a car,a motorbike, or a boat, whatever he wanted. There wasn't anything she wouldn't give him, it might not make up for what he'd had to live through as a child, but at least for the rest of his life he would be well taken care of.

"What are you thinking about so hard over there?" Christian asked. He'd kept his hold on her hand, and they walked side by side, the pad of his thumb brushing almost absently across her knuckles.

Lila hesitated but decided if they were going to build a future they had to be honest with one another. "I was just wondering how I could make up for everything you suffered. I have money. More than we could ever need. I can buy you anything you want. A house, a …"

Her words were cut off when Christian spun her around and crushed his mouth to hers in a powerful and steamy kiss that made her wish they were somewhere with a bed.

"Silly girl," he whispered against her lips. "Don't you know that I don't need things? What I need is your love. You and our baby. People. That's all I ever needed."

Choking down a sob, Lila carefully threw herself into

Christian's arms, not wanting to hurt his shoulder. "You have that," she cried, burying her face against his neck. "You have my love, you have our baby, you have both of us forever. We will always love you, we'll never hurt you, never judge you, never want anything but the best for you. I love you so much already, and we haven't even known each other for more than a couple of months. I can't imagine how much I'll love you tomorrow, next week, next month, next year, or a lifetime from now."

Betrayed by the people who were supposed to love and protect them had shaped both of them and the people they had become. Was love enough to undo that damage? Heal those wounds? Lila had to believe that it was.

"Sweetheart, I already love you and our little one more than I thought it was possible to love anyone. You two are my everything, and there isn't anything I wouldn't do to protect either one of you." Leaning back, he cupped her cheek with his large hand. His calloused palm reminded her how strong he was, a true warrior, yet his green eyes were almost impossibly gentle. "No one will *ever* hurt you again. No one. Not on my watch."

She believed him.

His fierce protectiveness enveloped her like a warm hug. Comforting and soothing. When he touched her like that and looked at her like that, Lila felt like anything was possible. She felt like she was starring in her very own movie, only this one wasn't pretend, it was as real as it got.

"I believe you, and it makes me love you even more," she admitted as she reluctantly took a step back. As much as she wanted to curl up in Christian's arms, she wanted them both safe, and the only way for that to happen was to get out of there.

As she moved, her bad ankle gave out, causing her to lose her balance.

It happened in slow motion.

Lila stumbled backward, her arms swinging wildly as she tried to regain her balance so she didn't land flat on her back.

Instead, her landing was wet.

And cold.

Christian had reached for her. She could almost feel the air move as his hand came millimeters from hers.

But he was a split second too late.

The river seemed to swallow her whole.

The cold stole her breath and froze her muscles, and Lila was completely helpless to stop it from sweeping her away.

CHAPTER FOURTEEN

November 20th
9:24 A.M.

Surf watched in horror as Lila's head went under the water.

The last thing he saw was her eyes, wide with pain and terror, too big and stark in her pale face.

Then she was gone.

Gone.

Lila had grown up in California, in a rich family, chances were even if she hadn't frequented the beaches much her family had had a pool so she should know how to swim. The biggest problem was that it was almost winter, and the water would be freezing. Being thrown in like that would shock her system and could render her paralyzed for a few moments while her muscles adjusted.

A few moments was all it would take for her to drown.

Surf had been a SEAL, and long before that, the ocean had been his safe place. Peaceful, quiet, and free from anyone who wanted to harm him. The water was as much his home as the land, and he dived into the river.

It had a reasonably fast-moving current, and already he'd lost sight of Lila.

With strong, confident strokes he glided through the water. It was as cold as he'd thought, but this wasn't his first time throwing himself into freezing water. Memories of Hell Week filled his mind as he went beneath the water, searching for any glimpse of Lila.

Nothing.

Rising above the surface, he scanned the river, but again couldn't see any signs of her.

No.

Wait.

Up ahead was a flash of purple.

Lila had been wearing a purple sweater, and the color wasn't one you'd find naturally in the forest, so there was zero doubt in his mind that it was her.

His shoulder protested slightly, but the pain was nothing compared to the absolute terror constricting his heart.

He couldn't lose her.

There was no way his heart could cope with that.

Yesterday he had bared his soul to her, told her everything he'd endured as a child, his darkest, deepest shame, and she hadn't rejected him. She'd held him, cried for him, and soothed him with nothing more than her presence and her love. There was nothing left between them, no secrets. She knew about his childhood and how his mom had pimped him out for drug money, and he knew that she had been sold by her parents to a man old enough to be her grandfather.

They were both free now.

Free from the chains of their pasts.

Just ahead of him, Lila disappeared again under the water. Her arms were thrashing, splashing water about, and he glued his eyes to the disturbances her panicking created and increased the speed of his strokes.

He had to get to her.

Neither of them was dressed for a dip in the icy water. Hypothermia wasn't just a major concern. There was no way either of them was walking away from this unscathed.

Especially Lila.

At least his fatigues protected him slightly, but Lila was dressed only in jeans, a t-shirt, a blouse, and a sweater.

There was no way her body could survive this temperature

much longer.

Hold on, baby. I'm coming.

The spot he'd been aiming for suddenly went still.

His heart lurched.

If Lila was no longer struggling to get to the surface it was because she couldn't. There was no way his girl would just give up. She didn't have it in her. Everything else life had thrown at her she had dealt with, she didn't back down, not even when she was scared.

You got this, sweetheart. Don't give up on me.

Pushing his body almost beyond what he could stand, Surf powered through the water, one single thing on his mind.

Lila.

Had to get to her.

Had to save her.

Couldn't lose her.

The words spurred him on, and he calculated where the currents would have dragged her since she disappeared and stopped moving and dived down.

His frantic gaze searched the water.

There.

Just up ahead.

Kicking harder with his legs, Surf propelled himself forward and if he wasn't holding his breath would have let out a sigh of relief when his fingertips brushed across the soft cashmere of Lila's sweater.

Yanking her closer, he fisted a hold of her clothes and pulled her up against his body. Then with her secured against him, he swam them both to the surface.

Lila didn't move.

A glance at her showed her skin was so pale it was near translucent, and her lips were tinged with blue.

He had to get her out of the river before he lost her forever.

Again, his shoulder protested his vigorous strokes toward the bank, but it was absolutely nothing compared to his fears for Lila.

Failure here was not an option.

The river wasn't terribly wide, and it didn't take him long to reach the bank. Lifting Lila out, he laid her down and scrambled to his knees at her side.

One of his hands reached for her neck, searching for a pulse as he leaned his face down so his cheek was above her mouth looking down her body.

There was no puff of air against his chilled skin.

Her chest didn't rise and fall.

Surf pressed his fingers deeper into her throat, desperate to feel the thump of her pulse telling him she wasn't gone.

There.

Faint but detectable.

Lila had a pulse, but she wasn't breathing.

Positioning himself at her side, he curled his hand around her chin. Tipping her mouth open, he pinched her nose closed, covered her lips with his, and breathed his own air inside her, willing her to live.

"Come on, baby, don't do this to me," he begged as he turned his head to check to see if she was breathing.

Nothing.

"Breathe, mama bear, don't you dare leave me. Come on, you can do this. Keep yourself and our baby bear alive." Surf didn't have nearly enough medical knowledge to know if their baby could survive this. There was every chance that Lila would miscarry, but he was going to believe that life wouldn't taunt them with this chance at happiness only to yank it away at the last second.

While they would both be devastated if they lost this baby, already they both loved it, and he knew it wasn't all that was holding them together. They could survive this loss, he just prayed they didn't have to.

Surf breathed into Lila again, willing her to take a breath.

He gave her another puff of air.

The longer she didn't breathe, the greater the chances she never would.

"Please, honey. Breathe for me. Breathe," he roared the word into the quiet forest as though by sheer force of will he could make Lila come back to him.

Beneath him, she tried to suck in a breath, choked, and began to cough. Surf rolled her onto her side so her lungs could expel the inhaled water.

"Thank you," he whispered to the universe as he kept Lila on her side with one hand and with his other stroked back wet hair from her face. Her skin was so cold, and he knew that even though she was breathing she was nowhere near out of the metaphorical woods.

Forcing his exhausted body into action, he gathered Lila into his arms and pushed to his feet. He had to get her somewhere warm and get her out of her drenched clothes. It was the only chance she had at surviving the fall into the freezing water.

Pain screamed through his injured shoulder as he took Lila's weight, but there was nowhere else in the world he wanted her right now. She didn't stir, her body had already been teetering on the brink of complete and utter exhaustion. Hypothermia on top of almost drowning was more than enough to push her right over the edge.

Time meant nothing as he stumbled through the forest looking for shelter.

Lila didn't stir.

His fear for her grew.

Fear for himself as well.

His own body wasn't much warmer than Lila's, but at least he was moving to generate some heat.

The world around him blurred a little, and he blinked to clear it.

If he had to guess, he wasn't much further away from

exhaustion than Lila had been this morning.

He had to find them somewhere safe and warm soon or he was going to pass out.

If he passed out there was no one to protect Lila.

Zara and Ross were still out here somewhere.

As was the man who had shot him.

Then there were the elements.

Danger seemed to surround them on all sides, and for a moment, Surf felt like he couldn't breathe.

Of course, with his job danger had always been lurking around the corner, but that was different. This time Lila was here, *she* was in danger, and that changed everything.

Surf stumbled and went down hard on his knees.

He swayed.

Struggled to stand.

Then he caught sight of a small cabin.

Warmth.

Knowing it could be the house belonging to the man who shot at him, Surf had no choice but to head toward it. Right now, Lila's dropping body temperature worried him more than anything else. He was still armed, he could defend them, and wouldn't hesitate to eliminate any threats.

Somehow, he made it to the cabin.

A glance in the window showed it was empty.

While sparsely furnished there was a fireplace and a bed.

All he needed.

There were no lights on inside it, and the fireplace was empty and cold, but wood was stacked on the porch.

Balancing Lila in one arm, he found the door unlocked and opened it, setting Lila on the floor just inside then kicking it closed behind them.

He stripped her out of her soaked clothes, then removed his own before scooping her up again and carrying her to the bed. After he'd tucked her in, he went to the fireplace and started a fire, laying their wet clothes out in front of it to help them dry.

Then Surf somehow made it back to the bed. Sliding in beside Lila, he pulled her against him, covered them both with the covers, and then the world disappeared around him.

* * * * *

November 20th
12:02 P.M.

Warm.

Lila felt blessedly warm.

Kind of floaty and not altogether there, but she remembered what had happened.

Losing her footing, the cold water stealing her ability to function, her head beneath the water, trying to get to the surface, unable to make it, fear, panic, drowning …

With a gasp she snapped fully awake, bolting upright in the bed.

Bed?

After going under the water that last time, her exhausted limbs unable to propel her back to the surface, everything was a blur.

Vague memories of Christian's cold body cradling her were all she had. Now she woke up to find they were no longer out in the forest, instead, they were in some tiny one-room cabin. There was no one else here so she assumed Christian had found this place and carried her here so she wouldn't freeze to death.

He was beside her, asleep in the bed, and the fact that he hadn't stirred when she woke up and moved worried her. Lila knew from experience that Christian was a light sleeper. Usually, the tiniest of movements or sounds had him snapping awake.

But not this time.

When she reached out and rested her palm against his cheek, his skin was warm enough so she knew he wasn't hypothermic, nor was it too hot indicating his bullet wound was infected. It was likely exhaustion that had him passed out.

Her own exhaustion tugged at her mind. Urging her to lie down, curl up in Christian's arms again and go back to sleep, but he'd taken care of her, saved her life by getting her out of the water and someplace warm. Now she needed to take care of him.

Before stripping them out of their clothes and getting them into bed, Christian had started a fire in the fireplace, but it was mostly out now. Lila had never tended to a fire in her life, but surely it couldn't be all that hard. The house she'd grown up in had had several open fireplaces, and she'd loved curling up in front of the one in her bedroom, but she'd never started it or tended to it. They'd had staff to do things like that for them.

Servants her mother had always called them, but that term seemed offensive so in her mind Lila had thought of them as the staff.

There had been an older man, probably similar in age to Ross Duffy, who had been with her family for as long as she could remember. He'd always started a fire in her fireplace for her any time she'd asked, and she'd watched him do it plenty of times while he'd asked her questions about a book she was reading, or a drawing she was working on, or how her cello lessons were going. She'd appreciated him taking the time to ask about things that interested her rather than the career her family forced on her.

Climbing slowly out of bed, her head swam for a second before clearing enough that she could move. Pure agony shot through her ankle at that first step, and she shoved a fist into her mouth so she didn't cry out and wake Christian. He needed his rest.

If her ankle hadn't been broken in her original fall or from overusing it, falling into the river could very well have snapped the bones. It was swollen to at least twice its usual size and a horrible mix of black and blue.

Hobbling toward the fire, Lila grabbed the fire poker, and

prodded at the logs and sticks still in there before adding another couple along with some kindling. At first, she thought she'd smothered what little flame remained but then the kindling caught, and a few seconds later the new logs she'd added were burning brightly.

For a moment, she stood there and watched the flames dancing. How nice would it be if instead of injured, exhausted, and running for their lives they were in a little cabin on a romantic getaway? She'd never been camping, but it seemed like fun. She could see her and Christian sitting around a fire maybe doing a little fooling around after they'd tucked the kids into their sleeping bags.

As she turned to face the bed, Lila pressed her hand to her stomach. Was her baby okay? How much more trauma could her body sustain before it self-terminated her pregnancy? There was no blood between her legs, so she had to believe that, for now at least, her little one was hanging in there.

Tough like its daddy.

Tough like its mommy, too. Maybe?

She'd survived her childhood, she'd survived Ross' assault and the aftermath, and she would survive this too.

That perfect family future she'd always dreamed about was within her grasp.

Limping back to the bed, Lila hoped that Christian didn't see her as a spoiled princess now he knew the truth about her. They hadn't had a chance to really talk about that yet, but she hoped he still saw her as the same woman he'd been getting to know before he broke things off now he knew all her secrets. Just like she still saw him as the same man who had captured her heart that first day.

While it hadn't been love at first sight, there had been a deep understanding somewhere inside her that Christian was hers. It was the only reason she would have agreed to go on a date with him right then and there even though she was always cautious when it came to men.

Chilled after spending too long out from the cozy pile of blankets and the man who owned her heart, body, and soul, Lila slipped carefully back into the bed, doing her best not to wake her sleeping knight in shining armor. He looked so adorable like this, free of stress, worry, pain, and even free of the humor he used as a shield to protect himself from more pain.

Lila wished he could be like this forever.

Peace.

That was what she wished for both their futures.

"Where'd you go, mama bear?" His voice was rough, sleep laden, and almost impossibly sexy.

"Stoking up the fire. I thought you were asleep." Reaching out, she ran her fingers through his dark blond locks. Despite the fact they hadn't showered in days, his hair was soft and silky, and she twirled the short strands around her fingers as her palm brushed across his temple.

"Babe," the word rumbled through his chest. He grabbed her wrist, his long fingers circling it, strong and sure, and lowered it, touching his lips to the sensitive skin on the inside of her wrist, and just like that she was wet for him.

No. Not wet. Drenched.

Drenched for this sweet, sexy knight in shining armor who meant everything to her.

Trying to be the strong one, Lila tried to pull her wrist from his grasp. "You need rest."

"I need you." Tugging on her wrist, he pulled her up and over so she was straddling his muscled thighs.

Pain pulsed through her ankle, and despite the rest her muscles and joints still ached, but nothing could erase the ball of need sitting inside her.

"You're right, we shouldn't do this. You need rest and you're in pain." Anger, worry, and concern warred in Christian's forest green eyes, and Lila reached out to smooth a fingertip across his brow, easing away the lines there.

"I need you," she echoed his words as she reached out and grabbed his erection, curling her fingers around it and running her hand from tip to base and back up again.

"Lila," Christian warned, trying to pull her hand away but she tightened her grip.

"Come for me, Christian," she begged. She wanted to watch him fall apart, lose himself in pleasure for just a short while. He carried such a heavy weight of pain and responsibility, and she wanted to shoulder that weight and let him rest, let him enjoy being free.

With a nod, he reached between her legs and found her already quivering little bundle of nerves, playing with it as she continued to play with him. His hands were magic, applying just the right amount of pressure to have feelings building inside her, sensations that had no words to truly describe them.

In her hand, Christian seemed to grow bigger and harder, his length jerked and trembled beneath her ministrations, and she could see he was holding back.

"Inside … me … now," Christian ordered, shifting his hands so they spanned her waist and lifting her as effortlessly.

One smooth movement was all it took for him to spear himself inside her and then he was thrusting at a near frenetic pace. Lila felt that same desperation, that same crescendoing of sensations inside her.

Bracing her hands on his forearms, she held on as he maintained his grip on her hips and pumped into her.

"Come, baby, now," he ordered tightly, and those words were all it took for her world to burst into a mass of fiery confetti as pleasure consumed every inch of her body, soaking down into her very soul.

Christian's own release exploded inside her.

She loved that there was nothing between them, she was already pregnant so a condom wasn't necessary, and she knew their love was the forever kind, so she never wanted to use one with him again.

All her life she'd wanted someone to see the real her, and now someone had.

Someone who saw her, loved her, and wanted to claim her.

Christian Bailey was better than a prince charming or a knight in shining armor. He was real, and he was hers.

Forever.

CHAPTER FIFTEEN

November 21st
8:33 A.M.

Damn, she was beautiful.

Heart-stoppingly gorgeous.

Surf couldn't get enough of looking at her.

Right now, all Lila was doing was sitting at the table preparing some fish he'd caught for them in the same river that had nearly claimed her life, and she was just stunning. Their clothes were still drying so she was gloriously naked. Her smooth skin was still too pale for his liking and married with cuts and bruises, but her delicate hourglass figure, curves he had touched and tasted every inch of, were the stuff men dreamed of.

Add in the long blonde mane that hung down her back like spun gold, long-lashed blue eyes that she kept peeking at him through, plump pink lips that were the most kissable things he'd ever seen, and it was a wonder he could think of anything but burying himself in her tight, wet heat. Drawing breathy moans from her as he thrust inside her and hearing his name fall from her lips as she surrendered to the pleasure.

"You keep looking at me like that, and I'll forget all about being hungry," she said, giving him a shy, sweet smile. Lila still lacked a little confidence when it came to her body, at least until he put his hands—or his mouth—on her, then she turned into a veritable sex kitten.

Surf laughed. Part of him wanted to take what he knew she would willingly offer, but the other part was filled with a deep need to take care of her. And not just sexually. Sure, he could give her a quick orgasm, and they could go back to preparing the fish, but they hadn't eaten in over twenty-four hours, and he wanted to take care of all of her. Which meant food first, sex second.

There were still a couple of MREs in his pack, but he thought they might as well take advantage of having the fire and eating some fresh food. While he could whip them up a fire while they were out in the forest it increased the chances of them being spotted, something he didn't want to risk.

"Later I'll get my fill of you. Right now I'm feeding you," he said as he dropped a kiss to the top of her head.

They'd lost a good day and a half already. If his team were alive and unhurt, they would be going crazy with worry for him and Lila, but yesterday they'd both been too exhausted and needed the rest. His plan had been to spend the morning in the cabin, then after another fresh meal for lunch head back out into the forest.

Last night was the night he'd promised her they'd be back at the mansion. Instead, she still had at least today and tomorrow to go, maybe longer. Her ankle was bad. She wasn't complaining, but he could tell she could hardly bear weight on it, meaning he might have to carry her.

"I've never cooked over a fire before," Lila said.

Since he hadn't wanted to use any of the supplies whoever owned the cabin had stocked there, he'd caught them enough fish for breakfast and lunch. Lila had seemed excited by the idea of cooking it over the fire, and he also got the impression that she wanted to show him she wasn't some spoiled little rich girl. Not that he'd thought she was.

"You're going to love it," he told her.

"I know I will. Maybe once everything dies down, and you have Zara in custody and anyone else working with her, and it's safe again, we could go camping. I've never been, but it looks like fun."

Warmth rushed through him, and it had nothing to do with desire for his gorgeous woman. Despite their vastly different upbringings, they had so much in common, and he couldn't wait to get the shackles of this damn conspiracy off their backs so they could start the rest of their lives together.

Standing behind her, he pressed one hand to her stomach while the other rested on her shoulder. "It's a date."

Her breathy moan and the way she slightly tilted her head as though silently begging for his lips on her neck unraveled his control.

"You want this, darlin'?" he asked as he kissed the spot just behind her ear he knew would make her shiver.

"Mmm, I *always* want your lips on me."

"Yeah?" Surf trailed a line of kisses down to the curve of her shoulder and back up again. "What else do you want?"

"Your hands touching me."

"Touching you where, sweetheart?" he asked as the hand on her stomach drifted higher to claim one of her breasts.

"Mmm," she moaned again. "Touching me there."

"Where else?" The hand on her shoulder swept down her arm and settled on her hip, his fingers cresting the dip between her thighs.

"B-between my legs," she murmured.

"Right here, baby?" Her legs parted, and he brushed a fingertip across her center. "Already so wet for me."

"Mmm. Yes. Please, Christian, touch me there," she begged.

"Like this?" He brushed his finger through her juices again, coating it in her arousal before sliding it inside her.

"Yes, please …"

"You need more, sweetheart?"

"More. Yes. Please."

Somehow her begging seemed to make her even sexier, and he slipped another finger inside her. His length stood to attention, practically begging to be allowed to be the one buried in Lila's heat, but for now this was about her girl. She'd been such a trooper, walking on a likely broken ankle for days, no complaining, holding on even though she was scared and tired, the least she deserved was a mind-blowing orgasm.

"Oh … that's … so … good," she panted when he started working her hard little bud.

"Come on, baby, let me watch you fall apart." Stroking as deep as he could, his thumb pressed hard on her bud, and she blew apart.

Her internal muscles clamped around his fingers, her hips undulating, riding out the wave of pleasure as he continued to apply pressure on her bundle of nerves dragging things out for as long as he could.

"So beautiful," he whispered, dropping another kiss to the top of her head.

"I agree. She's stunning when she's coming," a crude voice mocked from the doorway.

Their heads whipped around to find a man dressed in flannel and a thick woolen coat, with a fur hat on his head standing there looking at them.

Surf withdrew his hand from Lila's body and lunged for his weapon while simultaneously throwing his body between hers and the threat.

"Uh uh." The man shook his head, his own weapon aimed at them. "I don't think so."

He weighed his options. He could make a move for the weapon, but that would risk Lila getting hurt. With her ankle, she couldn't run even if he caused a distraction, and while he'd take a bullet for her any day, he needed to be able to protect her.

This was his fault.

He'd gotten complacent.

No one had come back to the cabin the day before, and he'd allowed himself to believe they were safe here. That whoever owned this place was likely tucked away in a house in a nearby town, that this was just a cabin used on occasion, not someone's permanent home.

He had lowered his guard, and because of that, they were now both being held at gunpoint.

"Easy," he said, holding up his hands. There was something familiar about the man, and he was almost certain this was who had shot at them, but he had to see if there was a way he could talk them out of this. "My girlfriend is hurt, she fell in the river. We just came here to warm up. I'm happy to pay you whatever you want as compensation for us using the cabin overnight."

"Oh, I'm going to be compensated all right," the man said with a tone Surf didn't like one bit. Lust glittered heavily in his eyes, and Surf hated that Lila was naked and so very vulnerable. "Girlie, move over to the cabinet, grab the rope and tie your man up. Don't want him trying nothing."

Instead of moving, Lila stayed right where she was. He could feel her fear like a living, breathing entity filling the cabin. Keeping her safe was all he cared about, and one distraction was all it would take to eliminate this threat.

"It's okay, honey, get the rope," he told her.

Still, he felt her hesitate.

"Do it or I shoot your man," the man ordered.

Behind him, he felt Lila get to her feet and heard her hiss of pain as she took a step, but as she moved out from behind him and into their attacker's line of vision, as he had known it would, the man's gaze swung toward her.

There wasn't a man alive who wouldn't focus his attention on a naked woman.

Taking advantage, Surf pounced.

Slamming his body into the man's, they both hit the cabin floor hard, in a tangle of limbs. Surf got in a blow to the man's abdomen and then one to his head before the man had a chance to retaliate.

Playing dirty, the older man—who was more resilient than he looked—aimed a blow directly at the bullet wound on Surf's shoulder. Still recovering from hypothermia on top of being shot his strength wasn't what it usually was.

The blow caused enough pain that he momentarily lost concentration.

One moment was all it took.

The man threw a punch that connected with the side of Surf's head, stunning him slightly.

"Lila, run," Surf ordered. She was naked and injured, but she had to get out of there. Facing the elements would be better than what he knew this man had planned for her. She knew what direction they'd been heading in, all she had to do was keep going, and eventually, she'd get to the mansion.

Surf just managed to dodge the next blow to the side of his head, and instead got the other man in the gut again. The older man heaved as air was shoved from his lungs, but in a last-ditch effort, he swung the weapon and slammed it into Surf's temple.

Just like that it was lights out.

* * * * *

November 21st
8:58 A.M.

"No!" Lila screamed as Christian sagged against the floor.

Whoever this man was he was big and strong. If Christian hadn't been shot, lost blood, and then battled hypothermia because he'd had to jump in the river after her, he could have taken him easily.

But weakened as he was the man had managed to knock him out.

Red rage blinded her for a moment.

This man had hurt her man.

That was not in any way acceptable.

The fury was enough to send her flying across the room toward him. There was no pain in her ankle, she was beyond feeling pain. The anger that this man had attacked them, hurt Christian, and was staring at her naked body like he wanted to take something he knew she wouldn't give him, was enough to wipe everything else away.

Christian wouldn't be pleased that she was putting herself in danger instead of trying to escape, but they both knew she didn't have the strength to escape right now. With her ankle she wouldn't get very far, and she was naked, the elements would claim her far too quickly if she had run while Christian and their attacker were fighting.

Slamming her body into the man's, she hit with enough force and with the element of surprise on her side that she actually took both of them to the ground.

Lila had no plan. All she knew was that she wasn't letting anyone hurt her man. He'd been through enough, and no one was messing with the happy ever after they both deserved. Christian had saved her life when he'd tackled her and taken a bullet for his trouble. He'd saved her again by jumping in the river after her, she loved him, was protective of him, and they were in this together.

A team.

Now and for the rest of their lives.

Knowing she was too weak to deliver a blow hard enough to stun him. Instead, Lila did what she could. She kneed him in the groin and got a very satisfying howl of pain, then she followed it up with a strike to his nose, much like the one she'd given Ross the day she escaped.

The man cursed at her, and hoping he was distracted enough not to stop her, Lila scrambled for the weapon he'd dropped when she tackled him.

Her fingers curled around it, and she swung it up and toward their attacker, fully prepared to shoot to kill. She might never have touched a gun before a few days ago, and she had never tried to hurt someone before she'd attacked Ross to get away from him, but this was about survival.

Her life, Christian's life, and their baby's life.

There wasn't anything she wouldn't do for them and the life they wanted.

Just as she was moving her finger to the trigger, pain exploded in her head.

Another blow came to her hip, and then her thigh, and her chest when she slumped sideways.

The gun fell from her hand, and she could hear a steady stream of curses coming from the man as he kicked her several more times.

Dizziness and pain swamped her, and she was aware of footsteps moving away from her.

Vainly she tried to push up onto her feet.

Christian was counting on her.

"Lila?" his weak voice called her name.

"Christian!" she cried back. It did not take a genius to figure out what this man had in store for her, and as much as she was afraid and sick about it, what scared her the most was knowing it would kill a piece of Christian. Even if they survived, he would never be the same, and she was afraid that having to watch her live out both of their worst nightmares right in front of him would break him.

"Oh, no you don't," their assailant muttered as he grabbed Christian's arms and yanked them behind his back, binding them with rope.

"Leave him alone," she said, moving closer and trying to knock the man's hands away from Christian.

Swatting at her like she was nothing but an irritating fly, he sent her tumbling sideways. Her entire body hurt so badly, new bruises on top of old ones, and one night of sleep in a bed wasn't enough to wipe away the exhaustion of the last few days.

Although she did her best to pull herself out of his grip, when the man picked her up and carried her toward the bed she couldn't stop him.

Just like she couldn't stop what was coming next.

Any satisfaction she got at seeing blood on his face was hollow as he threw her onto the mattress and proceeded to grab her limbs and one by one tie them to the bedposts. The rope tore at the skin on her wrists and ankles as she fought against them. He'd tied the ropes tight, and the pain in her likely broken ankle was excruciating.

Still, she would take it every time over what was coming next.

"Touch her and die!" Christian roared. When she looked at him, she could tell that his head was clearing, he looked furious and deadly, and she had no doubt that given enough time he could get himself out of those ropes.

She also had no doubt he would follow through on his threat with zero remorse.

Lila was sure this was the man who had shot at them the other day. Somehow, they'd found his cabin, and now he was here to finish what he'd started.

After he raped her.

"Don't think you're in any position to be doing any killing," the man mocked. He spoke English clearly although his Swiss accent said Switzerland was his home.

His leering gaze was fixed on her breasts and then traveled slowly down her body. She wished more than anything that she had put her clothes on this morning. Because they were still damp, she and Christian had decided to let them dry by the fire until they were ready to go. He had been partially dressed because he'd gone out to go fishing, but she was completely naked.

Completely vulnerable.

Completely helpless.

"Don't touch her," Christian said, his voice low and dangerous, and she could see he was straining against his bonds, desperate to get to her.

When the man's hands touched her body, Lila squeezed her eyes closed. "Don't watch, Christian, please," she begged. Their chances of surviving this were slim, but if they did, she didn't want him to have to live with the images of her rape inside his head.

"I don't mind an audience," the man said with a laugh as he unzipped his pants and climbed onto the bed.

His body was heavy, and it smelled bad. His breath was hot against her neck, and when his lips touched her skin it took everything she had not to throw up.

But worse was when his thick length pressed between her spread legs.

Tears leaked out the corners of her eyes, and she kept them scrunched closed, not wanting to see his face as he violated her.

"I'll kill you! I will rip you to shreds!" Christian was screaming, but Lila let her mind wander.

Maybe she could hide inside it and avoid the worse of the assault.

Was that possible?

Lila didn't get a chance to find out.

Just as she felt him prodding at her entrance, the door to the cabin banged open, and the sound of a gunshot cracked through the small room.

Something wet splattered all over her, and then the weight of the man's body was crushing her against the mattress.

"You," Christian growled, and Lila's eyes snapped open.

In the doorway stood Ross and Zara and a couple of their henchmen. Ross had a gun in his hand, and she realized he'd shot the man who owned the cabin.

"I don't share," Ross said as an explanation even though no one had mentioned anything. As she watched, he stalked across the room. Despite the fact that he and Zara must have been hiding out in the forest for as long as she and Christian had, he looked clean and refreshed, dressed in a dark gray suit with a gray woolen coat.

When she noticed his nose was swollen and he had two black

eyes, she couldn't help a smug smile.

She'd done that.

She might not have much power right now, but she wasn't completely helpless.

There was nothing that would make her give up. She would fight. Christian would fight. And somewhere out there was his team. Lila had to believe they were okay and would be looking for them.

"We have them now. Can we hurry up and get out of here?" Zara snapped. "At least you killed the old man so we don't have to pay him."

"Don't do this, Zara," Christian said. "My team will be coming for you and if you kill us all of Prey will be out for blood."

Zara laughed. "I don't want you dead. Not yet anyway. Not until you and the rest of your team watch the women you love die in front of you like you made me watch Kristoff's murder. Only then will I kill you. For now, you're coming with us."

With a nod at their bodyguards, two men moved, one toward her and one toward Christian, who was still fighting against the ropes binding him. Both of the henchmen pulled out syringes and small vials.

The intention was clear. She and Christian were going to be drugged and abducted. Held until Zara had possession of all the men on Alpha Team and their partners. Then they would be executed.

Except maybe for her.

From the look Ross was giving her, she wondered if he planned to keep her for himself.

His own personal sex slave.

Lila wasn't sure which option was worse.

CHAPTER SIXTEEN

November 21st
9:52 P.M.

His damn head hurt.

Even as his brain struggled to fit all the puzzle pieces together, Surf knew he had failed.

Not himself, but the two most important people in the world to him.

Lila and their baby.

That sense of failure ran deep. Deeper than any pain, deeper than any drugs, deeper than any lingering sense of confusion.

It was soul-shattering.

Heartbreaking.

Crushing to the point where he almost couldn't focus.

No.

Giving into the pain and devastation wasn't going to help anything right now. What he had to do was focus. Pull it together. If he gave up on his girl, she was as good as lost to him.

Which was not acceptable.

Surf dragged in a breath and shoved the fogginess right out of his head. He needed to clear it, figure out what had happened, and how he was going to get himself and Lila out of this mess and home safely.

As he forced his sluggish brain to cooperate the memories came back, in a trickle at first, but then a flood that left him near breathless.

A protective rage unlike anything else he had ever experienced barreled into him almost hard enough to knock him to his knees if he hadn't already been sitting down.

The man who had shot him had shown up at the cabin. Not at one hundred percent, Surf had been overpowered and knocked unconscious. Something he would never forgive himself for. Because Lila had been tied to the bed and assaulted.

As clearly as though it were playing out before him, he remembered her naked body bound to the bed. The terror in her eyes as she'd looked at him, the devastation in her voice as she'd begged him not to watch.

Helpless.

Overwhelming helplessness had flooded his system as he fought against the ropes binding his wrists and ankles. His girl had been assaulted right in front of him, and he hadn't been able to do anything to stop it.

Hadn't been able to protect her.

Hadn't kept the promises he'd made that he would keep her safe.

That she could trust him.

Damn, Lila must hate him.

A howl of rage echoed through the space, and it took Surf a moment to realize it was coming from him.

Shoving open his eyes he looked around. He was in a small, dark room. Likely a basement if the dank smell and concrete walls were anything to go by. There was no way to know if they were still in Switzerland or if Zara and Ross Duffy had transported him someplace else after they knocked him unconscious. Since there were no windows, he couldn't tell what time of day it was or how much time had passed since they were taken.

Was Lila here somewhere too?

He struggled to get to his feet, and it wasn't until he looked down that he realized it was because of a metal cuff around his right ankle. It was attached to a heavy metal chain currently tangled around his feet. It ran to a metal ring embedded in the concrete floor in the middle of his cell.

Memories of being held hostage in Somalia along with his team assaulted his mind.

Naked, injured, humiliated, controlled, it had reminded him so much of his childhood that when he and his team had finally been rescued, he'd felt completely hollowed out and empty inside.

There had been only one way he could cope.

The same way he had coped as a teen when he was finally too big to be pushed around by the men his mom brought home. Sex. With as many different women as he could find. All that had mattered to him was that high of an orgasm, knowing no one but himself was in control.

Now it wasn't sex he craved. That high was of no good to him. If he survived there would be no procession of nameless women in his quest to heal.

All he needed was Lila.

The helplessness he'd felt those couple of weeks was nothing like he felt now. Then his life and the lives of his team had been in danger, and while he loved every one of them, they were his brothers in every way that mattered, they'd all signed up for this life knowing full well the dangers they were facing.

But Lila hadn't signed up for any of this.

She was just a sweet woman who had been unloved, used, and manipulated her entire life.

She deserved freedom and happiness, not to once again be at the mercy of someone who didn't care about her and wanted only to cause her pain.

"Hold on, honey, I'm coming for you," he vowed as he shoved at the chain to straighten it out.

Once he had, Surf shoved to his feet, examining his body for injuries. There were a couple of bruises, and from the pounding in his head and the lingering dizziness, he likely had a concussion on top of the drugs that had been pumped into him.

When the old man had entered the cabin, he'd been partially dressed. Wearing his pants, socks, shoes, and shirt, all of which he still had on. He was missing his warmer layers, along with his tact vest, but at least he wasn't naked.

Patting his pockets, Surf wondered whether anyone had searched him. Despite being Kristoff Mikhailov's partner he doubted an actress like Zara knew much about anything outside her safe little world. The men that had been guarding the mansion in Switzerland had been highly trained, and he assumed whoever she had here was as well, there was every chance they had thought to go through his pockets even if it had never occurred to their boss.

Still, he could hope.

A grin broke out on his face a moment later when he found exactly what he was looking for.

Ever since Somalia, he'd been paranoid about himself and his team being caught again. He hadn't been sure he could survive a repeat of that captivity and torture, so he'd sewn a little insurance into the inside of every pair of combat pants he owned.

The kit was small. It contained lock-picking tools and a Swiss army knife, all he thought he could reasonably hide, but all he really needed to get out of almost any situation.

Certainly, something he could use to get out of this.

Palming the kit, he circled his cell looking for weaknesses. The walls were concrete, there were no bars, no exterior windows, just walls and a door at one end. The door did have one small window, but when he looked through it all he could see were more doors like the one trapping him in his cell.

"Lila?" he called out, praying she was nearby. Not only did he want to reassure her that he was conscious, uninjured, and able to get them both out of this, but *he* needed the reassurance of hearing her voice.

He needed to know that she was alive, yes, but he also needed to know if she hated him for not protecting her. If Ross and Zara hadn't arrived when they had, then the old man would have raped her.

As much as it killed him to admit it, that was what would have happened.

It felt wrong to be grateful to Ross Duffy for anything, given he was at least part of the reason Lila had been taken, but in this he was thankful for the man's obsession with and unwillingness to share her.

The door wouldn't budge, and there was no way to get his arms through to the other side to pick the lock, so he was going to have to play this a different way.

Returning to the corner of the cell where he'd woken up, Surf sat down and opened the kit. There was nothing in his cell, no toilet, no mattress, no blanket, but he knew that Zara wanted him alive until she had abducted the rest of his team and their partners.

That meant sooner or later someone had to enter his cell to bring him food.

When they did, he'd be ready and waiting for them.

It didn't take him long to pick the lock in the metal cuff binding him to the chain, and he immediately breathed a sigh of relief at having the cuff gone. His wrists and ankles were a little worse for wear from the ropes the old man had used, but he felt stronger than when he'd woken, ready to fight.

The cell had a single bulb hanging from the ceiling. If he broke the bulb, it would alert whoever came to bring him food that something was up, but there was no way they could know about the kit he'd had sewn into his pants. If they knew of its existence, they would have taken it so they wouldn't be expecting him to be free of the chain.

Swinging the chain at the bulb, he smirked with satisfaction as it shattered, raining small shards of glass down on the floor.

Surf had the knife in his pocket ready to go, and he held the chain in both hands. Before he killed the unlucky man who would come to feed him, he needed intel. He also needed a way to contact his team. If he was lucky, the man who came would have a radio on him he could use.

Settling himself into the corner, Surf now had nothing to do but wait.

Wait and let his fear for Lila's safety fuel the fires of his fury.

* * * * *

November 22nd
9:21 A.M.

Lila paced around the bedroom.

She felt like a caged animal.

She had woken up in this room when the drugs she'd been given in the cabin had worn off. No one had been in to see her, so she had no idea how long she'd been here. At least one night, it had been bright, probably afternoon when she'd woken up, and she'd watched through the window as the sun sank and the moon came out. Unable to sleep, she'd then watched as the moon slowly crossed the sky and the sun rose once again.

The not knowing was the worst.

Where she was, what was going to happen to her, whether Ross was here too, and his crazy wife Zara.

But the worst was not knowing about Christian.

Was he here too? Was he okay? Had he been hurt?

Fisting her hands, she paced another circle, stopping by the window. Wherever they were it looked remote. All she could see were trees for miles. Still in Switzerland? Or had they crossed the border into a neighboring country? Or had they hopped on a plane and flown halfway around the world?

Not knowing made the knot of fear in her chest tighten.

At least she was dressed again. Although knowing someone—almost definitely Ross—had put their hands on her while she was unconscious churned up her empty stomach. If it wasn't empty, she likely would have made good use of the toilet in the adjoining bathroom.

Tired as she was, there was no way she was going to go and lie down. After what had happened at the cabin, how close she had come to being raped a second time, there was no way she could handle a bed.

Not unless she wanted to completely lose it.

If Christian was there to lie beside her it would be different. His body warm and strong pressed up against her, his arms wrapped securely around her, his heart beating beneath her ear, reassuring her she wasn't alone, then maybe she could face a bed.

But not now.

Not alone here in this room.

Not when she had no idea if Christian was all right.

"Where are you? Are you okay?" she whispered to the empty room.

When she started another circuit of the room her ankle gave out, and she stumbled, throwing her hands out against the wall so she didn't fall. The joint was still swollen and black and blue, and constantly walking on it wasn't helping.

What she should be doing was taking this opportunity to rest it and try to regain a little of the strength her body was so badly lacking. If she couldn't go near the bed, she could at least curl up in the comfortable-looking armchair by the window and rest there.

But Lila was afraid.

Afraid that if her eyes closed again, she would wake up in a worse situation than she was already in.

Zara had been upfront about her plan to keep both of them alive until she had the rest of Alpha Team and their families. That meant she didn't have to worry about being killed just yet, but that wasn't her biggest fear.

Nope, her biggest fear was Ross touching her.

So much had happened in so few days that her mind hadn't had a chance to process it yet. The abduction, waking to find Ross there, being forced to put her mouth on him, having him almost put his mouth on her. Running and falling, walking for hours through the forest, the gunshots, the cabin, the old man.

It was so much …

Too much.

Air began to puff in and out of her chest in harsh gasps.

Great.

She was going to lose it.

Fall apart when she needed to be holding it together.

The feeling of hands on her skin was so real that she slapped at herself, desperate to rid her body of the sensation.

Hot air on her neck.

An intrusion inside her.

Squeezing her legs together did nothing to erase the phantom feelings.

Memories.

Past and present.

Merging together.

White spots danced in front of her, and she wanted so badly to give in to them. Allow unconsciousness to wipe everything away.

Only if she gave in to the urge, she'd be completely helpless.

The white dots grew, likely would have claimed her, but the sound of shouting voices came from outside her room.

Grateful for the distraction, Lila shoved away her fears and the memories that haunted her and hobbled toward the door. Balancing on her good foot, she pressed her ear against the wood.

"She's mine. That was the deal," Ross screamed.

"Idiot. Do you really think I was going to let you keep her? She's not a pet."

"Of course, she's not a pet. She's a woman. One who I bought fourteen years ago. She belongs to me, not you."

"Stupid man." Zara's voice was haughty and pure ice. There was an evilness that hadn't been there before. In the mansion before she'd run, Zara had seemed content to watch whatever

Ross wanted to do to her, more focused on her own plans.

What had changed?

"You really are a fool."

"Don't insult me, Zara. It won't go well for you," Ross said. While there was an edge of anger to his tone, it was nothing like Zara's. Ross was a bad man, a rapist for sure, and he'd gone along with Zara kidnapping her, but he wasn't evil. Not in the same way Zara was.

"You really think you're in control here, don't you?" Zara sounded amused now. "You were never in control, Ross, and you were never getting the girl. She's mine. They're all mine. But you're going to be the one who gets the blame."

"What do you mean?"

"Are you really so stupid you haven't figured it out?" Zara scoffed. "You are the fall guy, you ridiculous moron."

"Fall guy? For what? I don't understand."

"Of course you don't. It's why you're so perfect for the job. When Lila turns up dead, and there's evidence of her being at the mansion in Switzerland that you own, you don't think her family is going to go public with the fact that you raped her as a teen?"

"They wouldn't. If they do they expose themselves and the fact they gave her to me."

"And who's going to corroborate that story? You? Is anyone going to believe you after you killed her?"

"I would never kill Lila." Ross sounded outraged by the notion.

"No, but I would. I will. I'm going to. And then I'm going to turn my husband in. Tell the cops how you went crazy. Went after the girl you were obsessed with. I'll make sure it's known that she was involved with one of Prey's Alpha Team, so when they find all their dead bodies, they'll think you killed them for trying to take your girl away from you," Zara sing-songed the last as though she were excited about her plan.

Zara obviously had no idea that Prey already knew she was

Kristoff Mikhailov's Dark Beauty. Her plan would never work, but the woman didn't know that, and Alpha Team wasn't here. That meant nothing was stopping the woman from killing her now.

"No one will believe that."

"Course they will. I'm an actress. My husband is crazy," Zara's voice changed, filled with fear, laden with tears. "He took my poor friend Liliana. He's obsessed with her. She fought him and he got angry. He killed her. There were men, they tried to save Liliana, but he had them all killed too. I was so afraid he was going to kill me as well. See?" Zara's voice returned to normal and now she sounded pleased with herself. "No way they won't believe me. And then I'll have a platform, a reason to come forward to fight against the government. They don't protect us, they don't care about us, they bow down to the wealthy. I'll step in, bring about change, and show people a new way."

"A way that gives *you* all the power," Ross snapped. "I won't let you use Lila."

"Too late."

Sounds of a scuffle came from the hall, and Lila took a step back. There was a grunt of pain she knew came from Ross, and then everything went silent.

Too silent.

The kind of eerie silence that said something was about to happen.

Something bad.

The sound of a key in the lock had her stumbling backward.

When the door swung open to reveal Zara flanked by half a dozen heavily armed guards, in her hurry to get away from them, Lila fell, landing heavily on her backside, her injured ankle screaming out a protest.

"Hello, friend." Zara's smile was creepy. "You get to be the sacrifice to bring in a new age."

Not just a sacrifice for Zara to bring about whatever plans she and her insane lover had cooked up, but bait for Alpha Team and punishment for them killing Kristoff.

CHAPTER SEVENTEEN

November 22nd
11:47 A.M.

He was getting impatient.

Surf was antsy. His strength had returned, his head was clear with the drugs out of his system, and now he wanted to get out of this cell, get his girl, and get her someplace safe.

It felt like hours had passed since he first woke up, his best guess was at least twelve, and so far nobody had come to see him.

Even though he knew sooner or later they would, Zara wanted him alive so wasn't going to let him starve to death, he was starting to struggle to hold onto any semblance of calm.

The longer he was stuck in there, the more his concerns for Lila grew. She hadn't replied to any of his calls, so he had to assume she wasn't being held down here in the basement with him. The other cells were most likely there to house the rest of his team when they were lured out here.

At least he knew they were alive.

Before having him drugged back at the cabin, Zara had spoken of her plans to collect each member of his team like they were chess pieces. That meant they hadn't been killed in the explosion at the Swiss mansion. It was a relief, a weight off his mind to know they were alive, but he felt antsy without them by his side.

They were a team, and he hated not having them at his back.

A change in the atmosphere alerted him to the fact that someone was coming before he heard any sounds.

Shifting his body so his weight was on the balls of his feet, he waited in the dark back corner of the cell like an animal ready to pounce.

And he *was* ready to pounce.

More than ready.

The footsteps came closer, echoing in the empty space. There was only one set, so it was going to be no trouble taking out the man. Hopefully, he was armed and also had a radio on him.

With the room almost completely dark when the man stopped outside the door, Surf could see him tense. With the hall's light backlighting the man he could get a better look at him than the man could get at him. At worst he'd be nothing but a shadow. At best he'd be completely invisible.

A key slid into a lock, and then a moment later, the door swung open.

"Breaking the light's not going to change anything," the man said, chuckling like he was so confident that he had the upper hand.

Arrogance was going to get him killed.

Timing was everything, and Surf watched and waited while the man continued to laugh to himself as he set down a tray with some food.

His knife was in his pocket, his hands wrapped around the chain, ready to use it as a weapon.

Before the guard could straighten, Surf lunged.

Since the man wasn't expecting him, he had the chain around his neck, his body yanked up flush against his before he even thought to fight back.

Surf felt surprise ripple through the man's body before he snapped to it and began to struggle. His struggles were useless, Surf had all the leverage, plus he had a whole lot of anger raging inside him and only one person here to outlet it on.

Applying pressure with the chain, he cut off the man's oxygen supply, stopping only when his body began to sag.

"Where are we?" he growled in the man's ear.

Instead of answering the guard tried to fight again.

"You're not going anywhere. I can make it quick or slow. Your choice. Where. Are. We?"

"Switzerland," came the sullen reply.

Good, so they hadn't left the country. His team wouldn't have left without him and Lila which meant they were close by. "How far from the mansion?"

There was a pause. The man's body tensed, but then the fight seemed to drain out of him as he accepted that he wasn't walking away alive. "Approximately one hundred kilometers." The man rattled off a location.

A doable distance if he could get his location to his team. All he needed to do was get to Lila, hide her somewhere safe, then wait for his team. "How many guards?"

Another short pause. "Twenty-five of us."

This guy would be dead within the minute, meaning there were another two dozen to go. Not great odds but not terrible either. Especially since he had the element of surprise on his side. Plus, the guy had a weapon on him. "Zara and Ross Duffy still here?"

The man squirmed slightly, but Surf got the impression it wasn't because he didn't want to answer. "They're here, but we work for her."

"She's Kristoff Mikhailov's partner," he said. They suspected, but he wanted confirmation the actress was Dark Beauty.

"Yeah."

"Is Lila Angeletti still here?"

More squirming. "She's here, but Ms. Duffy's plans have changed."

Surf stiffened. "Changed how?"

"She's impatient, tired of waiting."

"How does that affect Lila?" He was getting a bad feeling in his gut. The plan seemed to be that Zara would keep them alive until she had all of Alpha Team and their families, then kill them all, making him and the guys watch as their women were killed. He'd also assumed part of the deal was that Ross got access to

Lila. He'd been afraid she'd be raped, but he hadn't thought her life was in immediate danger.

"She is to be a sacrifice."

"A sacrifice?"

"To bring in a new world. Lila is a celebrity. Her death at the hands of her rapist will cause widespread unrest. Ms. Duffy intends to use it to her advantage."

"You mean she's going to set up her husband and then try to use that to destroy the government and stage a coup."

The man's silence was his answer.

With one swift move, he snapped the man's neck and let the body drop. Changing out of his clothes, he put on the ones the guard had been wearing, then put his clothes on the man and snapped the metal cuff around his ankle. Hopefully, if anyone else came down here, this would buy him a little more time.

Locking the door behind him, he switched through channels on the radio until he found the one his team used. There was a chance they would be out of range, but he had to try.

"PAT5," he said into the radio, using his Prey security code. Each team member from all of Prey's teams had a unique one they could use if they were on an insecure line and needed to identify themselves.

"Surf?" Bear's voice replied moments later.

Relief hit him hard at the sound of his team leader's voice. "Yeah."

"Report."

At Bear's order, he rattled off an extremely brief recount of the last few days and then his location. "I need you guys here sooner rather than later. Seems like whatever Zara Duffy's plan was, it's changed. Lila likely doesn't have long." As much as he hated admitting that, he was free, he was going after her, and his team would already be preparing to come after them. An hour tops and they'd be here.

"Hold on, man, we're on our way," Bear assured him.

"I have to go after Lila."

"Wait until we get there," Bear said.

"I can't, man. If it was Mackenzie, would you be able to sit back and wait?"

It was a rhetorical question, but still Bear muttered, "No. I'd do whatever it took to protect her, keep her safe. I love her."

"And I love Lila. Plus, she's pregnant with my baby."

"Don't get yourself killed."

That was one order he was determined to follow.

There was a door at one end of the corridor, and Surf headed toward it. His plan was to find Lila and get her out of there, or at the very least hide her somewhere. If he couldn't do that, he'd cause some sort of distraction, something to keep Zara's little army busy until his team showed up.

As he made his way up a staircase and into a large kitchen, he found the house quiet. If he didn't know that Lila, Zara, Ross Duffy, and two dozen armed men were here, he would be positive that the place was empty.

Careful to keep his head down, praying the uniform was enough to assure anyone who saw him thought he was just one of the guards, he began a search of the house. The kitchen opened into a large ornate dining room with a table that had to seat at least twenty. That opened off onto a large entrance foyer with another half dozen doors.

Was Lila behind one of them?

Was she waiting for him to come to her?

Where are you, honey?

Letting his gut lead him, Surf picked a door, one that was slightly ajar, and headed for it.

As he approached, he could hear someone talking. He would swear it was Zara. Was she in there with Lila?

After a quick glance around to make sure no one was watching, he peeked through the crack.

His heart dropped at what he saw.

Lila *was* in the room, along with Zara. She was standing on a chair, a rope around her neck looped through one of the beams in the ceiling. Zara was circling her, ranting about Kristoff and the new world they had planned.

One nudge of the chair and if the rope didn't snap Lila's neck it would crush it, cutting off her air supply, slowly suffocating her.

* * * * *

November 22nd
12:39 P.M.

Zara was a lunatic.

Lila had no idea how she'd never seen that before. Perhaps because as a kid, she hadn't liked being made to act, hadn't been interested in it, and hadn't felt like she had anything in common with any other kids she worked with. She had made no attempt to get to know Zara particularly well, but from what she had known, Zara took acting seriously, wanted to be good, and wanted to make a career out of it.

What had happened to that girl?

How had she gotten mixed up with someone like Kristoff Mikhailov?

She supposed the why didn't matter.

Not now.

Not when she was standing on a chair, her arms tied behind her back, and a rope around her neck.

Zara was ranting and raving, carrying on about how much she hated Christian and the rest of Alpha Team and how much she was looking forward to killing them all. The rant was interspersed with various monologues about how she was going to fulfill her plans with Kristoff and take over the government.

None of it was important as far as Lila was concerned, and she wasn't paying much attention. Instead, she was wondering how she was going to get herself out of this mess.

Right now, she wasn't coming up with many options.

"Are you listening to me?" Zara paused in front of the chair, her pretty face marred with a vicious snarl.

Before Lila could offer an answer, something thumped outside the room, drawing both of their attention.

What was that?

As much as she would like to believe it was help, Lila wasn't going to put any of her eggs in that basket.

There was no way out of here.

Zara was going to kill her.

The entire mansion was crawling with armed guards.

Even if she somehow managed to get off the chair without killing herself, there was no way she was getting out of this house alive.

"What was that?" Zara snapped like Lila would have any answers. She knew what Zara knew which was nothing.

When she didn't say anything, Zara huffed in irritation and stalked over to the door, throwing it open.

"Hey," she yelled out. "What's going on. I told you I didn't want to be disturbed."

There was no answer, and Zara huffed once again and stalked out into the hall, giving Lila a small reprieve.

Still, she'd take what she could get right about now.

Letting out a slow breath, she tried to control her fear. She'd accepted that she was going to die here, but it hurt so badly to know that her baby was going to die right along with her.

That didn't seem fair.

Her baby hadn't done anything wrong, it wasn't even born yet. That it would die before even getting to live seemed like a gross injustice.

Zara claimed she wanted a new world, a better world, but really all she wanted was money and power for herself.

That her baby was going to die for some crazy actress to make a power grab filled her with anger.

But it was pointless anger.

Anger, sadness, it didn't make any difference, it wouldn't change what was going to happen to her.

Movement outside the double glass doors on her left caught her attention, and she gasped when a figure slipped into the room.

It was dressed like the rest of the guards here, but it moved like …

"Christian." His name came out on a sob as a barrage of emotions hit her at once. She'd tried to be strong and hold it together, but knowing she was facing certain death was terrifying, especially knowing what the death of her and their baby would do to Christian.

"Hey, sweetheart," he whispered as he came toward her.

Lila scanned his body in search of injuries. He seemed to be moving easily, and his handsome face had no new wounds. She so badly wanted to grab hold of him and kiss him until all her fear receded and she could breathe normally again.

"What did you …? How did you …? Are you okay?" she asked.

"Fine, darlin'," he assured her. "More worried about you. Did they hurt you?"

"No."

"Did Ross …?"

"He didn't touch me. They just left me in a bedroom until a couple of hours ago when Zara had me brought down here."

She noted his broad shoulders slumped briefly in what she assumed was relief. His green gaze met hers as he reached out and touched a hand to her stomach. "Our little baby bear?"

"No bleeding, so I think it's hanging in there." At least she prayed it was. Until she was examined in a hospital and told by a doctor that her baby was okay, she was afraid to believe it.

"Tough like its mama," Christian said as his fingers caressed her stomach. "Come on, let's get you out of here."

"Where were you?"

"Basement."

"How did you get out?"

"I'll tell you everything once we're safe. I want you to wrap your legs around my waist, and I'm going to get this rope off."

Christian's large hands spanned her waist, and he helped her lift her legs and curl them around his hips. It was awkward to keep them there with her bad ankle, but she locked her feet together as best she could, and gritted her teeth so she didn't cry out in pain.

The last thing they needed was someone to come in and find Christian here.

It didn't take him long to untie the rope around her neck and she let out a sigh as the scratchy material was gone. Exhausted down to her very bones, she sagged against him, letting her forehead drop to his shoulder.

"Almost done, baby," he murmured soothingly as he sat on the chair she'd just been standing on and set her on his lap.

While she rested, he pulled out a small knife, cut the ropes binding her wrists, and slowly moved her hands around in front of her. Her shoulders ached from hours pulled in an unnatural position, and her wrists were so thankful not to have rope tied tightly around them.

"It's going to be okay. I'm going to get you home." The words were softly spoken but with a firmness that said he would not allow any other option.

"Get *us* home," she corrected. After a taste of what it was like to be loved by an honorable man who would protect her from anything, there was no way she could live without him.

Instead of answering, Christian held her hands in his, massaging them gently to restore blood flow.

"Christian?" There was something he wasn't telling her, and she didn't like it.

"I want you to run."

Lila's mouth dropped open. Surely, he didn't mean … "On my own?"

"I was able to contact my team, they're on their way, but Zara will be back any minute, and I don't want you hurt. I want you to run, find a place to hide. I'll come for you."

Of course he would.

That wasn't what she was worried about.

What she was worried about was Christian sacrificing himself for her and their baby. She wanted all three of them to live. He'd been through so much, she had too, it was time for them to get some happiness.

"No, I can't leave you."

"I'll be right behind you. Promise. As soon as my team gets here and we have Zara and Ross in custody, I'll come and get you."

"But the guards …"

"I can take the guards. And all I need is to hold them off until my team arrives."

"But …"

"It will be okay, honey. I promise."

She wanted so badly to believe him, but things just seemed to keep getting worse. Now he expected her to run and hide like a coward while he took on a crazy woman and her army.

"Christian, I can't take you …" Damn, she couldn't even say the words. Couldn't even think them.

Crushing her mouth to his, she kissed him like she was a dying woman, and he was the air she needed to live.

In a way he was what she needed to live.

Ever since she'd run from her old life she hadn't really been living, just existing. Now she knew what it felt like to live life to the fullest and that chance at happiness was being dangled in front of her like a carrot.

The universe couldn't be mean enough to snatch it away, could it?

One of his hands tangled in her messy hair and he kissed her back as fervently as she was kissing him.

A sound behind them had him standing and setting her on her feet behind him.

The door to the room swung open, and a couple of guards stormed in.

Christian didn't hesitate.

He fired, taking down one first and then the other.

"Run, Lila," he ordered.

She hesitated for only a second, knowing that if she stayed, she wasn't helping she was impeding his ability to do what he had been trained to do.

Even though it broke her heart, she turned and ran as fast as her bad ankle allowed out into the gardens, heading for the forest, praying Christian survived the gunfight she could hear raging behind her.

CHAPTER EIGHTEEN

November 22nd
1:08 P.M.

Come on, guys. Any time now would be good.

Surf fired off another shot and another guard dropped.

These guys were good but weren't nearly as trained as he was. Already he'd killed at least six, but there were still another eighteen to go. He was just waiting for them to realize that all they had to do to take him down was circle around and come at him from both sides.

Thankfully, they hadn't figured that out yet.

The door behind him was still open from where Lila had fled, and he prayed her ankle held out long enough for her to get away, find herself somewhere safe to hide and wait for him.

At least all the guards were focused on him, so he hoped no one had followed her.

Nothing mattered more to him than getting Lila safe. If he had to give his life to ensure that she and their baby lived, then that's what he'd do, trusting that his team would take care of his family for him.

Family.

The word had always been a sour one to him, given what his own family was like, but now, when he thought of Lila and their child, it was sweet.

The sweetest word that existed.

This is why he would do everything in his power to stay alive so he could spend the rest of his life with them.

Movement caught his attention through the glass.

They'd finally figured out that there was no way he could effectively shoot at the men coming through the door from the hall, and men coming in through the garden.

Looks like he might not get that sweet ending after all.

Bullets began to pepper the wall behind him. He'd knocked a huge oak desk over and taken cover behind it. It had protected him so far, but it wasn't going to be able to save his life from a full-on assault.

Not that he was giving up without a fight.

If they wanted to take him down, he wasn't going to go easily.

More bullets attacked the desk, and he popped up to fire and heard another body drop, but then the bullets continued, and he could hear them moving slowly toward him, sure they had him right where they wanted him.

And they did.

He'd given it everything he had, but it didn't look like he was walking out of this room alive. He prayed Lila was somewhere safe. That no one would find her until his team got there.

I'm sorry, baby.

Just as he was about to accept his fate, the sound of bodies hitting the floor gave him a rush of hope.

Could it be?

The room went quiet.

Cautiously he stood, weapon up and ready to fire.

Then he lowered it and grinned.

"Needed a hand here I see." Arrow grinned.

"'Bout time you guys showed up." Surf relaxed now that his team was here.

"Hey, you were the one who decided to take his girl for a stroll through the forest," Mouse teased.

"I had everything under control." He shrugged but couldn't be more grateful that they were there. He had no idea how they'd made it so quickly, but he was glad they had.

"Sure you did." Bear rolled his eyes, but then he sobered. "You okay?"

"A little banged up," he admitted. The gunshot wound in his shoulder ached, and he had a lingering headache. There were bruises from his tussle with the man at the cabin, but there was nothing he was concerned about.

"Lila?" Arrow asked, scanning the room that was littered with bodies.

"Told her to run. She's hurt, think she has a broken ankle. Plus, she took a dip in the river and stopped breathing." Just thinking about it had his heart clenching.

"We'll get her to the hospital," Arrow assured him.

"First, we need to make sure the house is clear," Bear added.

"Zara Duffy?" Domino asked.

"She was in here with Lila. I don't know where she went. Her plans have changed," he informed her team. "Originally, she wanted to get all of us here, kill our women in front of us then kill each of us. Now she's getting impatient. She was going to kill Lila as some sort of sacrifice to start up her campaign."

"She can't have gone far, probably holed up here somewhere," Brick said.

Surf hoped so.

Because the alternative was that once again she had taken a few men and disappeared at the first sign of trouble.

The woman might want to instigate a war so she could overthrow the government, but she didn't have the stomach to do what actually had to be done. She was a coward who prioritized herself, letting others do her dirty work.

"For now, your girl is probably safer out there until we've cleared the house," Mouse said.

"Then let's get clearing." He wanted this over. He wanted Lila safe, checked out, and in a hospital receiving the medical treatment she needed. Then he wanted to take her home and spoil her rotten, do everything he could to make up for all the horror she'd been through the last few days. All the horrors she'd been through in a lifetime. He wanted to soothe each of those old hurts along with all the new ones, and make sure she knew he would always take care of her.

Together his team moved through the large house, clearing room after empty room. It wasn't until they got to a bedroom on the third floor that they found a locked door.

Zara?

His gut said she wouldn't hang around, that when she'd heard the gunfire she had fled, but they had no proof.

With a nod, Bear prepared to break down the door as the rest of them were ready to fire at any threat that presented itself.

One well-placed kick was all it took to splinter the door.

Inside was Ross Duffy.

The man was naked and tied to a chair. There were bruises littering his torso, his nose was swollen, both eyes black and one was swollen almost shut.

His one good eye was wide and full of fear as he stared back at them. There was a ball gag in his mouth, and even though he knew they couldn't understand anything he tried to say he was yelling at them.

There was a distinct sense of satisfaction at seeing the man who had hurt Lila trussed up and suffering. No amount of suffering was ever going to be enough for what he'd done to her, but at least he was paying.

"Ross Duffy," he said slowly as he stalked toward the chair, noting the way the man flinched and tried to press back into the seat as though there was some escape to be found. "Do you know who I am?"

The old man nodded frantically.

"Then you know I have every reason to hurt you given what you did to my woman. You know who they are?" He inclined his head at his team who had his back.

More nodding.

"They aren't going to care what I do to you. They care about

Lila too. You get my meaning? This can go easy, or it can go hard. That's up to you. Personally, I'm torn. I want to hurt you, cause you even a tenth of the pain you caused Lila. But I also want to go get my girl and get her the hell out of here. So, you answer my questions, we cuff you and hand you off to the cops, and you won't need to take a beating. Another beating," he added with a snicker.

When Ross nodded frantically again, Surf stepped up and removed the gag. For now, he'd leave the man cuffed to the chair. He didn't think Ross Duffy was any sort of threat, but it paid to be safe, especially when he wanted to get out there and find Lila.

"She's crazy," Ross blurted the second the gag was off.

"Who is?" Surf asked.

"Zara. She wants to kill Lila. When I told her that wasn't our deal, she had this done to me." The man looked down at his battered body. "Lila is … okay?"

"She's none of your business. You don't talk about her, you don't say her name, you don't even think about her," he growled.

"What was the plan?" Bear asked, arms crossed over his wide chest as he stared down at the old man making Ross shrink further in on himself.

"I … I always wanted Lila, but she had proof I …"

"Raped her," Surf supplied with a snarl, still hating that word in conjunction with the woman he loved.

"I … she was given to me."

"She's not a possession, she can't be given away. She's a person," Surf hissed.

"I love her. I wanted her back. Zara has some issue with your team. You killed her boyfriend. She said it was a win-win. She could use Lila … umm …" Ross trailed off shooting him a nervous look. "I mean … her … use her as bait. The rest of you would come. She'd keep you all prisoner, take your wives, make you watch as she …"

"Yeah, yeah, we got that," he snapped. "What changed?"

"I don't know. Zara is edgy and impatient, she was talking about some plan she and her lover had to take over the government. I didn't know anything about that. I swear. Just that she wanted revenge on you. I was supposed to be able to keep Lila after as long as I kept quiet and let her use the Swiss villa. Zara is insane, dangerous, and obsessed. She won't stop until you're all dead, until she gets everything she wants."

"And that all starts with killing Lila," he said. The need to get to her flooded his system.

"I know you don't believe me, but I do love Lila, I always have. Don't let my wife hurt her. Please," Ross whispered brokenly.

There was no way he was letting anyone harm a hair on Lila's head.

It was time to go get his woman.

* * * * *

November 22nd
2:36 P.M.

Lila cried out as she tripped on something and went down hard on her hands and knees.

Her ankle was a burning, throbbing mass of agony and she wasn't sure she could get back up on it even if she wanted to.

And she wanted to.

She wanted to put as much distance between herself and the house as she possibly could. There was a part of her mind that recognized the further she went the harder it would be for Christian to find her, but there was some primal part, some flight or fight part, that was compelled to keep moving.

Distance equaled safety.

That was all her mind could cling to.

The compulsion to keep moving was strong, stronger than she

could control right now. So even though her body was weak and exhausted, running on nothing but fumes, Lila pushed up until she was standing.

Gritting her teeth, she cautiously placed her bad foot on the ground, but as soon as it bore her weight it collapsed.

Another cry fell from her lips as the pain in her ankle intensified until it was almost unbearable.

Still, she had no choice but to bear it.

Tears blurred her vision, and she sank to rest against the cold ground. The sticks and rocks were scratchy against her cheek, but she barely registered it. Her whole body was one painful, uncomfortable, exhausted mess. A little more discomfort was nothing.

It would be so nice to close her eyes, sleep, and let everything else fade away.

Rest.

Just for a moment.

She was so tired.

Lila had already started drifting off, her wiped-out body almost completely drained of energy.

It was only fear that made her stir.

What if Christian's team didn't arrive in time?

What if Zara's guards killed him?

What if they were already out here searching for her?

There was no way she was going back there. She wasn't going to let Zara kill her, using her as a prop for her twisted plans. Nor was she going to be used as a prop in her games of revenge against Alpha Team.

She wasn't going to die out here in Switzerland. Wasn't going to lose her baby and the man she loved.

Not going to happen.

But it seemed highly unlikely that she was going to be able to walk any further.

Okay, if she couldn't walk, she could always crawl. Or maybe it was time to hide. Christian had told her to find a place where she could hide away and wait for him to come for her.

Lila had to believe he was alive and he would come.

Allowing herself to think—even for a second—that Christian was already dead would open up room for her to give up. And she couldn't give up, not when her baby was counting on her. She'd failed her first child, hadn't been strong enough to stand up to her parents and deal with her trauma. There was no way on earth she was going to let this baby down as well.

She had to be strong.

Scanning the area, she spotted what looked like a cave up ahead. One similar to those Christian had found for them to stay in when they'd been together. But now it was just her. There would be no MREs, no thermal blanket to snuggle under, no big solid presence to make her feel safe.

Just her.

Alone.

There was no way she could get back on her feet, her ankle had done all it could and now it needed rest, so she was going to have to crawl over to the cave.

In theory, that sounded easy enough, but her arms were shaky and wobbled precariously, wind sent her hair whipping around her face, and there wasn't a single angle that didn't put pressure on her ankle. With each drag of her leg, it screamed out in agony, and by the time she managed to cross the forest floor and enter the cave she was breathing hard, sweating, and a fresh wave of tears were stinging the backs of her eyes.

But she'd done it.

She was here and somewhat safe. All she had to do was curl into a ball, try to conserve some body heat so she didn't freeze to death, and wait.

Carefully shifting around so she was sitting on her bottom, Lila winced as she shuffled backward until her back rested against the rough rock of the cave. If Zara and her army found her, she wasn't going to be able to run from them. Her ankle was too painful. Lila hated admitting it, but it was the truth. The only thing left for her to do was wait here and pray Christian found her first.

Another wave of exhaustion rolled over her, and she tipped her head back. Never in her life had she felt this drained. She hadn't even realized a body could be this level of tired and still function.

Well, semi-function.

As wonderful as sleep felt, she didn't want to pass out and have Christian walk right past her. He knew how to track someone, but the wind was continuing to pick up speed, and she was worried that it was blowing the leaves and sticks around, wiping out any trail she would have left.

As weak as she felt right now, Lila wasn't sure she could survive a night out here in the cold.

Stay awake, she had to stay awake.

Counting.

She could count.

That was simple and something she could do pretty much on automatic, but it should be just enough to keep her brain operational.

"One, two, three …" *Would Christian be here before she reached ten?*

"Four, five, six, seven …" *Maybe before one hundred?*

"Eight, nine …"

"How cute, you're counting."

Lila screamed at the sound of the voice. That scream quickly morphed into a cry of terror.

Zara was there.

And she wasn't alone.

One of the bodyguards she remembered seeing on the plane, and at both of the mansions was with her. The man was always close to Zara, and she assumed he was her own personal bodyguard while the rest of the men were her army.

With her back pressed against the cave, solid and unbreakable, there was nowhere for her to go.

No escape.

Just a destiny she had tried so hard to avoid.

A destiny that kept coming for her no matter what.

"Of all the caves you could have crawled into you picked this one. Practically did my work for me," Zara continued gleefully, and Lila saw that Zara and the bodyguard were behind her in the cave.

Zara had that right. Of all the caves she could have collapsed outside of, it had to be the one where the woman who wanted her dead was hiding out.

Destiny.

Sometimes you just couldn't fight the universe's plans for you.

Her future was now sealed. She'd be killed and used as a weapon by Zara to put her plans in motion. Lila accepted that, all she hoped was that Christian knew she'd done the best she could.

"Your stupid boyfriend and that team of his keep messing everything up. I don't know how he did it, but he escaped his cell, got you out, and killed most of my men." In the shadows of the cave, Zara looked positively evil. There was something in her eyes, something unbalanced. It was like Kristoff Mikhailov's evil insanity had somehow rubbed off on her.

Zara took a step toward her. Lila was too tired to even make an attempt at shifting away. The bodyguard had a weapon in his hand, one which was aimed directly at her. There was no way she was lucking her way out of this, and fighting her way out was completely impossible.

"But they won't stop me from killing you." Zara smirked and reached out to tug on a lock of Lila's messy blonde hair. "*Nothing* is going to stop me from …" The woman trailed off as they heard the sound of voices nearby.

"I didn't think she could make it this far."

Relief hit her hard.

Christian.

That was Christian's voice.

"She's tough," someone else said. Arrow. She was sure that was Alpha Team's medic.

"Not arguing about that, brother, but you didn't see the shape she was in. She's faced everything like a champ, no complaints, walking on that ankle for hours, but she was close to tapped out," Surf said.

"Don't give up on her," Arrow said.

"Never." The strength in Christian's voice sent an infusion of strength through her. If he hadn't given up on her then she couldn't give up either.

Lila opened her mouth to scream, but a hand covered her mouth.

Not to be deterred, she sank her teeth into the palm, and Zara hissed and snatched her hand back.

Before she could suck in a breath and scream for all she was worth, Zara's voice whispered in her ear.

"You scream, and Aleksei here kills them. He was Kristoff's right-hand man you know, he'd love nothing more than to shoot your precious boyfriend. In fact, he's been waiting for an excuse to do some damage to the men who murdered his boss. Do you want to give him that excuse?"

No.

The answer to that question was simple.

There was no way she would risk Christian.

Not for anything.

Not even for a chance at saving her own life.

With tears streaming down her cheeks, she pressed her lips together and listened as Christian and Arrow's voices faded into the forest leaving her alone with two dangerous lunatics.

Destiny sucked.

CHAPTER NINETEEN

November 22nd
3:12 P.M.

This was gloriously, darkly delicious.

Zara was buzzed with excitement.

The look of utter defeat and acceptance in Liliana's eyes as she sat silently and waited for her only chance at rescue to disappear was everything.

Soon it wouldn't just be one pathetic washed-up actress whose life she held in the palm of her hand, it would be the entire country. Then one day the whole world.

She wasn't stopping until she had achieved everything she and Kristoff had planned.

Nothing was going to stop her from avenging the death of her beloved and making all of their dreams come true.

Pleasure built between her legs. Zara still wore the beautiful gift Kristoff had gotten for her, she kept it on every day, but most days it didn't have her body humming on the edge of pleasure, waiting for her man to give her permission to come like it had when she knew Kristoff was in control, tormenting her with beautiful pleasure.

Kristoff had owned her body as well as her heart and soul, and it hurt to live in a world without him. Hurt more than she ever could have imagined. Living without him was a kind of torture different from the games they would play. Then she had known that in his own twisted way, he would love and protect her, that he cared about her and wanted to bring her pleasure, but only when he knew the time was right.

Only when the darkness that lived inside both of them peaked.

Darkness was growing inside her now.

Now as she watched Liliana's heart and soul get crushed. Knowing she had done that brought about that look of utter desolation.

Kristoff would be proud of her.

"They're gone," Aleksei announced. The man had been Kristoff's personal bodyguard until her lover had assigned him to her. He had spent every second of every day for the last few years by her side. He was the one who would remove her chastity belt to allow her time to use the bathroom. He'd seen her naked, and even now, although Kristoff was gone and she didn't have to continue to wear it, she did, and she allowed Aleksei to keep control of the key.

It was the closest thing she had to Kristoff.

"Then it's time for us to leave. They'll be back." As nice as it would have been to take down the two Alpha Team members, they were skilled, and it was just her and Aleksei. She would get them but when the time was right. When the odds were in her favor.

"What are you going to do? Where are you taking me?" Liliana asked as Aleksei curled a hand around her arm and roughly pulled her to her feet.

"You, my dear, are going to be the bait that finally gives me Alpha Team," Zara replied.

Aleksei tugged Liliana along with him, but she made it no more than a step before she cried out and stumbled.

"Hurry up," she snapped. They didn't have time for theatrics.

"I can't walk anymore," Liliana said. Pain filled her voice and was etched into her features.

Huffing an irritated sigh, she waved at Aleksei. "Carry her. We have to get out of here."

With an annoyed growl, Aleksei threw the woman over his shoulder, and they both crept out of the cave. The Prey guys were good. Every time she thought she had them they did something to surprise her. With the one called Surf locked in her dungeon, Zara had thought that everything else was just a foregone conclusion.

She'd been wrong.

It wouldn't happen again.

Toying with the team had been the wrong move. It allowed a window of opportunity Alpha Team had taken advantage of.

This time she was going straight for the kill shot.

Not quite as satisfying, but in the end the men responsible for Kristoff's death would be punished.

Then it was time to move on to the next stage in her plan.

When the public learned that influential billionaire movie and TV producer Ross Duffy was not only a rapist who had killed one of his victims but was also involved in a plot to set explosives off around the country to destabilize the government they would go crazy.

That was when she would step in.

She already had a new presidential candidate waiting in the wings, and with her husband branded a pedophile, a psychopath, and a traitor, she would step in as the new First Lady. Kristoff had financially backed the man, who was already playing his role to perfection. With Ross out of the way, she could pretend to fall in love with the man who wanted to make their country a safer place.

While in theory, she would have no real control, she had enough blackmail material on the next president that she would be the puppet master. Kristoff had taught her you didn't need to be the face of something to be the one with all the power. He hadn't been the face of the Mikhailov Bratva, yet he had been the one in control. The two of them would have run the entire country from behind the scenes, she would play the dutiful wife, but she would belong to her lover always.

Zara had learned many things from her lover, another of which was to always have a backup plan for your plan, and a backup plan for your backup plan. Being prepared when you were playing such a high-stakes game was only good sense.

When they reached one of their hidden vehicles, Aleksei tossed Liliana in the trunk and opened the back door for her. Once she was buckled in, he climbed into the driver's seat and took them toward another property in the area she had rented under her husband's name.

She hummed to herself as they drove through the quiet, winding roads. That pressure between her legs was growing.

Maybe instead of being turned on by Kristoff, she was now turned on by the pain and suffering of others.

Knowing Liliana was terrified and in pain in the trunk of the car, accepting her fate and knowing there would be no last-minute reprieve had her squirming in her seat.

When she had first begun to plan this whole thing out with Kristoff, he had been the one to want the control. She'd wanted the money and prestige that would come with it. Perhaps she was becoming more like her lover since he was murdered because now she just didn't want the money and prestige, she wanted the power and control as well.

Got off on knowing that she could play others like the puppets they were.

By the time they reached their destination, it was starting to get dark. Perfect. It wouldn't be long to wait until she could make the call.

"Bring her inside, Aleksei," she ordered as he opened her door for her and she slid out.

"Yes, ma'am."

"Always so polite." Zara smiled in admiration. A bodyguard who knew his place was everything. So many people didn't know their place. How many servants had she had who thought they could talk to her however they pleased or try to rebuke her or control her in some way?

Too many to count.

But not Aleksei. He was submissive and loyal, the two attributes that had not only earned his place as Kristoff's personal protection, but also the job as hers. He would be rewarded for his loyalty.

After her lover's murder, Zara had this place built. It was a replica of the building on the Mikhailov property where those who had been disloyal received their punishment. Where Kristoff's life had ended. It had seemed only fitting that this be where they died as well.

"String her up." Zara waved a hand at the ropes in the middle of the room. This was where she had intended to kill off each of the Alpha Team member's women, making them watch from where they would be chained to the metal tables spread throughout the room. Once they had watched their loved ones die, as she'd had to do, they would be killed slowly, painfully.

Now she was going to have to go with fast.

She needed these men dead. They were too focused on her, too determined to try to stop her. There was no choice but to eliminate them.

"What are you going to do to me?" Liliana asked as Aleksei secured metal cuffs around her wrists.

"So full of questions," Zara said, amused.

"I deserve to know how I'm going to die."

Liliana's words sent a bolt of anger through her. "You deserve nothing." Stalking closer, she backhanded the woman. "Do you think you matter? You are nothing but an insignificant pest. One whose only purpose is to bring in the men I must see pay for what they did."

"Is that all you can think of?" Liliana demanded. Aleksei was crouched by her feet, fitting metal cuffs to her ankles, and as the loyal guard he was, he tightened the one around her bad ankle at the woman's disrespectful tone, causing Liliana to cry out.

"Thank you, dear," she said, patting Aleksei's head.

Blue eyes glared at her defiantly. "You were insignificant too, weren't you, Zara? Always every director's second choice for the role, always in the shadows, not as good as the other girls. Not as good as me. How many times did I beat you for a part? How many times have you come in second for an award?"

Anger seethed inside Zara.

She wasn't second.

Kristoff had chosen her.

She was going to be the new First Lady.

The new puppet master in control of the most powerful nation in the world.

Control.

She had to grasp her control back.

"Strip her," she ordered Aleksei who was pulling on the ropes so they would lift Liliana, suspending her in the air. "She doesn't need clothes for this role."

Liliana's already pale face drained of color. There was hunger in Aleksei's eyes as he took out a knife and began to cut her clothes from her body. Her loyal soldier deserved a reward.

Meeting the other woman's gaze Zara held it, a smile curving her lips up. "When you're done, Aleksei, you may have yourself a little treat."

"Thank you, ma'am."

"Aleksei, use the remote," she ordered as he unzipped his pants.

He pulled the remote from his pocket, and a moment later, the toy inside her sprang to life.

As Zara watched, pleasure built inside her. Control, power, she was in charge here. She decided who lived and died. She alone was judge, jury, and executioner. She was going to be the ruler of the world, and she owed it all to the man she loved more than anything.

Zara came in a rush, Liliana's cries ringing in her ears.

CHAPTER TWENTY

November 23rd
12:00 A.M.

Surf was well past the point of frustration by the time his cell phone buzzed with an incoming call.

They'd scoured the forest surrounding the house where he and Lila had been held, but so far they hadn't found her. At first, he'd found a trail to follow, but bad weather—wind and then freezing rain—had caused him to lose it. He knew Lila had to be out there somewhere, but she was weak and exhausted, injured and in pain, and he was afraid she'd passed out somewhere, unable to hear them as they searched for her.

He was sure there was no way she could survive a night out in the cold.

Which meant if he didn't find her soon, he'd lose her forever.

"I've got a call from an unknown number," he called out to the others. After searching for Lila for hours they had regrouped at the house. Ross Duffy had been taken into custody by local cops and would be sent Stateside later in the day. They'd searched along with the local police department for miles around the house, now they were trying to come up with another plan to find Lila.

Deep in his gut, Surf feared he knew the reason she hadn't been found, he just wasn't ready to go there yet.

"Put it on speaker," Bear ordered as his team gathered around him.

"Took you longer than I would have thought to answer. I thought you were anxious to find your woman," a voice he immediately recognized came through the phone.

"Zara." Fear warred with anger as he had no choice now but to accept that the greatest threat facing Lila wasn't hypothermia.

No.

It was this psychopath.

"In the flesh so to speak," Zara said, then laughed at her little joke.

"Where is she?" he growled.

"Oh, I'm going to give you the location, don't you worry your pretty little head about that. I want you to find her," Zara told him.

"Don't, Christian," Lila's voice sounded further away as it came down the line. "Don't come, please. It's a trap."

They all knew that.

"Thank you for that interruption, darling," Zara drawled. "I think your man is smart enough to figure that out. But he's going to come anyway, even knowing it's a trap, aren't you?"

There was nothing that would stop him from going after Lila. Even if it killed him, he would risk everything for a chance at saving her. "I'm coming."

"No," Lila cried out, and he felt her pain in that one word. It was the same pain echoing inside him. He didn't want to die, and certainly didn't want to lose the woman he loved and their baby, but he couldn't stay away.

"I knew it," Zara sang, sounding delighted.

"She strapped a bomb on me," Lila cried. "It's set to go off in one hour."

"That was supposed to be our little surprise," Zara said, obviously to Lila, and he heard the sound of flesh hitting flesh, and even though Lila didn't cry out he knew Zara had hit her.

"You'll pay for that," he growled.

"You'll be dead soon. How exactly are you going to make me pay?" Zara taunted.

"Please, Christian, please don't come. I don't want you to die, please," Lila sobbed.

"I'm coming for you, sweetheart. Nothing on earth could keep me away." If nothing else, then he would ensure that his woman didn't die alone.

"Perfect. I'm sure you won't mind that I'm not here to greet you," Zara said, then tittered a little laugh. "I'll text you the address. Enjoy one last moment with your girl before you both go kaboom." The line went dead, and a couple of seconds later, a text with an address came through.

"That's almost an hour away," Mouse said.

"She wants us to show up just before the explosion goes off," Arrow added.

"I'm so sorry. This is all because I killed my brother," Domino said, looking tortured.

"Not your fault," Bear said firmly.

"You guys shouldn't come. If we can't stop this then I don't want you dying. I … I have to go, even if it's pointless. I can't let her die alone." The thought of her afraid, sitting there waiting for the bomb to go off all alone made his stomach cramp.

Five offended faces glared back at him.

"If you think we're letting you go in alone then you hit your head harder than I thought," Arrow snapped.

"You guys have families. There's no way I could ask you to risk everything for me and Lila."

"You didn't ask," Brick said.

"We live as a team we die as a team," Bear said, fire dancing in his brown eyes. "And who said anything about dying today?"

"You heard what she said. The bomb is rigged to go off in an hour, it'll take us most of that time to get there, and those people love bombs. It's not going to be an easy one to disarm, she wants us dead." As much as he wanted to believe they could save Lila he wasn't sure that they could.

"Never underestimate Alpha Team," Mouse said. The man had never met a bomb he couldn't disarm, but would there be enough time for him to figure out how it was set up before it blew and took them all out with it?

"Are you guys sure?" Surf knew they were stronger together but asking them to risk their lives was something else.

"You shouldn't even have to ask." Arrow grinned then slammed a fist into his shoulder, hard enough that Surf stumbled backward.

"Let's go save your girl," Bear said.

They bundled into an SUV, Surf at the wheel. With the address programmed into the GPS, he didn't even bother to pretend to follow a single road rule. It was the middle of the night, the roads were empty, and nothing mattered to him except getting to Lila as quickly as was humanly possible.

If he wanted a chance at saving her, he had to give Mouse as much time to work on that bomb as he could.

It was Lila's only chance.

The only chance for all of them.

Because he wasn't leaving Lila's side, and he knew his team would have his back until the end.

No matter what.

They flew across the roads and made excellent time and had a full ten minutes by the time they reached the address.

Surf couldn't even remember if he turned off the engine, all he knew was that he had to get to Lila.

Behind him, the others checked to make sure they were alone, but he already knew they were. Zara wanted to kill them in an explosion, she had a thing for them, or Kristoff Mikhailov had a thing for them. Their plan involved bombs, and Zara wanted to take them all out with one.

"Lila," he called out as he stepped into a large shed. She was in the middle of the room, strung up with chains by her wrists and ankles. There was a suicide vest strapped to her chest, and she was naked.

Red rage burned inside him, but he stowed it and ran toward

her.

"Christian," his name came out in a sob, and she shook her head. "You shouldn't have come. Why did you come?"

"Always going to be there for you, baby. That's what I promised you." Reaching her, he cupped her cheek in his palm and stroked his thumb across her temple.

"I don't want you to die." Tears streamed down her cheeks, and he saw her gaze shift to something behind him and she stiffened. "You all came? No! You have to leave! You all have partners, kids, I don't want anyone dying for me."

"Not your choice to make," Bear said firmly.

"We're a team. We face things together," Arrow added.

"And no one is dying today," Mouse vowed as he shifted to stand behind Lila where he could better see the bomb.

"I've never had a team before," she said. Although tears were still tumbling down her cheeks, there was a hint of awe in her voice, like she couldn't quite believe she was worthy of them all risking everything for her.

"Well, you do now," he assured her. As much as he wanted to cover her, hold her, gather her up, and never let her go, he didn't want to do anything that might set the bomb off. He had no idea how stable it was, and Mouse needed full access to the vest so no one died tonight.

"Christian, if it gets close to zero promise me you'll leave." Lila's blue eyes pleaded with him, and while he hated to disappoint her, that was one promise he couldn't make.

"No, baby. I'm not leaving you. Ever."

Resignation filled her face. "Your team has to leave. I appreciate the sentiment more than you know, but I won't hurt Mackenzie, Phoebe, Piper, and Julia."

"It's going to be okay, my sweet mama bear. Try to have faith." His hand remained on her cheek while his other brushed lightly across her stomach beneath the vest.

"I'm trying, but I'm so tired."

"I know, baby, but I need you to hold on just a little bit longer. Can you do that for me?"

Determination flared in her eyes. She was down, but she wasn't out for the count. "Yes."

"There's my girl." Keeping his gaze fixed on Lila, willing his strength into her, he asked the one question they all were desperate to know the answer to. "Mouse? Can you disarm it?"

* * * * *

November 23rd
12:52 A.M.

Lila held her breath as she waited for Mouse's answer.

Live or die?

As scared as she was to be blown up, she was more scared knowing that other people might die along with her. The thought of the women she hardly knew but had welcomed her so openly and warmly losing the men they loved, the fathers of their children, gutted her.

"I got this," Mouse said.

He sounded so confident, and Lila wanted to believe him, she really did, but so far every time she thought things were improving, finally looking up, something else bad happened.

Why should this time be any different?

"Hey." Christian increased the pressure with his thumb as he continued to sweep it across her temple in an attempt to soothe her.

It wasn't working.

"Trust Mouse. He knows what he's doing," Christian assured her.

This wasn't about not trusting Mouse or believing in his skills, it was that destiny still had its claws dug deep into her skin, and she wasn't sure it was going to loosen its hold.

Still, she wanted to reassure Christian so she nodded. "I trust him."

From the small quirk of his lips, she knew she hadn't convinced him. "It's going to be okay, sweetheart. We're going to get you out of here."

"Area is clear," Bear announced, coming over to join them.

Everyone was gathered around her, and although they had their weapons hanging across their bodies, in their hands they held tools. They looked like bolt cutters, and she assumed that they were to cut her free from the chains that held her suspended in the air the second Mouse got the bomb disarmed.

Assuming he got it disarmed.

A tremor rippled through her body. The large space was freezing, and she didn't have any clothes on. She'd be embarrassed about being in front of Christian's entire team completely naked, but to be honest, she was too exhausted for another emotion.

"Not long, honey," Mouse assured her.

"We got this, baby," Christian said. "Hold on just a little longer."

She wanted to, but she was so tired.

When would this finally be over?

"How many minutes left on the timer?" she asked. If it got too close, she was going to insist they all leave. The last thing she wanted was to have the deaths of six good men on her conscience as she took her final breath. She'd tell the guys they had to take Christian with them. She wouldn't let him die for her.

She loved him too much for that.

No one gave her an answer.

"How long?" she repeated.

"Three minutes left, but I'm almost there," Mouse finally replied.

One hundred and eighty seconds.

That wasn't much. Barely long enough for the guys to get far enough away from the bomb before it blew. If Mouse didn't have the bomb disarmed before it hit two minutes, they would have to leave.

"Christian …" she started.

"It's going to be okay, don't give up faith."

Lila closed her eyes and tilted her face into his hand, soaking up what could be her last moments with him. It was so unfair, she wanted the future with Christian and their baby that she'd been dreaming about, and they were so close to having it.

But bemoaning the unfairness of the world wouldn't change anything.

"How long left?" she asked again.

"Mouse," Christian warned.

She knew he was trying to protect her, but she needed to know. For days now everything that had happened to her had been completely outside her control. Now she needed the only control she had left, which was knowing exactly how many seconds she had left to live.

"Please, Mouse," she whispered.

After a brief hesitation, he replied, "Two minutes."

One hundred and twenty seconds.

It was time.

"You guys have to go. I appreciate everything you've tried to do for me, I really do, but I don't want to make your wives widows, and your children grow up without their fathers. Leave. Please," the last was a broken plea she prayed convinced them.

The men stood stiffly.

Unmoving.

But Christian nodded at them.

"Go. Neither of us wants to break your family's hearts," he said.

"You too," she told Christian as the others reluctantly moved away.

"No way in hell, mama bear. We either both walk out of this

room alive or neither of us do."

There was determination on his face. The steely kind that said arguing was futile.

She loved him so much it hurt.

Hurt knowing that love was going to get him killed.

"Please," she begged.

Instead of answering, he crushed his mouth to hers in a kiss that started fiery and passionate but morphed into something deeper. The fire and passion were still there, but there was also tenderness, sweetness, and love.

An entire lifetime in one moment.

"Never leaving you, sweetheart, because you're the other half of my heart. I don't want to live in a world without you in it."

His words cracked the shell of her control and tears began to roll down her cheeks as she nodded. If they couldn't be together in life, they would be together in death.

Nodding as though understanding that she had accepted he wouldn't leave her, Christian kept his gaze locked on hers as he spoke to his friend. "Mouse?"

"Sixty seconds."

"You need to go, man."

"Almost got it," Mouse responded.

"Don't want you dying in here. Phoebe and Lolly need you."

"Got no intention of leaving my girls any time soon."

"Christian, I love you," Lila murmured. She wanted so badly to touch him, hold him, wrap her arms around him, rest her head against his chest, and take her last breath wrapped in his embrace. But chained as she was, she couldn't do anything but use her words and eyes to express how much he meant to her.

"Love you back, mama bear, more than anything."

"You would have been an amazing father to our baby bear."

She saw him flinch, but then his face broke out into a breathtaking smile. "Thank you, you don't know how much those words mean to me. You already are the best mommy our little one could have asked for."

"Thank you."

"Mouse?" Christian asked.

"Thirty seconds."

"Time for you to go. Thank you for trying to save her."

"Not going anywhere."

"If you don't run now you won't make it."

"Said I almost got it."

"Kiss me, Christian."

"Run at ten," he said to Mouse. Then his lips found hers, and he was kissing her with every bit of love he felt for her branded in his touch.

Lila let go of everything else. The pain, the fear, the regrets. All that mattered was that she had found her soul mate and he loved her enough to give his life to be with her until the end.

The world around them faded.

Then all of a sudden she heard a smug chuckle. "Told you no one was dying today."

Christian pulled back, eyes wide. "You did it?"

"Eleven seconds to spare," Mouse replied.

"I … I'm not … going to … die?" Lila asked, wary of believing what she was hearing.

"Not on my watch," Mouse said, moving in front of her and grinning.

A slow smile slid over Christian's face, then he dragged his teammate in and hugged him hard. "I owe you everything. Thank you for saving her."

"Don't mention it," Mouse replied, slapping Christian's back.

"We need to …" Christian turned then froze. "You guys didn't leave?"

"Live as a team, die as a team," Bear said.

"And no one was dying here today," Arrow added.

"Thank you." Christian's voice was thick with emotion, and tears blurred Lila's vision.

These men had risked their very lives to stay with her and Christian. How could she ever thank them enough for that?

"Let's get her down," Arrow said.

Christian moved to stand in front of her again, one arm around her waist, while the guys made quick work of breaking the chains binding her. Once she was free, he swung her into his arms and knelt, gently lowering her to the floor.

"Get this thing off her," Christian said, and she felt his hands tugging at the vest.

Someone helped him remove it, then she was laid down flat on the concrete. People moved about her. Someone lifted her head and slipped something soft beneath it, she was covered in a blanket. Her vitals were checked, her ankle probed, and the prick on the back of one of her hands told her an IV was being started.

Through it all she felt fingers curled around her own.

Christian.

Her lighthouse in the storm.

Her safe place.

Her everything.

She wanted to tell him again how much she loved him, how grateful she was he hadn't left her to face death alone, but it was getting harder to think.

"Christian, I need to go to sleep," she murmured.

"All right, baby." He brushed a lock of hair off her cheek. "You close your eyes, sleep. I have you."

"You always have me," she mumbled.

"Forever," he agreed.

Unable to fight the darkness tugging at the corners of her mind any longer, Lila succumbed to it.

At the back of her mind, the thought registered that Zara was still out there.

Still a threat.

CHAPTER TWENTY-ONE

November 23rd
8:41 P.M.

He couldn't take his eyes off her.

Couldn't stop touching her either.

Surf hadn't left Lila's side since he found her chained up in that shed, a bomb strapped to her chest, her naked body pale and littered with bruises.

An image he would never be able to wipe from his mind's eye.

At least she was alive and mostly in one piece, and he was determined to keep it that way.

"Hey, man, we're ready for you," Arrow's quiet voice spoke from the door of Lila's hospital room.

He had to leave her now, just for a little while. He hated doing it, but it was his job, and the threat wasn't eliminated yet.

Even though he was only going to be down the hall, debriefing with the rest of his team and their boss, the thought of not having her in his direct line of sight left him feeling anxious and shaky.

He'd come so close to losing her.

Close enough he still felt that terror down to his bones.

Lila had passed out back at the shed before Arrow had even administered a sedative, and she was yet to regain consciousness. After she had been treated and was comfortable and settled in a bed, he'd allowed a doctor to check him over, but in the same room as her. He'd dozed in a chair at her bedside, confident in the knowledge that his team was watching over them and he could let go and focus on his woman.

Since she'd been out since they got the bomb disarmed, they

hadn't had a chance to question her on what had happened after Zara found her in the forest. But Surf had seen the bruises on her thighs, and he could make a pretty good guess on at least one thing she'd been forced to endure.

"She's doing okay, stable. Her body just needs rest," Arrow assured him. The medic crossed the room, picked up Lila's wrist, and checked her pulse. "Stable," he said again.

"I don't think I can leave her," he admitted. "Don't want her waking up alone and scared."

"Chances are she's going to be out for at least a couple more hours. She's been through a lot in the last week with zero time for her body to even begin recovering. What she needs now is exactly what she's getting, uninterrupted sleep. You'll be back before she wakes."

Surf knew all of that was true. Still walking away from her while she was vulnerable in sleep felt wrong.

Because he didn't have a choice, he stood, stooped to touch a kiss to her forehead, and followed Arrow out of the room and further down the hall to where Eagle had somehow managed to procure a room for them to use.

"How is Ms. Angeletti?" Eagle asked the second he entered the room.

It eased a little of his anxiety about leaving Lila to know that his boss' first priority was her wellbeing. Add in the fact that the man had left behind his pregnant wife and little daughter to come over here to support them, and Surf knew he was lucky to work for a company that wasn't just the best at what they did but also a big family.

"She's stable and sleeping," he replied, dropping into a chair and massaging his temples. He needed sleep too, but he wasn't going to be able to rest until he knew Zara was in custody.

"We'll get you back by her side as quickly as we can," Eagle promised.

"It just sucks that we know she's still out there. The woman is loaded, she could hide out anywhere in the world she wants to, and she won't stop coming after us." Surf rested his hands on the bed, which they were using as a makeshift table, and curled them into fists. He hated being helpless like this. Brought back memories of his childhood, the ordeal in Somalia, and all the times in the last week when he hadn't known where Lila was or whether she was okay.

"We cut the head off the snake when we eliminated Kristoff," Eagle reminded him, casting a glance at Domino whose face remained an impassive mask at the reminder of the brother he had killed.

"Lot of good it did," Surf muttered. If anything, it had made things worse for him and his team.

"It did do a lot of good," Eagle contradicted. "It sent Zara Duffy into a tailspin. She's not acting rationally right now. She's making mistakes and being sloppy."

"Sloppiest thing she did was leave her husband alive and behind," Bear said.

"She thought she could set it all up so we'd think it was him," Mouse continued. "She took Lila to Ross' mansion. She rented the other house where she took you two in his name and knew that the fact that Lila and Ross shared a dark history would make him look guilty of not just her death but ours as well. She was going to make it look like we were collateral damage in his quest to get back a woman he was obsessed with."

"That's what I mean," Eagle said. "Finding out Lila had a link to Alpha Team made her act in haste. She concocted this scheme spur of the moment, took advantage of what she thought was an opening to get all of you, and pin this on her husband. But that's not what happened."

"She tipped her hand too early," Bear agreed.

"Ross Duffy is singing like a canary," Brick said. "Telling everything he knows. I think the guy honestly believes he is in love with Lila because as soon as he knew that Zara was out to get her, he turned on her."

As much as he hated thinking about Lila's rapist believing he was in love with her, at least that meant Ross was willing to tell them everything he knew.

Exhaustion weighed heavily on him, but he shoved it aside. Lila needed to know that she was safe. It was the only way she could even begin to process and work through everything that had happened to her. "What's he saying?"

"Elaborated on what he already told us at the house, that the plan was for Zara to use Lila as bait to get the rest of us, but that he was supposed to get Lila for himself once we were dead," Brick said. "I focused on getting details out of him about what Zara's changed plans were."

"And?" he prompted.

"And Ross said that she was ranting about being the puppet master, gaining control of the most powerful country in the world," Brick continued.

Surf huffed out a frustrated breath. "We already knew that from Kristoff."

Brick shot him a reassuring smile. "I wasn't going to let you down, man. I may be the only one who doesn't have a family to care about, but you guys *are* my family, and I love your women and kids as though they were my own. I didn't stop until I got something we could use."

Of all of them, Brick was a master of interrogation.

The man might be quiet, keep to himself, a closed book, but he had their backs and always did whatever it took to get them the intel they needed. Surf had seen the man do everything from seducing information out of women to inflicting the kind of pain no man could endure and keep his mouth shut.

When he nodded at his friend, Brick nodded back then continued. "Ross said Zara was carrying on about being the next First Lady."

Eagle's eyes grew round. "She's targeting a presidential

candidate."

"Likely already has," Brick agreed.

"Kristoff would have the money to fund a campaign," Domino said thoughtfully.

"And I think it's safe to say your brother wouldn't have had any qualms about blackmailing someone into working with him," Arrow added.

Domino nodded his agreement. "Kristoff would definitely get off on that."

"He gathers information on a politician, then blackmails them into agreeing to his terms. Says he'll keep quiet and fund their campaign, but they have to answer to him," Mouse said.

"Then they get Zara's husband out of the way—likely the original plan had nothing to do with Lila—and she marries the politician while still remaining Kristoff's lover. Their plan was to destabilize the government so they knew what points to hit in the campaign all but ensuring their man was elected," Arrow said. "Kind of a genius plan for power."

"Crazy genius," Eagle corrected. "We need to find out which politician Zara and Kristoff were using."

That was important, Surf acknowledged that, but right now he had only one priority.

Finding and stopping Zara.

The election was still months away. They had time to find out who was working alongside Zara and stop them.

They might not have time to stop Zara before she made another attempt on their lives.

On Lila's life.

* * * * *

November 23rd
9:10 P.M.

"Mmm." Lila sighed as she blinked open her eyes.

Clean, warm, not in pain, not a bad way to wake up. After everything that happened this last week, she wasn't sure she would ever feel this way again.

"Christian?" Lifting her head took effort. Although the edge had been taken off her exhaustion by her nap, she still felt like she could sleep for a month, but when she didn't hear him respond she managed it. She glanced around the hospital room, expecting to see him sleeping in a chair beside her bed or in his own bed.

Instead, the room was empty.

A tinge of panic elevated her pulse.

She knew the bomb hadn't gone off. Remembered the fear of thinking that Christian and the rest of his team were going to get blown up along with her because they wouldn't leave her side. She also remembered the relief when the chains were removed and she was in Christian's arms. Exhaustion had quickly pulled her under, but the last thing she knew was him beside her holding her hand.

Now he was gone.

Had something else happened?

After making the phone call to Christian, Zara and her goon had left, so she assumed they were still out there somewhere. Had the guys gone after her? Had she hurt them?

Her pulse rate continued rising, and her body protested as she ripped at the IV in the back of her hand and swung her legs over the side of the bed. Her bad ankle had a cast on it, and there was a bandage on her arm where she'd cut it in the fall that day she'd run. Gauze was wrapped around both her wrists and her bare ankle, and bruises everywhere on the exposed skin on her forearms and shins.

She no doubt looked like an extra in a horror movie, and she certainly felt like one, but she needed to find Christian.

There was no way she was going to be able to rest until she knew where he was and that he was okay.

Probably wouldn't rest until he was there in the bed beside her.

Didn't he know he was human too?

He'd been shot, almost drowned, beaten and knocked unconscious, drugged and held captive, and almost got blown up alongside her. His body needed rest every bit as much as hers did.

Her man needed to get his sexy butt into bed beside her and hold her so they could both go to sleep safe in the knowledge they were together.

Whatever drugs they'd given her had stolen her pain. Temporarily, but it was better than nothing, and her ankle didn't protest too much as she hobbled awkwardly on the cast toward the door.

When she opened it, she found a cop leaning against the wall just outside. As soon as he saw her, he straightened and offered her a smile.

"You okay, ma'am?" he asked in accented English.

No.

She wasn't okay.

Likely wouldn't ever be completely okay.

But she was going to live her life to the fullest.

She was alive, and that was all that really mattered. Everything else could be dealt with in time.

"Do you know where the men from Prey Security are?" she asked. If he's been assigned to watch over her then he knew enough to know who was after her and that Prey was involved.

Understanding filled his warm brown eyes. "Your man will be back soon."

Her man. Lila liked the sound of that.

Christian Bailey was hers forever, and she was his.

Together they were going to raise this little one growing inside her. At least she hoped her baby was still alive. Since she'd been asleep, she hadn't spoken with a doctor, and Christian had left her alone, so she didn't really know if everything was okay with the baby.

"He wouldn't want you out of bed. You should go back, rest. Do you need help?"

Lila sighed. It was obvious he wasn't going to give her anything else. Likely Christian had told him not to tell her anything that might upset her.

They were going to have to have words about that.

It was sweet he wanted to protect her, but she wasn't some weak coward. Even though she had been terrified out there, she had walked on an injured ankle, fought off an assault, and even in the end accepted her fate and not wanted anyone to die with her.

She could handle whatever came next.

She just hoped what was next was Christian back in her room.

"No, I can make it. Thank you."

Letting the door fall closed behind her, Lila eyed the room's other door. She assumed it led to a bathroom, and now that she was up, she realized she needed to go.

Inside, she paused at the mirror and gaped as she took in her reflection.

Talk about looking a hot mess.

There were dark smudges under her eyes, bruises and a couple of scrapes on her cheeks, and her hair hung limply down her back. Someone had cleaned away the dirt she was sure must have been on her skin when she was brought in, but she didn't feel clean.

Lila eyed the shower, wishing she had enough energy to take one, although she wasn't really sure if she was allowed with her cast and bandages. Instead, she shuffled to the toilet, did her business, then washed her hands.

All of a sudden, the bed felt very far away, and she had to wonder how she was even on her feet. Christian better hurry up and get back here because she didn't want to go to sleep alone. She was scared of nightmares.

So much for her she wasn't weak or a coward pep talk.

She didn't feel very strong or brave.

Time.

Time, Lila. That's all you need.

As she opened the bathroom door, Lila prayed that was true. She didn't want to squander this chance. To all intents and purposes, she should be dead. Destiny had demanded her life, and yet somehow, here she was, alive and … mostly in one piece.

Movement caught her eye, and she relaxed. "Christian, you're finally here. Where were …" she trailed off when she realized the movement wasn't Christian.

Nope.

No way was she going to be that lucky.

Looked like destiny was ready to screw with her again.

A nurse was in the room, but Lila would know the face of the woman who had tried to kill her anywhere.

"Zara."

"Why won't you just die?" the woman hissed.

Anger surged through her.

Lila was *so* tired of people playing with her life. Even Christian had taken the choice out of her hands as to whether or not she could handle the threat hanging over his team's heads. Then Ross and Zara had kidnapped her, both wanting to use her in their sick games, and she was tired of it.

No more.

She was done.

She wasn't going to be a passive plaything to others ever again.

It was time to take back control of her own life.

"Why won't you just leave me alone?" Lila growled.

Zara took a startled step back at Lila's vehemence, but her surprise quickly morphed into rage. She pulled out a weapon and aimed it right at Lila, but instead of being scared it just made her angrier.

There was so much rage inside her there wasn't room for any other emotion, not even fear, and she stalked—as best as she could with a cast on—slowly toward Zara.

"I'm not going to be used as a pawn in your plot to kill the man I love," Lila snarled as she limped closer.

"Don't come any closer or I'll shoot you," Zara warned.

"Yeah?" Lila scoffed, knowing that wasn't going to happen. "If you shoot me then you alert the guard in the hall and the team of warriors somewhere nearby that you're here. With me dead there's nothing that's going to stop them from killing you."

"Not if I shoot them first."

That made her laugh. "You really are delusional, aren't you? You think you can take out six highly trained former special forces operators? Give it up. It's over. You either shoot me now or I'm taking you down myself."

"I'm going to rule the world."

"You were never in control of that plan. It was all Kristoff Mikhailov, you're just another of his puppets. He used you for your contacts and your body. Without him, you don't stand a chance at making your plans work."

"Shut up," Zara hissed, but the weapon wavered, and Lila knew she'd hit a direct score. The woman didn't like being told she was nothing, talk about delusions of grandeur. "Kristoff loved me. We were partners. If your man and his team hadn't murdered him, we would have ruled the world. They have to pay."

"Stop threatening the man I love," Lila screamed as she threw her body at Zara's, confident that Zara wouldn't shoot because then she'd find herself trapped in here. Plus, Lila didn't believe the woman had it in her.

Just as she connected with the other woman, sending them both tumbling to the floor, the gun went off.

CHAPTER TWENTY-TWO

November 23rd
9:23 P.M.

A gunshot.

Surf's entire body went ramrod straight.

There wasn't a doubt in his mind that it was related to Lila.

Without a word, he shoved out of his seat, vaguely registering that it clattered to the floor behind him, but he was already moving out the door.

They were only down the hall from Lila's room. The guard they'd left on her was on his radio, his weapon in hand. The man looked both worried and guilty, knowing he'd failed by allowing the person hunting the woman he was supposed to be protecting to get right to her.

When the officer went to open the hospital room door, Surf shoved him aside. He had no time to deal with the man, no interest in either reassuring him or reaming him out.

All he wanted was to assess the scene.

There was no way he could even begin to accept the possibility that it was already too late. That Lila was dead. There was no other exit, so if Zara Duffy was in there then they had her, they'd take her into custody, get the name of the politician involved, and all this would be over.

But if Lila was dead then it would be a hollow victory.

One that would have come at much too high a price.

His heart was in his throat as he threw open the door and saw Lila and Zara on the floor, tussling over a weapon.

"Lila," her name fell from his lips with no conscious thought, and he was already moving toward her when Zara took advantage of Lila's momentary distraction to drag her body up in front of her own.

A human shield.

Pulling Lila up with her, Zara got to her feet. Her back was pressed against the wall, Lila covered her front, and the weapon pointed at her head. Zara's eyes were wild, telling him as surely as any words could that she was dangerous and unpredictable.

Lila didn't seem to care about that. She was fighting Zara, trying to get out of the woman's grip, a thunderous look on her face, anger he hadn't seen before burning brightly in her baby blues.

"Stop fighting her, sweetheart," he ordered, panic clawing at his throat.

"I'm not going to be a victim again," Lila yelled, continuing to struggle against Zara's hold with no care that a gun was pressed to her temple.

She was going to get herself killed.

Panic was no longer just clawing at him, it was consuming him.

He wasn't going to stand there and watch her die right in front of him.

Not after everything they'd been through.

Everything they'd survived.

"Lila." He waited until she lifted her gaze to meet his. Surf tried to convey everything he felt for her in that one look, knowing it was the only way he could save her life. "Trust me."

Her body stiffened, and he could see that she was bucking against his words. She was tired, angry, and determined not to play the victim again, but this wasn't a one-person op, and he needed her to realize she wasn't fighting this battle alone.

It was time for her to trust her team.

Trust that they had her back.

Slowly, that thought seemed to resonate in her mind because he saw her relax and she gave him an almost imperceptible nod.

"Aww, how sweet," Zara mocked, grinding the barrel of the gun into Lila's temple, making her wince.

The flash of pain on Lila's face added fuel to his fury.

Anger that matched his own continued to shine in Lila's eyes, and he could feel his team's anger as they filled the small hospital room.

Zara was crazy if she thought there was any way out.

Her only bargaining chip was Lila, but if Zara killed her the woman would be dead before Lila's body hit the floor. If she thought she was going to talk them into letting her leave with Lila as a hostage, that was never going to happen.

"It's over, Zara," he said, his voice flat. If he was going to get his woman out of this alive, he had to shut down his emotions. He couldn't let himself be distracted by the fact that Lila was the hostage, the one who could be dead with one twitch of Zara's finger. This had to be just another mission.

Nothing more.

Focusing on how high the stakes were would make him weak.

Being out of control was his biggest fear, but you could never control others, no matter how hard you tried. All you could control was yourself. And he had no intention of letting his control over his emotions slip even for a millisecond.

"I told her that," Lila muttered under her breath, causing Zara to glower and press the gun tighter against Lila's head.

"It's not over. It won't be over until you're all dead," Zara yelled.

He could see Lila tense at Zara's words, and the look she tossed over her shoulder was almost sharp enough to kill. They were all sick of Zara Duffy and her threats. This ended here tonight.

"You only have one option here, Zara," he said, keeping his tone matter-of-fact. "You can only shoot one of us before the rest of us open fire on you. You kill Lila, same thing, we kill you."

Panic hit Zara's dark eyes as though she had only really

thought it through when it was spelled out for her. Eagle was right. She had been going off emotion, making spur-of-the-moment decisions because she was swamped with grief and a desire for revenge.

In her mind, she'd thought she could get into the hospital, take Lila again, and then play the whole baiting them game all over again.

Now she realized she was out of options.

There was no way Zara was walking away. She had backed herself into a corner and now needed to accept the consequences.

"You need to accept that this isn't going to work the way you wanted," he continued. Pushing her was a risk. She could either get frustrated and fire the weapon, or she could get annoyed and distracted and lower the weapon.

Millimeters.

That was all he needed to take the shot.

"Put the weapon down. Let us take you into custody. Maybe if you turn in whatever politician you're working with you can make a deal." Although he suggested it, Surf would be surprised if she'd be able to make any worthwhile deal. Not with the extent of lives lost and damage done by her and Kristoff's plot. Dozens of people had been killed in the explosions they'd set. She'd be spending the rest of her life in some prison cell in some hidden prison reserved for terrorists and traitors.

"Stop!" Zara shrieked. "Let me think!"

"There's nothing to think about," he reminded her. "This is it, the end of the road, you're not going to kill all of us, and you're not walking out of here. Body bag or handcuffs, those are your options." Personally, he hoped she chose the body bag. Surf knew both he and Lila, along with the rest of his team and their partners, would all sleep easier knowing the threat against them was permanently eliminated.

The wheels inside Zara's head were obviously whirring.

Then calm descended.

Surf got a bad feeling.

Whatever she had planned he knew he wasn't going to like it.

"You're right, I can't get everything I want, but I can at least kill the man who murdered my love, *moya lyubov.*" Without warning she spun and fired at Domino.

Lila took advantage and slammed her casted leg back into Zara's shin.

Zara cried out and stumbled, the weapon going off again as both women fell in a tangle of limbs.

He sprang into action, flying at the women and reaching for Lila.

Somehow, he managed to detangle her and yank her away from Zara.

As he whisked her to the other side of the room, he saw her eyes grow wide.

"Christian!"

Acting on instinct, as she screamed his name, he spun them so his body was between Lila and the shot he knew was coming.

The gun went off.

He braced for pain.

But it never came.

"It's over," Bear announced.

"Christian?" Lila asked, trying to lift her head.

Refusing to let her until he saw for himself that the threat was eliminated, he kept her tucked against his chest as he slowly turned around to find Zara's body slumped in the corner, a bullet wound between her eyes.

Domino was staring at Zara, his weapon still held out, and Surf assumed not only had his friend dodged the bullet Zara fired at him, but he had been the one to take the kill shot.

Given Domino's guilt over all of them having to give up their lives to hide from Zara because he'd killed his brother, being the one to eliminate that threat should hopefully help him move forward.

Free.

They were all free.

There was still a politician to find and stop, but at least his team was no longer being hunted.

"Christian, is it really over?"

* * * * *

November 23rd
9:34 P.M.

"Yeah, baby. It's over," Christian answered, tightening his hold on her.

Relief had her sagging against him, almost unable to believe they were all finally safe. "Over," she murmured as she pressed her face against his neck. She'd been trying to lift her head, see what was happening, but now she stopped fighting against him, letting his strength take the place of the anger that had been the only thing keeping her on her feet.

"Shh, it's all right," Christian soothed, his hands smoothing up and down her spine, and Lila realized she was shaking.

She had no idea why.

She should be happy, it was over.

That did mean what she thought it did, didn't it?

"Zara is …?" She lifted her head to meet Christian's eyes, needing to make sure he wasn't going to lie to her, tell her what he thought she wanted to hear. She needed the truth. Needed to know Zara could never hurt her or the people she cared about again. It was the only way she would be able to heal.

"Is dead," Christian finished her sentence, his green eyes holding her gaze, no wavers, no dips, communicating that he was giving her the truth.

So it was over.

Finally.

"Here," Arrow said, passing Christian a blanket that he quickly wrapped around her.

Right.

Because her entire body was trembling somewhat violently.

"I … I d-don't know w-why I'm sh-shaking," she stammered through chattering teeth.

"Shock, honey." Christian's hands rubbed up and down her arms, and she pressed closer, seeking his warmth.

"Your adrenalin is crashing now that it's over," Arrow added.

Over.

It's over.

Over, over, over, Lila repeated to herself.

Then a thought occurred to her. "Domino? Did she shoot him?" She scanned the room for the man she had been so sure that Zara was going to kill.

"He's fine," Christian answered just as her gaze landed on him.

He looked okay.

No blood.

Not shot.

Relieved, she shoved out of Christian's arms and hopped the couple of steps to where Domino was standing, throwing herself into his arms. Lila felt his surprise, but his arms quickly closed around her, returning her hug.

"I th-thought she g-got you," she whispered against his neck. If Zara had managed to kill Domino, Lila would have blamed herself because she hadn't been able to get the gun out of the woman's hands when they'd been wrestling over it on the floor.

"I'm all good," he assured her.

Summoning a small smile, she shoved away the fear and anger and allowed the reality that they were all alive and unharmed to take over. "G-good, I wouldn't h-have wanted to b-break the news t-to Julia that y-you got yourself sh-shot," she teased.

One side of Domino's mouth curled up. "My little flame is a handful."

"A handful?" Arrow snickered. "Julia is way more than a handful. But don't let her know I said that."

The guys laughed, and Lila felt herself relax a little more. There was still tension humming in the room, and she knew the body was over in the corner even though she couldn't bring herself to look at it. But Christian and his team no longer had a threat hanging over their heads, and that was worth celebrating.

"Can I have my woman back now?" Christian asked mildly even as she felt his hands reaching for her. He took her from Domino, cradling her in his arms.

Her body continued to vibrate with shakes, and she clenched her teeth together in an effort to still their chattering. It made sense that she would be in shock given that her system had gotten another scare, but none of the guys seemed affected by what had happened.

While she knew it was because this was their job, it was what they did, it still seemed unfair that she was a trembling mess, and they were standing around like it was all no big deal.

Then she felt a shudder ripple through Christian's big body, and she knew he wasn't unaffected at all.

He was every bit as scared as she was.

"Was so scared she was going to kill you," Lila whispered, nuzzling her face against his neck.

"Ah, baby, when I heard that gunshot …" he trailed off and another shudder rocked through him. Pressing closer, she tightened her hold on him and touched a soft kiss to the pulse point in his neck.

"I didn't want to be a victim anymore. I wasn't going to just go with her, wasn't going to let her use me to kill you."

Christian's arms tightened convulsively. "You don't ever risk yourself like that again."

Lifting her head, Lila narrowed her eyes at him. "If it comes down to protecting you, I absolutely will do whatever I can," she said defiantly.

"It's *my* job to protect *you*," he countered.

"Nu-uh." Lila shook her head firmly. "I love you. If you get to put yourself in danger for me then I can do it for you."

"Not sure I can take seeing you with a gun pointed at your head again, darlin'. About had a heart attack when I came in here and saw you fighting Zara, and when you were muttering taunts at her I almost lost my mind. I love you, sweetheart, and you're the mother of my baby. You don't get to be in danger ever again."

Giving him an indulgent smile because she totally got where he was coming from, Lila pressed a quick kiss to his lips. "I'm always going to have your back, and if I can protect you, I will. I won't ever be a victim ever again."

"But—"

"That's a battle you're not going to win, brother," Eagle said, slapping him on the back.

"Your woman's just giving you a taste of your own medicine," Mouse added.

"Exactly." Lila beamed at Christian. "We love each other, that means we always have each other's backs, no matter what."

"Amen," Arrow said.

"We're all a team, and we look out for each other," Bear added.

Lila's brow furrowed as something occurred to her. Alpha Team weren't the only ones who watched out for one another. "Where's Aleksei?"

"Who's Aleksei?" Christian asked.

"Why does that name sound so familiar?" Domino asked. Then almost immediately his eyes widened. "Aleksei was Kristoff's best friend."

"Now he's Zara's personal bodyguard," she said softly, a chill settling in as she thought of the last time she'd seen the man.

"He hurt you," Christian growled.

There was no use lying about it. "He … raped me. In the shed before Zara called you. He had some remote, I think it was for some toy … sex toy … that Zara was wearing because she started to moan like she was … turned on … and then she came, you know … orgasmed." Saying this stuff in front of a team of ultra-tough warriors was embarrassing, but she needed them to know how sure she was. "If Zara is here then Aleksei won't be far away."

The change in the men was instantaneous. They went from mostly calm and relaxed to focused and prepared.

Before any of them could react, the hospital door opened.

A man dressed in scrubs stepped in.

His eyes roamed the room, taking in the men with guns and the body lying on the floor, but instead of panic flaring in his dark eyes, there was anger.

"Ty ubil yeye. Yy umresh'," he yelled in what Lila assumed was Russian. The man reached for the waistband of his pants, hidden beneath his top, and pulled out a weapon.

A weapon he never got a chance to fire.

Christian turned, keeping her tight against his chest. One of the guys fired before Aleksei got a chance to.

She heard the sound of the body hitting the floor.

Even though she knew it was one of the bad guys, one she had every reason to want dead, she still flinched at the sound.

So much death.

So much pain.

"It's like a damn horror movie," Arrow muttered. "Every time you think it's over it's not."

"It's over now," Bear said.

"Damn straight," Mouse added.

Christian turned and nodded at Domino. "Thanks again, man."

Domino's dark eyes were turbulent, and she assumed he had been the one to kill Aleksei. "You're welcome."

Reaching out, she touched Domino's shoulder. He would never know just how much his ending the lives of Zara and Aleksei meant to her, but she hated that he'd been forced to take their lives in part for her. "Thank you," she whispered.

His gaze softened. "You're welcome. Now maybe you, Julia, and all of us can get some peace."

"And rest," Eagle Oswald added. "I want you back in bed," he said, pointing to her.
"You too," he said to Christian. "We're heading home tomorrow morning, and it's going to take me most of the night to get this mess sorted. So, all of you get some rest. Good job. All of you." Eagle's blue eyes met hers, and she saw respect and admiration in them.

She hadn't done anything.

She'd had to be rescued several times, and even though she'd fought both Ross and Zara, she didn't have the strength it took to save herself.

With a glance at Christian, Lila wondered if she had the strength to get through the trauma of the last week and have the happy ending with the man she loved that she so desperately craved.

CHAPTER TWENTY-THREE

November 24th
7:44 P.M.

Finally.

Surf had been waiting for days to get his beautiful woman home and all to himself, and now they were finally here.

Despite the fact that he knew without a shadow of a doubt that he loved Lila with every fiber of his being and wanted to spend the rest of his life with her, raising their baby, celebrating holidays, traveling the world, and enjoying one another, things felt almost strained between them.

Not distant perse. Lila hadn't been out of his arms since Domino shot Zara Duffy and then Aleksei. After settling in a new hospital room—one not stained in blood and death—they'd curled up on the bed together and slept. On the plane, he'd kept her tucked against his side the entire time. And even when Eagle had insisted on driving them to Surf's apartment himself Lila had been plastered against him.

Surf had even gone so far as to carry her the short distance from the street to his apartment building. Needing the slight weight of her in his arms had nothing to do with not wanting her to cause herself pain by using her crutches, it had everything to do with wanting the reassurance of feeling her body against his.

Lila hadn't spoken much, seeming content just to rest her head on his shoulder and let him hold her, and while he appreciated that she wasn't pulling away from him, he could tell she was holding something back.

Burying it inside herself where it could fester and destroy her.

Not that he had any intention of allowing that to happen.

Protecting the woman he loved didn't just mean keeping her safe from physical harm, it meant making sure every part of her was taken care of.

Including her mental health.

"Almost there, mama bear," he murmured, making sure his tone was pitched low and soothing. He carried her through the lobby, bypassed the lifts, and took the stairs instead. Surf was more mentally exhausted from the events of the last week than he was physically worn out. While his body was used to pushing itself to the edge, his mind wasn't used to someone he loved being at the center of a mission.

The toll of worrying over Lila, seeing her in danger over and over again, that was something he wouldn't get over anytime soon.

"Home sweet home," he said as he managed to balance Lila in his arms and pull his keys from his pocket, unlocking the door and then locking it behind them. While they hadn't discussed it yet, he wanted her to stay here with him permanently. Or if she preferred, they could live in her apartment or find a new place. Surf didn't care where they were as long as they were together.

Since this was his apartment and Lila didn't have any of her things here, Eagle had organized for his wife Olivia to pick up the things Lila had taken with her to the Prey safehouse and drop them off here. He wanted her to be comfortable and knew having her own things around her would help.

"Hey, baby, how you doing?" he asked as he set her on the couch and knelt beside her. When he reached out to smooth a lock of hair behind her ear, he let his fingers linger, caressing the still-bruised skin on her cheek. Thankfully, the only serious injury was to her ankle, which was broken, and would require surgery when she was stronger, but the most important thing was that she was alive, and so was their baby.

"I'm okay, Christian. Happy to be alive and back home." She

tilted her face into his hand, seeking more of his touch and he was happy to give it to her.

There were shadows in her eyes he didn't know how to chase away.

He wanted that fire back that had been there when she was fighting Zara in the hospital room. He wanted the spark back, the light, now her beautiful blue eyes were so dull that it broke his heart.

"Tell me what to do," he said, desperation leeching into his voice. "Tell me how to make you smile again." Did she know he would give anything to erase all of this from her mind? All the trauma, fear, and pain, he would take it in a heartbeat if he could.

A small smile curled her lips up. "You're doing exactly what I need. You're here. You brought me home with you rather than taking me back to my apartment."

Surf frowned. "Did you honestly think I wouldn't bring you back here?"

Lila shrugged.

"Sweetheart, I don't want to let you out of my sight, much less have you in a completely different building in another part of the city." Standing, he scooped Lila up then sat again, settling her in his lap. "This is where I want you. Forever. Right here in my arms. I don't care where we live, but I want us to live together." When she didn't offer any protests he asked, "Any objections."

Lips touched his jaw in a soft kiss. "Are you sure?"

"Positive. You're it for me. I knew it the moment I laid eyes on you. When I ended things, I prayed I would get the chance to win your love and trust back. Do I have your love?"

"Oh, Christian. You have every drop of love I have to give."

The next was perhaps a harder question and one that might be more important. "And do you trust me?"

"With my life, my heart, and my soul," Lila replied without hesitation.

"You don't know how much that means to me, baby. I'm not

worthy of your love—"

"You stop that right now, Christian Bailey," Lila said vehemently. Lifting her head so she could meet his gaze, he saw the same spark of fire he'd just been praying for back in her eyes. "I don't *ever* want to hear you say you aren't worthy ever again."

His heart swelled until it felt too big for his chest. No one had ever believed in him like that before. Still, lingering shame from his past made him feel like he could never be good enough for this former child star. "Lila, you know about my past."

"And you know about mine," she shot back. "Do you think less of me because of *my* past? I was raped by Ross when I was sixteen and was forced to give up my baby. Does that make me unworthy?"

"Damn it," he growled, his blood heating. "You know it doesn't."

"I was forced to put my mouth on Ross, he tried to put his on me. And Zara's bodyguard Aleksei r-raped me. Does that make me unworthy?" Lila's voice cracked and tears brimmed in her eyes. Her spark had faded again, and he knew she needed to hear him tell her that nothing could make him not love her.

"You are my everything, Lila. Do you even know how in awe of you I am? What you've endured, what you've dealt with, mostly on your own, I can't even believe that not only are you standing but you built a life for yourself. One where you help people on the worst days of their lives. You are worthy of everything. *Everything*. And I promise I will spend the rest of my life making sure you are happy, supported, taken care of, and most of all loved. I'll take your pain, baby, and while I can't absolve you of that burden, I can carry it with you. Never again will you cry into your pillow alone, no one to hold you as you weep. When you're afraid I'll be there, and when your eyes shine with happiness that's where I'll find my joy."

A few years trickled down her still-wet cheeks, but Lila smiled through them. "And that's exactly how I feel about you. I'll share your pain, your feelings of unworthiness, and your joy. The good and the bad, both sides of the coin, I'll be there by your side, holding your hand, through both. We both suffered so much when we were younger, but that's all behind us now. Nothing but smooth sailing from here on out."

Framing her face with his hands, he touched a kiss to her forehead. "Smooth sailing."

Her smile faltered. "I feel dirty, Christian," she whispered. "I don't know how to make it go away. I don't know how to process everything that happened these last few days. What if I'm not strong enough to get through it? What if I can't be the woman you deserve? Or the mom this baby deserves?"

Stowing the anger thinking about someone raping his woman, Surf kept his touch light, his tone gentle, infusing every bit of love he felt for her into his words. "You are strong enough to conquer the world. On the days you feel like you don't have what it takes, you tell me, and I'll give you whatever you need."

"You know I'll give you the same."

"I know, baby. It's one of the many reasons I love you. I can completely be myself with you. I want it all with you, Lila. I want to live with you, I want to marry you, I want to raise this baby with you, I want to spend the rest of my life with you. There is no question about it, no doubts in my mind, I love you with everything I have to give, and I promise you right here and now I will give you all of myself. Now and forever."

* * * * *

November 24th
8:00 P.M.

Christian's words washed over her like a warm caress.

His love meant everything to her right now.

Her world was spinning out of control. Too much had

happened in too short a space of time and she was struggling to process it all.

How could you process even one of those traumas let alone all of them back-to-back-to-back?

Just having the man she was falling in love with unexpectedly dump her and then find out she was pregnant would have been enough to send her world into a tailspin, and yet it had turned out that was the most minor of her problems.

Lila wanted to work through it all, wanted to be strong and have herself put back together by the time their baby came along, but she was floundering as to just how to do that.

Sensing her inner turmoil, Christian's thumbs began to stroke her cheekbones, and he touched kisses to her forehead, her cheeks, the tip of her nose, and then finally her lips. "What do you need, baby?"

Helplessness washed over her. "I … don't know."

It was hard enough sorting through the mess of emotions and fears inside her own head, let alone able to articulate it and express it out loud to another person.

Despite their conversation, there were still lingering feelings of dirtiness and unworthiness.

Probably always would be.

She knew from experience that those feelings would never completely go away, but they would fade enough that she could function. With Christian by her side, she also knew she would more than function, eventually she would thrive, and experience happiness and peace in a way she never had before. Then these days would be just dark memories and pale scars.

Lila just didn't know how to get to that place.

Overwhelmed, she locked her gaze onto Christian's, silently begging him to tell her what she needed.

His caress of her cheeks never stopped as if he knew maintaining physical contact was important. "We'll make an appointment for you to see someone tomorrow. You know Piper is Prey's on-staff psychiatrist. If you want you can talk to her, I'm sure she'd be happy to see you."

"No. Piper and Arrow are part of your family, part of my family now, and I don't want to do anything to muddy that. I want Piper to be my friend, not my shrink."

"Then I know someone you can see. Arrow and then the rest of us decided not to see Piper after we were held captive in Somalia. Arrow had already fallen for her, and when she told him she wouldn't date him because he was a patient, he fixed that real quick." He threw her one of his easy-going grins, and Lila felt a small part of herself relax.

"Then definitely not Piper. But … I think maybe I should talk to someone." She hesitated, then decided she may as well just say it. "Maybe it would be good for you too. I don't think you've dealt with what happened to you as a child and given what I've just been through—what we've both been through—I think maybe we both need it."

Christian's entire body tensed, and for a second his thumbs ceased smoothing across her skin. He dragged in a slow breath, and she could see his internal struggle. His alpha side likely rebelled at the notion that he needed to talk to a shrink while his practical side likely knew that he needed to work through it to finally heal.

Wounds like theirs didn't heal easily, and they left behind jagged, messy scars, but she was determined that they would fight their way through this.

Side by side there wasn't anything they couldn't do.

"Please," she whispered.

His gaze softened, and he leaned in to feather his lips across hers. "Okay."

"I want you to do it for you, not for me." The only way to heal was to want to for yourself. If he did it only for her and the baby then she was afraid it wouldn't work, and some day he would be consumed by his past.

"I want it for all of us. For our family."

"Thank you."

"I'm so proud of you, honey. Do you know that? Look at you, everything that you've been through, and there you are worrying about me. You're so strong. So strong," he murmured again.

Tears blurred her vision. "I don't feel strong. I feel one gentle breeze away from being knocked down. If I get knocked down, I'm scared I won't be able to get back up," she admitted.

His torment at not being able to fix this for her was evident in his beautiful forest green eyes. Against the sides of her head, where he still framed her face, his fingers curled into fists, further indicating his helpless frustration. "You're killing me, baby. You won't fall, I won't let you fall, and if you stumble the only place you'll land is in my arms."

Leaning forward, Lila rested her forehead on his. "I love you so much. I hope you know that. I just feel so … out of control."

"What is making you feel the most out of control right now?"

She hesitated briefly. "Sex," she mumbled, embarrassed. "We're just at the beginning of our relationship. You'll expect sex … what if I can't give it to you?"

Christian growled. "I'm not with you for sex."

His impassioned plea made her smile. Placing her hands on his cheeks, she stroked his cheekbones with her thumbs as he'd been doing to her. "I didn't mean it like that. I *want* to have a sexual relationship with you, I want our relationship to be normal, I want to give you everything. I'm just scared I won't be able to. I'm scared I'll let you down."

"Baby, you can't ever let me down, don't you know that?"

"I know."

"It will happen in time."

"I want it to be now."

"What can I do to help?"

"I don't … can I touch you?"

"Babe, you never have to ask me that." Shifting her slightly, he unzipped his jeans but didn't push them down his hips, then he leaned back against the couch and spread his arms out, resting them on the top of the couch, showing her with his actions he was no threat to her.

Her hand trembled slightly when she reached out, but she stroked along his length through the denim. At her touch, she felt him twitch, and she liked knowing that he responded to her touch.

That her touch could bring pleasure.

Pleasure, not pain, that was what touch was supposed to give.

Increasing the pressure, she stroked him until he was bulging against his jeans, and she realized she wanted more. When she reached up to slip her hand inside his pants, Christian grasped her wrist.

"You don't have to, baby, we can stop right there."

"I want to," she said firmly.

"Can I put my hands here?" he asked,placing his palms against her thighs.

For a second her pulse increased.

His fingers brushed her inner thighs, so close to her center.

It's Christian, she reminded herself.

He would never hurt you.

"Yes," she whispered breathily. Sensing his doubt, she slipped her hand inside his jeans, shoved aside his boxers, and claimed him. He was hot, hard, and big against her palm, and she could feel him pulsing.

Focus on this.

On the here and now.

Forget everything else.

You're safe with Christian.

Always.

Her pep talk was enough to keep her touching him, stroking him, watching his face as he watched hers. Knowing he was examining her closely for signs of distress even as he felt pleasure building inside him wrapped her in the sweetest sense of protective love.

No matter what, Christian would always be looking out for her. Putting her needs above his own.

She wouldn't have thought it possible, but in this moment, her love for him grew.

Increasing her speed and the pressure of her hand, Lila stroked him until he came apart, his hips thrusting into her hand as he came all over her.

Marking her.

Claiming her.

Making her irrevocably his.

"Can I touch you, honey? Just through your clothes," he added when she hesitated.

"Yes."

"You say the word and I stop."

"I know. I trust you."

He held her gaze as his fingers drifted to her center, stroking her through her clothes. Lila shut everything else out of her mind, focused only on the fact that this was Christian, she was safe in his home, and if it became too much all she had to do was say the word and he'd stop.

While her mind continued to offer itself reassurances, her body was well and truly on board, and she noticed her hips had begun to undulate against Christian's soft ministrations.

"More."

Lila thought he might have asked her if she was sure, but he didn't. Just slipped his hand inside the waistband of her yoga pants. It was like he understood before she did that if he questioned her, made it seem like he doubted her then it would give her cause to doubt herself.

He knew her better than she knew herself.

Christian kept her panties between her and his fingers as he lightly traced around her entrance before sliding up to sweep across her bundle of nerves.

Sensations built, growing quickly.

"More," she pleaded.

Again, he didn't hesitate to comply.

Pushing aside her soaked panties, he dipped one finger inside her, thrusting in and out slowly as his thumb worked her bud.

"I'm close," she said haltingly, her hips moving, seeking more.

"What do you need to get there?"

"I … I'm not sure." Teetering on the edge, so close, but afraid she couldn't get there. What if she'd lost her ability to orgasm?

As always, Christian seemed to read her mind and sort through her jumbled emotions with more ease than she could. He leaned closer and captured her lips.

Every single thing he felt for her was in that kiss, and his love was the final push her body needed. Lila came hard and fast all over Christian's hand.

Pleasure seemed to linger, lazily making its way throughout her body, and she felt like she was floating on a hazy cloud.

While she was under no illusions that just because she'd been fine with getting Christian off, and letting him touch her, that all her problems were solved, a sense of peace had settled inside her.

She could do this.

She would do this.

With Christian by her side, they would conquer their demons.

"Thank you," she whispered.

"For what?"

"For being the first person to love me, and for loving me so completely I feel it down to my soul."

CHAPTER TWENTY-FOUR

November 25th
10:51 A.M.

Surf could absolutely stay like this forever.

Home, in his bed, safe, warm, and comfortable with his woman tucked into his embrace, held snugly against his chest where he knew anything that tried to hurt her would have to go through him first.

As he lay there, he stroked a hand down her spine, almost in awe of the fact that he had her back where she belonged. Ending things with her in an attempt to keep her safe had been the worst decision he'd ever made, and a mistake he would never repeat.

From now on he was keeping her close.

There was not a doubt in his mind that he was the luckiest man alive. To have a woman like Lila, to have won her trust back after breaking it, to have her love after he'd made her believe she meant nothing to him. It was no small thing in his mind, and he intended to hold onto this feeling right here.

Glancing at the clock, he reluctantly eased Lila out of his arms. She didn't stir and after he'd slipped out of bed, he carefully tucked her back in, then took another moment to admire her and how right it looked to have her in his bed.

His team would be here any minute, still he stooped to press his lips to her forehead, letting them linger there, breathing in her soft scent.

Since he hadn't wanted to make her uncomfortable, instead of sleeping in a pair of boxers like he usually did, he'd slept in sweatpants and a t-shirt. When he'd offered Lila one of his t-shirts to sleep in instead of her pajamas, she'd quickly agreed, and he'd caught her holding the shirt to her nose, breathing in his scent when he'd come back from the bathroom before they'd both climbed under the covers.

Surf hoped being wrapped in his clothes and then in his arms gave her a measure of safety. A security blanket of sorts.

Damn, he loved the sight of her in his clothes.

With a last kiss, he quickly changed into jeans and a clean shirt and headed out of the bedroom, quietly closing the door behind him. Just as he entered the living area of his apartment, he heard movement at his door.

Wanting to open it before they knocked, he hurried over and swung it inward, leaving Arrow standing there, his fist in the air, prepared to knock.

Arrow grinned. "Morning."

"Lila's still asleep so you guys need to be quiet," he said in way of a greeting.

"How's she doing?" Piper asked as everyone ushered into his place, taking seats on his couches.

Surf dragged his fingers down his face and dropped into an empty spot at the end of one sofa. "She's hanging in there but had nightmares last night." When she'd woken him whimpering and crying out in her sleep, knowing she was suffering in the one place he couldn't be there for her, it had left him feeling so helpless. Almost as helpless as being trapped in his own dreams, where he'd been powerless to save the woman he loved as he watched her get raped over and over again.

"It'll take time, Surf," Mackenzie said, her eyes full of empathy.

"You got a strong woman there," Julia added from where she was nestled on Domino's lap. "And she's got all of us."

"Damn straight," Bear said.

His team's unwavering support was why he admitted, "I had nightmares too." Part of him expected his friends to laugh that off, tell him he had Lila back and it was time to focus on the future. He didn't know why given that no one who served in the military like they had, or did what they did with Prey, escaped without the odd nightmare.

"I had nightmares after Mackenzie was almost killed by her brother," Bear readily admitted.

"I think my nightmares were worse than Phoebe's or Lolly's after they were taken," Mouse added.

"Lolly definitely bounced back the quickest," Phoebe said, rubbing her swollen stomach. "I hope this little one has as much spunk as that kid does."

"Domino and I both still have nightmares about his brother," Julia spoke up, earning her a scowl from Domino. "They know you're human, Dom, like the rest of us mere mortals." She rolled her eyes then laughed and kissed her fiancé's cheek. "Even superheroes have nightmares, Surf."

"After what I did to Piper when we first got together, I was terrified my nightmares were going to come back and I'd wind up killing her," Arrow said softly, his arms reaching out for Piper who quickly moved closer, pressing her body up against her fiancé's.

"But we got through it together," Piper said, likely as much for Arrow's benefit as for his. "You and Lila will get through this too. You have each other, you have all of us, it will take time, but you *will* get there. Have you made an appointment for her to speak to a professional? I'd be happy to do it if she needs me."

Surf reached out to take Piper's hand and squeeze it. "Thanks for the offer, but I called Dr. Devereaux this morning and made an appointment for Lila for tomorrow. Today she just needs to rest and start rebuilding her strength, so she can have the surgery she needs on her ankle."

"Good." Piper looked completely satisfied. "She was great with Antonio, and I know you guys all liked her. She helped me too. I think knowing all of our history she's the perfect person for Lila to talk to."

There was a clunk in what sounded like the bedroom and Surf immediately jumped to his feet.

"That better not be my stubborn woman trying to get herself out of bed," he grumbled as he stormed off in the direction of the bedroom. When he'd carried her into the room last night, he'd made it clear he didn't want her walking around and causing herself pain.

She'd walked on that broken ankle more than enough.

The thought of her in unnecessary pain was too much for him right now.

"What exactly do you think you're doing?" he growled as he opened the door to find her hopping about trying to put clothes on.

Obviously, he caught her by surprise because Lila tried to turn but lost her balance. As she fell, her arms windmilled as she tried in vain to catch herself.

Instead, he flew across the room and caught her just before she hit the ground.

"Christian," she rebuked, smacking his arm. "Don't scare me like that again."

"You're not supposed to be up and standing."

"The doctor said I can use the crutches."

"Only you weren't using them," he reminded her.

"I was only getting dressed. I heard voices."

"My team is all here, the wives too. Do you want me to ask them to leave?" If she needed more time with just the two of them then he'd go out there and tell his team. He knew they would understand.

"No, it'll be nice to spend some time just hanging out with your friends."

"*Our* friends," he corrected.

"Right." There were still shadows in her eyes, but she seemed calmer today.

"Here, let me help you get dressed." Setting her down on the side of the bed, he grabbed a pair of leggings and eased them up and over her cast before sliding her other leg in. "Hold onto me," he ordered as he stood her up so he could pull the waistband over her hips. Then he sat her back down, grabbed a sweater and put it on her. Kneeling before her, he slipped both her feet into fuzzy socks, then looked up to find her watching him, eyes soft, a warm smile on her lips. "What?"

"You're just so sweet, taking care of me like this."

Leaning up, he whispered a kiss across her lips. "I will always take care of you, sweetheart. I'm your man that makes it my job."

"I love you, Christian."

"Love you more."

"I don't think that's possible."

He gave a dramatic sigh. "Okay, it's a tie."

She was laughing as he scooped her up and carried her through to the living room where she exchanged hellos with everyone. It wasn't until he sat down with her on his lap that he noticed Brick was off to the side, slowly lowering his cell phone from his ear.

"Everything okay, Brick?" he asked.

When the man turned to face them, his dark eyes were shocked and filled with pain. The look was enough to quiet everyone as they all looked expectantly at the most restrained, self-contained member of their team.

"That was Eagle. They think they got a lead on the politician working with Kristoff and Zara," Brick said, his voice heavy with emotion. "I know the family. Used to be best friends with the daughter. Eagle wants me to make contact, use her to try to get close to her father and gather evidence." Brick looked positively sickened by the idea.

"Are you going to do it?" Bear asked.

"Don't have a choice. If Hemmingway Xenos is involved, he has to be stopped, he's the last link to this plot, and we can't leave him to follow through on Kristoff and Zara's plans," Brick said tensely.

"Are you going to be *able* to do this?" Surf asked. From the looks of things, he wasn't sure Brick was up for the job.

He looked around the room at Bear and Mackenzie and their baby Mikey. They looked relaxed knowing that now their son could be raised without a threat hanging over their heads. Likewise, Mouse and Phoebe looked like a weight had been lifted from their shoulders. Now they could focus on the upcoming birth of their baby in just a couple of months. Arrow and Piper could finally get married, and Domino and Julia didn't have to live with the weight of knowing the whole team was in danger because he had killed his brother.

Surf held his future in his arms. His gorgeous woman who would soon become his gorgeous wife sometime before their baby entered the world. They might have a long road of healing ahead of them, but he already knew their happiness was written in the stars.

Brick, on the other hand, looked more alone than Surf had ever seen his friend. He looked like he was about to walk into Hell, and Surf couldn't help but wonder just what Brick's relationship with Hemmingway Xenos' daughter had been, and how badly it was going to hurt him to have to use her.

Even if it was for the greater good.

Sometimes life sucked, but sometimes it gave you everything you wanted and a whole lot more. Surf could only hope Brick somehow got the happy ending he had just been blessed with.